LOVE STORIES: UKRAINE

AN ANTHOLOGY OF SHORT STORIES FROM
YOUR FAVOURITE WOMEN'S FICTION AUTHORS

ADELE PARKES ALEX BROWN
AMANDA JENNINGS BERNICE BLOOM
CATHY BRAMLEY CESCA MAJOR
CHRISSIE MANBY CLARE SWATMAN
EMILY KERR GILL PAUL GILLIAN MCALLISTER
HOLLY MARTIN ISABELLE BROOM JANE CORRY
JANE FALLON JESSICA FELLOWES JOSIE LLOYD
KATE GREY KATIE FFORDE
KIRSTY GREENWOOD LOLA JAYE
MILLY JOHNSON PAIGE TOON
PERNILLE HUGHES PHOEBE MORGAN
RACHAEL LUCAS RACHEL EDWARDS
TAMMY COHEN TASMINA PERRY
VERONICA HENRY

This edition published by Sunflower & Co 2022

ISBN 978-1-911297-33-8

'Love Stories: Ukraine' is part of The Sunflower Seed Project. For every print book sold, Sunflower & Co will plant a tree in a part of the world with high levels of poverty, to restore the forests and create employment opportunities. While all profits from 'Love Stories: Ukraine' will go to the DEC Ukraine Appeal, the sale of this book also means that a tree has been planted in Haiti.

INTRODUCTION

TASMINA PERRY

Thank you for buying a copy of Love Stories: Ukraine. Like everyone else, I've been watching the events unfold in Ukraine with a mixture of dismay and helplessness, but the past weeks have shown that we can all do something, however small. Hundreds of bake sales, auctions, collections, concerts and donations have already been organised to raise money for the humanitarian relief effort. At a time when humanity can seem so dark, the collective power of good has been awe-inspiring.

When I sat down to think about how I could help, I realised two things. I knew how to publish books and I know lots of fabulous authors. Adele Parks was the first author I pitched the idea of an anthology to. When she pointed out that Ukraine's national flower is the sunflower and my publishing imprint is called Sunflower & Co, it felt like a sign to press full steam ahead.

The collection came together in less than two weeks. Many of the stories here were written from scratch, some were unearthed from a 'bottom drawer', but they were all given – fittingly - with love. Some of the contributions are romances – actual love stories – others are about the love for siblings or children or even finding a way to love yourself. Other stories are just wonderful examples of writing – stories to love. I'm really proud of the collection we have pulled together, especially in such a short space of time.

I've always believed in the power of storytelling. Whether it is a neighbourhood book club or a global best-seller that captures the imagination of the world, stories unite us, stories can help us escape. Stories help us understand the world. Today I hope we can use the power of stories to help raise funds for the DEC's Ukraine humanitarian appeal.

Only a month into the conflict and millions of people have been displaced, billions of pounds worth of property have been destroyed and thousands of lives have been lost. Every penny counts in the humanitarian relief effort, so please, if you enjoy the anthology, tell a friend so they might think of buying one too.

Thank you to all the authors who didn't hesitate when I asked them to get involved. Thank you to every person who buys the book.

I really hope you love our stories.

Tasmina Perry
March 2022

All profits from 'Love Stories: Ukraine' will be donated to the Disasters Emergency Committee Ukraine Appeal in support of humanitarian aid required due to the conflict in Ukraine.

www.dec.org.uk

CONTENTS

THE INVITATION

ADELE PARKS

Binita's transfer from the Liverpool office to the smaller office in Chester had come along at exactly the right time, and she knew she had to maximise the opportunity. She'd promised herself that she'd accept every social invitation that fluttered her way. So far, this meant she'd had to dig out flat shoes and amble around Westminster Park (commenting on the impressive landscaping), go to the Monday quiz night at The Crown (to answer questions on sport and politics), and get up early on a Sunday morning to play badminton (even though she hadn't held a racquet since she was in the sixth form). She had not allowed shyness or even personal taste to get in the way.

In Liverpool, Binita had been stuck in a rut – emotionally and professionally – for far too long. The place was rammed with haunting memories of her ex, Peter, even though they'd divorced three years ago. She had occasionally dated since then because everybody from her mother to her best friend said she ought to, but her broken heart just wasn't in it, and the men she went out with soon became aware of this. A clean start was exactly what was required.

She needed to know that she could confidently walk around Waitrose without bumping into Peter and his new wife. She wanted to be able to go to a bar or restaurant without being bludgeoned with memories of times when she'd visited the same place as half of a happy couple.

The only problem was, despite the undoubted efficiency of the company's relocation department, a clean start required a lot of effort. The relocation manager had shown Binita four equally lovely one-bed apartments, and she'd settled on the one nearest the park because she was thinking about getting a dog, or a bike, or something that would indicate that she had a life. The relocation manager registered her at a doctor and a dentist's surgery; she even supplied a list of decent hair salons. No, the difficulty was acquiring new friends. Binita realised that she had to make some, but she secretly felt a little bit old for it. It was easy when you were eight: you simply shared your Curly Wurly or offered a turn on the skipping rope. Not so easy at thirty-eight. The relocation manager couldn't help her with that one.

At work, a woman called Louise took Binita under her wing. Binita gratefully snuggled there because they were the same grade of middle management, the same age, and when they selected their lunches in the canteen, it transpired that they had the same taste in yoghurts. Binita hoped it was enough to kick-start a friendship. The notable differences between them were that Louise was married with two sons, and she lived in a large townhouse. She was so proud of her husband, boys and house that she threw elaborate dinner parties every Saturday to share her good fortune and no doubt showcase it too, Binita thought, as she tried not to feel aggrieved by the glaring disparity.

Anyway, Louise invited Binita for dinner. All week she

chattered excitedly about the menu and the other guests. She was planning on serving monkfish and scallops with wood-roasted vegetables. She would also be serving up an eligible man for Binita's delectation. Binita knew the dinner party formula: three couples, her and a spare man. The marrieds looked to the singletons for entertainment: would they or wouldn't they share a taxi home? Her married pals in Liverpool had done the same thing: potential boyfriends were recruited with unseemly enthusiasm. Binita knew their intentions were good and that a happily married woman like Louise would also be unable to resist match-making. It didn't stop Binita from dreading the evening.

It turned out to be exactly as expected. The food was marvellous, the guests were pleasant but not profound, and the spare man was disinterested. The conversation centred around children's schools and the difficulty in securing a trustworthy builder. They drank moderately because no one wanted a hangover, and they couldn't afford to lose their Sunday mornings to such messiness. Binita went through the motions; these concerns weren't hers, but she was sympathetic and familiar enough with them to make the appropriate comments in the correct places. The only surprise was Louise's husband, Ned.

Binita had been expecting a middle-aged guy, fighting his paunch and the weight of his mortgage. But Louise's husband was quite exceptionally striking: classically tall, dark and handsome, with cheekbones you could cut yourself on. Binita would never, ever look at a man who was taken – she herself had been on the wrong end of infidelity - but she couldn't fail to be impressed. Until she talked to him. Ned was dull. He was perfectly pleasant, not rude or aggressive or overwhelmingly cocksure - frankly, any of those alternatives might have been more exciting - he was simply boring. Ned spoke for fifteen uninterrupted minutes about the best garden weedkiller available on the market. Louise beamed throughout his monologue, seemingly unaware that her guests had nodded off. When they said good night, Louise pulled Binita into a hug and whispered, 'I know that one day you'll find someone just as wonderfully dependable as my Ned.' Binita appreciated the sentiment and therefore bit her tongue, resisting commenting that she'd prefer to stay single than suffer a slow death by tedium, even if her killer was so utterly handsome. Each to their own, she thought, as she got in the back of the cab.

The next invite Binita received was from Sharron in accounts, who asked her to join a gang of colleagues for a drink in town. When Louise heard that it would be at Hooper's bar, she looked concerned.

'It's a cattle market. That place attracts the wrong sort.'

'Which sort, exactly?'

'People just out for a good time, if you know what I mean.'

Binita thought that people just out for a good time would be a welcome break from people who had forgotten how to have a good time and so promptly accepted Sharron's invite.

As she pushed open the door to the packed wine bar, she was hit by the smell of bodies and booze, by loud music and equally loud shirts. Everyone there was clearly jacked up on irresponsibility, a powerful aphrodisiac. Binita hadn't been to this kind of bar, full of intensely alluring types, for ages. It was in a place like this that she'd first met Peter, a lifetime ago. She was just thinking that she might very well enjoy herself for the novelty factor alone when she saw him, sitting at the bar surrounded by a bevvy of young blondes, clearly having the time of his life. Ned.

She didn't stay long after that. Just long enough to see

Ned slide his arm around the most attractive girl's waist. Binita's blood froze. Poor Louise, poor trusting, content, loving Louise. After Peter had left Binita and the storm of tears and regret had finally subsided, two of her friends came forward and said they'd long since suspected him of having an affair; one said she'd actually seen him with the other woman. Binita had felt betrayed all over again. Why hadn't they told her? Warned her? Prepared her? Her friends had muttered something about messengers being shot. She hadn't understood at the time, but now she did. She didn't want to be the one to bring the bad news to Louise's door.

The following week Binita reluctantly agreed to a blind date with her new dentist's brother. Her reluctance was fuelled by the fact that she doubted the success of this particular path to true love – it usually led to a dead-end – but she acquiesced because every invite had to be honored. As she scampered into the restaurant and out of the rain, she bumped into Ned. This time he was with a brunette, who was throwing her head back and screaming with laughter. Binita couldn't imagine what Ned might have said that was so funny.

'Sorry,' he murmured to Binita as she wobbled with the force of their collision. 'You OK?' He flashed the most charming smile and it didn't falter even when he stared right at her. In fact, in the moment when he must have registered who it was he'd bumped into, Ned's smile broadened a fraction further. The rat. Binita was struck dumb by his audacity and watched helplessly as he hailed a taxi and drove away with his brunette.

Naturally, the blind date was unsuccessful, especially as Binita was in turmoil over Ned. Louise's husband was not just having an affair; he was a serial philanderer! Poor Louise, those poor boys. What could Binita do? After lengthy consideration, she decided that when she next spotted Ned, she'd tackle him. Make him see that his careless womanising was unacceptable. That it was in fact, a declaration of war.

She didn't have to wait long. The following Thursday, she agreed to go for a drink with a group of women from her yoga class. They selected a quiet wine bar where it was possible to hold a conversation; mellow lounge music floated past the enormous potted plants, and there was a menu of wines to savour. Binita thought it was a great find until she spotted him.

This time Ned was with a stunning redhead. It was heinous to admit they made a striking couple, yet brilliant to note that the date was clearly going badly. Ned kept looking at his watch, and the redhead seemed more interested in the menu than him. Binita slunk behind a potted plant and bided her time. After a few minutes, the redhead stood up, coolly kissed Ned on the cheek and said her goodbyes. Binita felt a jolt of delight and relief that tonight, at least, Ned hadn't got lucky. Would he now scuttle home to Louise? It wasn't a comforting thought, but what was the solution? As Ned waved for the bill, Binita seized her courage and the moment.

She stood in front of him, hands on hips. 'How could you?' she demanded.

'Sorry?' Ned had the nerve to look unperturbed.

'What do you think you are playing at? In a small town such as this, you were bound to be spotted sooner rather than later. Not that you seem to be making much of an attempt at discretion.'

'I really think that—'

Binita cut him off. She'd heard all the excuses and clichés when she and Peter split; she didn't want to listen to them again. She wouldn't allow another woman to suffer in the same way she had. So Ned was amazingly good-looking, and, considering how he'd been chatting to the blondes in Hooper's and the brunette at the restaurant, quite clearly gifted with some charm she'd evidently missed at his dinner party. Well, good looks and charm shouldn't automatically lead to infidelity. Ned didn't even have the decency to look ashamed. He appeared unconcerned, although mildly confused by Binita's outburst.

'It's the blatancy, the cruel indifference to Louise that I find most shocking.'

'Oh, you're a friend of Louise's.' Ned's face cleared.

'Ned, we met at your house. Am I that forgettable?' she demanded angrily.

'You're very memorable. And now I see you are also loyal, feisty and beautiful.' Binita was incensed. Was Ned hitting on her too now? How dare he?

'But I'm *not* Ned,' he said. 'I'm Ben, Ned's twin brother. His *single* brother,' he added with a deliciously slow smile that thumped Binita in the chest.

'Oh. I thought...' Binita faltered, embarrassed, delighted and excited all at once.

Ben's smile broadened a fraction further, 'Yes, I can imagine what you thought. Now, I wonder, would you like a drink?'

Binita accepted. After all, she had promised herself that she'd accept every invite that came her way. It would be wrong not to.

Adele Parks MBE was born in North Yorkshire. She is the author of 21 bestselling novels, including most recently, the Sunday Times and ebook number one bestseller 'Both of You'. Over four million UK editions of her work have been sold, and her books have been translated into 31 different languages. Her recent number one bestsellers 'Lies Lies Lies' and

'Just My Luck' were shortlisted for the British Book Awards and have been optioned for development for TV. Adele is an ambassador of the National Literacy Trust and the Reading Agency. She has lived in Botswana, Italy and London and is now settled in Guildford, Surrey. In 2022 Adele was awarded an MBE for services to literature. Her latest book 'One Last Secret' is released in July 2022. Find Adele on Twitter @adeleparks, Instagram @adele_parks and Facebook @OfficialAdeleParks or visit www.adeleparks.com.

THE BEACH WALK

ALEX BROWN

Claire Lucas loved this time of year. Not quite summer but warm enough to stroll on the beach at sunset with a floaty wrap draped around her shoulders as the breezy evening air cleared her thoughts for the day. Then, later as the plump sun dipped onto the horizon, smudging the sea with streaks of red and amber, she would slip off her sandals and savour the soothing sensation of the sand, soft beneath her feet. She sighed in contentment as she went through the wooden gate that led from her garden directly onto the beach. Her late husband, Tony, had loved it here too. 'Our little bit of paradise, my love,' is what he used to say as they climbed over the grassy dunes and out onto the sandy beach beyond. He'd extend a hand to her as they reached the top of the biggest hill, and then she'd tumble down and into his arms for a quick kiss, followed by a nice cup of tea from a flask as they sat side-by-side and watched the tide roll away.

Claire smiled at the tender memory as she watched the frothy waves ebb and flow, back and forth as they bubbled over the sand sparkling as if sprinkled with gold glitter. The melodic rhythm was comforting as she remembered Tony's face. His kind brown eyes - crinkly around edges from the years of gardening in all seasons. His wide smile - always with a pleasant word for everyone who met him. Reading the newspapers and doing the crossword together, listening to the radio and debating the current Archers storyline. An evening at the bingo in town with their friends, Sally and Bill. A cuddle on the sofa. His happy-go-lucky way.

They had just celebrated their thirtieth wedding anniversary when he passed away three years ago. They'd had their ups and downs like most married couples, but they had never lost sight of their deep love for one another. It was the simple, daily pleasures that she missed the most. Yes, the bingo evenings had continued, and she didn't often feel lonely now, but it wasn't the same without Tony sitting next to her with his dabber poised, ready for the 'eyes down' command from the bingo caller.

Claire walked further on along the shoreline. A young family were playing on the sand up ahead, and the sound of laughter reminded her of when her daughter, Emma, had visited last year from Australia, where she now lived with her husband and children. Her granddaughter Poppy was nearly seven years old now – didn't time fly? And baby Jack, who would be two next month, already with the same kind brown eyes as his granddad. Claire's mobile buzzed in the back pocket of her jeans, breaking her reverie.

'Ooh, hello love, I was just thinking about you,' she said on answering, 'funny how that happens, you must be telepathic.' With a broad smile on her face, Claire turned and headed up towards the grassy dunes, searching for a nice plump tuft to sit on as she caught up with Emma. It would be early morning in Australia. The children would still be fast asleep, with Emma's husband, Matthew, pottering around before heading off to the British embassy offices where he worked.

'Ah, Mum, all nice thoughts, I hope!' Emma replied, her voice bearing the hint of an Australian lilt these days.

'Of course,' Claire nodded as she sat down. 'So, tell me your news, darling. Anything exciting going on? How did you get on with the rainbow layer cake for the bake sale at school?' She crossed her fingers as baking wasn't her daughter's forte.

'Oh, it was great, Mum. That recipe you emailed was perfect – I followed it to the letter, and there wasn't a soggy bottom in sight ... just as you promised, so thank you. Everyone loved it.'

'Well, that's wonderful,' Claire replied, letting out a little sigh of relief.

'And that's not all, Mum. I have exciting news.' Emma's voice rose an octave. 'We're coming home!'

'Coming home?' Claire repeated and then held her breath, wondering if this announcement was what she hoped. When Matthew was first offered the post in Australia, Emma had been very reluctant to go. She hadn't wanted to live so far away from everyone and everything she knew, but Claire knew going to Australia was the opportunity of a lifetime, and even though she'd miss her daughter and family dearly, she hadn't felt it fair to put pressure on them to decline the offer.

'Yes, that's right, Mum, but not immediately. Matthew's office in London has asked if we could return by Christmas, so it's a bit of a way off yet, and it means we'll have to live near London when we get back, but at least we'll be in the same time zone as you,' she laughed.

'Oh, darling, I'm so delighted. That's the loveliest news I've had in ...well, since last summer when you were here,' Claire's heart swelled as she looked out over the waves, knowing her family would be back soon.

'Oh, Mum, I've loved our time here and experiencing the

Australian way of life,' Emma continued, 'But nothing beats being at home.' Claire nodded; her daughter had always been a home bird, never a fan of sleepovers like her friends were and had even gone to university in the next town, so she hadn't had to move out. Tony had driven her to lectures for the first year until Emma had passed her driving test. 'And we'll be able to visit every weekend ... that's if you're free. You might be busy ...,' Emma ventured.

'Busy? Don't be silly; you know you are all welcome any time,' Claire chuckled, but she had a feeling she knew where this was conversation was going. For the last year or so, her daughter couldn't resist playing cupid.

'I know, but wouldn't it be lovely if you had a boyfriend?' Emma teased, and Claire shook her head gently and laughed. 'For evenings out, meals, day trips and such like,' Emma said, seeming to have it all figured out.

'It's a lovely idea, darling, and I do go out, you know. I'm not lonely, so you really mustn't worry about me.' Claire tried to sound upbeat, but if the truth be told, there were occasions when a companion would be nice. A friend to accompany her to the weekly bingo sessions would be wonderful.

'You should give online dating a go, Mum; it's what everyone does these days,' Emma suggested.

'Hmm, it's not really my thing, sweetheart. Anyway, I'm fine,' Claire quickly added, fiddling with the trim of her wrap. It felt a bit strange chatting to her grown-up daughter about dating. Of course, they'd had many chats about boys back when Emma was of that age ... a teenager and then a twenty-something, all giddy in the first throes of romance. But still, Claire was a mature woman now, and she hadn't heard any of her fellow widows talking about online dating at the lunch club she sometimes went to.

'I know you're fine, but it would be lovely if you had a

nice gentleman friend? A companion. And Dad wouldn't mind. He'd want you to be happy.' Claire smiled at her daughter's enthusiasm. She'd always had a persuasive way about her. As a little girl she'd had her father wrapped around her finger, but that had been his own fault, really. Tony had doted on Emma, adored her from the moment she was born, with her soft downy hair and delicious new baby smell of talcum powder and wonder.

'But darling, I'm happy enough.'

'Well, yes, but ... happier, is what I meant. And I could set you up with an online dating agency from here. We'll pick a lovely picture of you to share, and any man would be very lucky indeed to enjoy your company. That's what Dad used to say!'

'We'll see. For now, I'm just so happy to know that you're all going to be coming home soon. I imagine Poppy and Jack are quite grown up these days.' Claire waved at the man she often saw around this time in the evening, walking his dog on the sand near the water's edge. He reciprocated by waving the dog's bright orange ball thrower in her direction.

'They sure are, Mum. I'll email some more photos to you when we come off the phone. But in six months, you'll be able to see the children whenever you like.'

'I can't wait, sweetheart.'

'Me too. Ooh, I can hear Jack calling; I had better go. I'll call you at the weekend, and we can choose a picture for your dating profile!' Claire began to protest, but her daughter had ended the call before she had a chance.

Standing up, Claire brushed the sand from her jeans and sauntered down towards the sea. The tide had gone out, leaving a long stretch of shiny wet sand in its wake. It was such a gloriously warm evening that she felt it a shame to leave the beach just yet, so she unbuckled her sandals and dangled them by the straps as she walked, pondering on

Emma's news, thrilled that her family would be coming home soon.

Claire had been walking and enjoying her thoughts for a little while when a very wet chocolate Labrador came bounding towards her, its tail wagging jauntily in the air.

'Hello, you,' she said as the Labrador got nearer. 'Did you enjoy your swim?' As she went to stroke the dog's ear, it did an almighty wriggle, spraying Claire with sea-water. She laughed as she instinctively put her hands out to protect her clothes from the impromptu shower.

'Are you OK?' a male voice called out behind her. Claire quickly pivoted to see the man she often waved at hurrying across the sand towards her and the dog.

'Oh yes, I'm fine, thanks. No harm done,' she smiled, shaking the excess water from her wrap before swinging it back around her shoulders.

'I'm so sorry; he doesn't usually do this.' The man reached down and retrieved her sandals from where Claire had dropped them. He shook his head in exasperation and gave the dog a withering look.

'Thank you,' she said, taking the sandals. 'How old is he?'

'He's nearly two, so really should know better by now. I'm Jonathan, by the way.' And he held out his hand to Claire. 'I've often seen you strolling on our wonderful beach.'

'Yes, I live in one of the beach houses.'

'Ah, which one? I'm on the end nearest the sailing club,' and he pointed towards it.

'The white weatherboard house at the other end,' Claire smiled, turning to him as they walked on.

'The one with the beautiful garden. I've often admired it on my way past.'

'My husband was a keen gardener. He passed away a few years ago now.'

'I'm sorry to hear that. I lost my wife two and half years ago.' Jonathan lifted the ball thrower high in the air to catapult the ball across the sand. They laughed as the Labrador hurtled after it.

'He's a lovely dog,' said Claire.

'Yes, he was a gift from my son ... a great companion, he told me. A good reason to get out of the house. He worries about me getting lonely, you see.' Jonathan laughed.

Ah, yes, my daughter worries about me too,' Claire smiled. 'What's your dog's name?'

'Bingo! My wife and I used to enjoy a game together....'

Alex Brown is the bestselling author of thirteen books including 'A Postcard from Paris' and the 'Bridget's Bicycle Bakery' series. She lives by the sea on the south coast of England with her family and two glossy black Labradors. When she isn't writing, she can be found walking on the beach, binge-watching a boxset or enjoying a French martini cocktail. She loves chatting to her readers on social media @alexbrownbooks

POCKETS

AMANDA JENNINGS

Emma North would describe herself - if anybody were to ask her - as an unremarkable person. In the primary school nativity she was unnamed, third from the left, obscured from view by a patchily-painted newspaper palm tree. She never won a school prize, not even one for progress. She wasn't on the party lists of the pretty girls and cocksure boys. She didn't meet her tribe at university, where she never missed a lecture or fell behind in her work or raised her hand to ask a question. In three years, she didn't do anything wild. There were no stories to regale her grandchildren with, innocent eyes wide with vicarious thrill, drinking in her tales. Not that grandchildren were on the cards. First, she would need children for that to happen. And for children, she'd need a partner, and Emma had discovered those were elusive. Of course, there had been dates; she wasn't unattractive. A couple of dates had resulted in a second, and there had even been a boyfriend. His name was David and Emma met him shortly after leaving university. He hadn't stolen her breath. In fact, if he hadn't been so persuasive, she most probably wouldn't have given him a second thought. Emma always expected to fall in love with someone warm and sunny and with a generous personality. Someone who smiled easily, who would take her hand and stroll. No, David wasn't a man to stroll. He walked from place to place with purpose, and if he ever had cause to smile, it seemed unnatural, as if his features had adopted the required shape of a smile under duress. Everything about David was serious. He wore dark-coloured turtleneck sweaters and neatly pressed corduroy trousers, an inch too short to reveal grey-ribbed socks, the type one might find on a school uniform list, described as 'regulation'. But he was nice-looking and fastidiously clean and asked permission to kiss her. Though the request took Emma aback, she gave it nonetheless and the resulting engagement - though perfunctory and lacking in fireworks - wasn't wholly unpleasant. When he then asked her out for dinner, she agreed. They talked about books, well, the ones he enjoyed; he made it clear her love of fantasy books was far from ideal. She could still recall with startling clarity the look of horror on his face when she admitted she'd never read Voltaire. David told her in great detail about the cities and sights he'd visited around Europe, and she found herself wondering if - despite the lack of attraction - David might lead her one step closer to a slightly more remarkable life. So she accepted his invitation to 'come up for coffee' and when he politely asked if he might 'touch down there', she didn't say no. David and Emma were together for thirteen months and twenty-six days. In that time, he didn't once suggest a trip to Paris or Rome or Reykjavik. When he finished with her, he told her by text.

I've met someone else. Granted, she isn't as pretty as you, but I think she's more 'me'. She has more substance to her. My mother always said, 'sometimes you must trust in fate'. Sorry about the text, but I'm no good with girls crying.

Emma had no idea what to write back, so sent a 'thumbs

up' emoji instead then went to bed even though it was only five in the afternoon. That was the last she ever heard of David. Ten years on and she hadn't found another boyfriend. It was as if that part of her had shut down.

Was she unhappy? It was a question she often asked herself, usually while inputting data at work or resting her head against the bus window on the commute home as the world on the other side of the glass rushed by without her. No, she wasn't unhappy. Just rather unremarkable.

As her thirty-fifth birthday approached, her friend Imogen asked what she wanted to do to celebrate.

'Celebrate?'

Imogen laughed. 'Yes, celebrate. It's what people do? They celebrate birthdays.'

But Emma couldn't think of anything she'd rather do less. Birthdays were an annual reminder that time was marching on without her. She pictured herself as a two-dimensional drawing in a dusty colouring book, a black and white outline that had never been filled in.

'You need to grab life,' Imogen said. It was something she said often.

'I'm not sure I know how to.'

'Well, first of all you need to kick that devil off your shoulder. Stop listening to him. Take some chances. Second, you need to stop worrying about being single. It's the twenty-first century. Nobody needs a man to be happy.'

'And what would Anthony say to that?'

Imogen groaned. 'Sometimes, I wonder if I'd be better off without him.' But then she smiled, her mind drifting, Emma suspected, to Anthony.

'Anyway,' said Imogen, jolting back into the here and now, 'What you need, Emma North, is a makeover. Not for any man but for you. When did you last shop for clothes or get a haircut?'

So on Emma's birthday, Imogen planned a day out. They ate lunch and got their nails done. Emma selected a bottle of nude pink nail polish, but Imogen laughed and swapped it for fuchsia. Afterwards, they went to a vintage clothes shop Imogen loved. As they walked through the door, the musty smell of old stories hit the back of Emma's throat. There were rails of clothes - dresses, shirts, trousers, skirts - hanging patiently waiting to be rehomed. Emma ran her fingers along them, wondering what tales they could tell.

'Wouldn't it be good if you could try something on and be transported to the life of the previous owner?'

Imogen laughed and shook her head. 'You're funny,' she said. Then she grabbed a dress and held it up. 'What about this?'

It was lightweight and floaty, with orange and yellow flowers decorating a scarlet background, a fitted waist and scooped neckline.

'That wouldn't suit me,' Emma said, her eyes floating over to the greyscale knitwear she felt probably did.

'Who cares?' Imogen smiled. 'It has pockets!' She pushed the dress into Emma's hands. 'Try it on. For me?'

Emma went to the changing area at the back of the shop, which consisted of nothing more than a rudimentary curtain to give the illusion of privacy, and a small mirror hanging from a nail on the wall. The dress fitted like Cinderella's slipper. Emma pulled back the curtain and did a twirl for Imogen.

'Stunning,' her friend said. 'It really is. You look amazing. And, pockets!'

Emma smiled and slid her hands into both pockets. She felt something. A slip of paper. She pulled it out expecting a dry-cleaning ticket or an old receipt, but when she looked down, she saw a piece of paper torn from a notepad. On it was written, in very neat handwriting, a telephone number and a name.

Alan Fisher.

Emma was about to screw it up when Imogen grabbed her hand. 'Emma, no! You've got to call it.'

Emma furrowed her brow. 'Whatever for?'

'Because what if it's fate?'

Emma laughed. 'You think Prince Alan is the man of my dreams?'

Imogen's eyes twinkled. 'You never know.'

'What happened to me not needing a man?'

Imogen shrugged. 'You never know,' she repeated.

On the way home, Emma clutched the dress in its carrier bag to her chest and rested her chin on her arms.

Fate.

From nowhere, she heard David's mother's voice - a woman she hadn't ever met – in her head: 'Sometimes you must trust in fate.'

Back at her flat, Emma sat on her sofa and stared at the number in her hand. She dialled a couple of times, but each time hung up before the call connected. She tried once more but threw the phone down on the sofa in frustration, then collapsed her head backwards and swore. But then something seemed to take hold of her. A calm resolve.

Grab life.

She retrieved the phone and dialled.

'Hello?' The voice was that of an elderly man. Emma wasn't sure which emotion took charge: relief or disappointment. 'Who's this?' he asked quietly.

Rather than hang up, Emma told him.

'And you found my number in the pocket of a dress?'

Alan didn't know anything about the dress or how his number might have ended up in its pocket, or who might have owned the dress before it found its way into the vintage clothes shop.

'I'm a piano tuner by trade. Perhaps someone gave her my number?'

'Yes, perhaps. I'm sorry to bother you.'

'It's no bother. Your friendly voice has cheered me up.'

Emma paused.

'Alan?'

'Yes?'

'Do you believe in fate?'

'I don't know about fate, but I know it's a lovely evening, it's your birthday, and you have a nice new dress. So why not go for a walk and enjoy it?'

So that's what Emma did. She put on her dress and went out. It was a beautiful, summery late afternoon. The streets buzzed with people leaving work. The air felt warm and optimistic, and as she walked, she felt a little bit of colour seeping into her outline. She smiled and slipped her hands into the pockets of her dress, pushed her shoulders back and tipped her chin a fraction higher. She passed a cafe and decided to buy herself some cake. It was her birthday, after all.

She pulled open the door and walked up to the counter. There was a man already standing there. When she drew up beside him, he smiled.

'You order first,' he said. 'I can't make up my mind.'

Emma did a double take. There was something about him, a softness in his eyes and an ease about his smile. It was as if he'd been born smiling.

'A slice of carrot cake,' she said to the woman behind the counter.

'That sounds nice,' the man said.

Emma glanced at him with a shy smile. 'It's my birthday.'

'Happy birthday,' he said. 'By the way, I love your dress.'

'Oh, thank you. It has pockets!' She immediately felt ridiculous. Why had she said that? Her cheeks flushed with heat, and she dropped her eyes to the floor. As she did, she noticed his trousers fell to the perfect length. She lifted her head. 'This might sound weird, but would you like to join me for a slice of cake?'

His face broke into a wide smile. 'Actually, I'd love that. You know, I nearly didn't come out for a stroll tonight. But now I'm very glad I did.'

Amanda Jennings has written six psychological dramas and numerous short stories, published both in the UK and abroad. Her latest, 'The Haven' is set in the wilds of Bodmin Moor where a group of friends move to an off-grid farm and discover utopia isn't quite as they'd hoped. *The Financial Times* called it 'hypnotic', while Lisa Jewell said it has a 'spine-tingling ending that will take your breath away'. Amanda and her husband have three daughters and live in Oxfordshire with a menagerie of animals.

A DAY OUT

BERNICE BLOOM

Margaret was a solidly built woman with wild hair piled messily on top of her head, so it resembled nothing so much as a birds' nest.

'You must both be quite mad to want to spend your Sunday here,' she said, opening the big wooden door and ushering us inside. 'Really - quite mad.'

We followed Margaret into the reception area and down the wide corridor through the centre of the home, practically running to keep up with her giant strides in her sensible shoes. A strong smell of overcooked vegetables and disinfectant hung in the hallways. I imagine that every old peoples' home, in every part of the world, smells the same.

'We could be in the pub now,' whispered Susan. 'In the pub, flirting with Jack Sheridan. Remind me why we're here again?'

'Sshh... you know exactly why we're here,' I said. 'To help out.'

Margaret swung open the door to reveal a room dominated by a big old-fashioned television. The room was so sweltering I felt that my face might melt.

'Just let me know if it's too cold for you,' joked Margaret, as I am sure she had many times, before delivering a snorting laugh and walking to the front of the room.

'Ladies,' she said, clapping her hands and raising her voice to be heard over the television. 'The King and I' was playing at a volume more commonly associated with rock concerts.

'Come on, chop-chop, Mary and Susan. Come to the front.'

We rushed into the room, which looked like it had been beamed down from the 1940s. Half a dozen old ladies were sitting staring at us. A lady with a tight, grey perm raised her hand. 'It's not more wartime singing, is it? Can't we just watch Yul Brynner?'

Susan tugged at my sleeve.

'I told you we should have gone to the pub,' she whispered. 'Jack Sheridan's going today. He hasn't been down for ages.'

Jack is a guy I've fancied forever. He's gorgeous. He used to join us all in the pub every Sunday to watch the football but hasn't been down for months.

I looked out at the old ladies in front of me.

'Would any of you like to play any games or anything?' I asked.

'Can we go for a trip?' asked a lady in brown tights and slippers (actually, that does nothing to identify the speaker - all the ladies had brown tights and slippers).

'Yes,' I said. 'Of course. We can take you for a trip.'

'Come on Gladys,' said the brown tights lady. 'Let's go to *you-know-where*. I'll ring *you-know-who* to come and meet us.'

'Is there one on today though, Ethel?' said tight grey perm lady, who I assumed was Gladys. She had the voice and size of a little bird. In fact, all the women in the room were small. Are all older people small? Have you ever seen a fat old person?

'Gladys and I would like to go out please,' said the one called Ethel.

Then she turned to the called Gladys: 'If we don't go, we won't know.'

I had no idea what they were talking about, but I figured taking them out somewhere would be better than staying in this hot, oppressive room.

'Oh dear,' said Margaret. 'I'm afraid you've drawn the short straw here. We're giving you Ethel and Gladys to look after for the afternoon. Best of luck. They can be quite a handful.'

Susan glared at me as if this were all my fault. Which, of course, it was. I'd had this bright idea of 'giving something back' to the community after seeing the heart-wrenching footage of people in Ukraine carrying all their worldly possessions as they walked towards safety. I wanted to help. I gave some money and donated some clothes, but I still felt I could do more, so in a wild moment of eagerness to help mankind, I offered to come to the old people's home and help for the afternoon. When I told Margaret I was a teacher and Susan used to be a nurse, she welcomed us with open arms.

'We'll get Gladys and Ethel ready, and they'll meet you in reception,' said Margaret, guiding the two women away to their rooms.

'Check your texts,' said Susan while we waited. 'Look, Claire has sent a message, it says: 'Jack's here and he's single'.'

'Just forget about Jack,' I said, but I'll be honest, it felt like a kick to the guts that he was single, and I wasn't there. Before Susan could say any more, we were distracted by a small commotion. Margaret's angry voice called out: 'You can't wear those tights.'

'I'll wear what I like,' came the reply, as Gladys and Ethel shuffled into view.

They were dressed in their finest clothing as if they were going to ladies' day at Ascot. Ethel wore a red dress and a straw bonnet with a big flower stuck inelegantly to the side. The offending tights were fishnets, and she wore a fox fur stole, a pearl necklace, and so much red lipstick that it covered most of the lower half of her face.

'I think you look lovely,' I said.

Ethel was marginally more demure in a purple dress and matching jacket. She too favoured elaborate headwear - a bright blue beret on the side of her head and a chunky gold necklace. Her shoes looked like they had been a gift to mark the end of the first world war. Both of them carried small bunches of flowers.

'Where would you like to go?' I asked although I was slightly dreading hearing the answer after all their talk of going '*you know where*'. I feared they might want to go drinking or gambling.

'The crematorium, please driver,' said Gladys.

'Ahh, of course. You want to lay your flowers. I completely understand. That's no problem at all.'

Gladys and Ethel exchanged conspiratorial glances as I guided them towards my car. What on earth were they up to?

As we pulled into the crematorium, there was great excitement in the back of the car. Gladys was the first to comment. 'Oooh,' she said, gazing up at the smoke as it billowed out of the chimneys. 'Look...there's a crem taking place.'

Ethel was excited too. She craned her neck to look out of

the window and gasped in awe and wonder. There were smiles and nudges. 'I love a good crem,' said Gladys.

'Wonder who it is?' said Ethel, squinting to focus, as if the clue to the deceased's identity would be hidden in the smoke trailing through the sky.

'We'll work it out,' Gladys said, as she pressed random buttons on the car door to open the window. Clearly, we had to smell the smoke as well as see it.

'Mourners!' shrieked Ethel, and both of them sat bolt upright like Marines on parade. These same old women who had shuffled along in the home were now displaying the speed and flexibility of greyhounds.

'We need to know whether it's a man or woman who has died,' said Ethel, taking a comb from her bag and running it through the front of her hair, teasing the grey curls upward. 'We need to know whether we are dealing with a widow or widower.'

'What?' said Susan, the penny dropping. 'You come here to flirt with men whose wives have just died?'

'Yes. This is what dating looks like when you're the wrong side of 85,' said Gladys.

'We've met lots of nice men by coming here and going to wakes, haven't we, Ethel?'

'Oooh, yes. We've met some lovely people. Remember Donald, who had his own teeth? He was very handsome. Can we get out of the car now?'

'Sure,' I sighed, accompanying them to the small chapel on the site. I noticed how they offered condolences to every man they passed, completely ignoring the women. When they reached the chapel door, Ethel saw the deceased's name: Robert Eves. A man. This was instantly disappointing to the lovelorn octogenarians. 'There are too many women mourners,' said Gladys, shaking her head. So, unable to gate-crash a wake, Ethel and Gladys had to content themselves with walking around the crematorium, laying flowers for everyone they knew.

'I wish I knew as many people alive as I know dead,' said Ethel, without a hint of sadness.

'Well, at least you know them dead,' replied Gladys, taking Ethel's hand and leading her through to the rose garden for a sit-down.

'You know that Ethel's meeting someone here, don't you?' said Gladys. 'It's her young fancy man.'

Oh, Good Lord above, no.

'You haven't really arranged to meet anyone here, have you?' I said. 'I'll get in such trouble, Ethel.'

'She always meets her fancy man here.'

I looked over at Ethel's face as she smiled at her friend. She was still an attractive woman. The years had taken the smoothness of her cheeks away, but her lovely bone structure and smiling eyes remained. Despite the garish clip-on earrings and liberally applied face powder, she had a quiet dignity.

I tried to relax; after all, it hadn't been a bad afternoon at all, in the end. Quite amusing, in many ways - I hoped that I would be sneaking off to meet men when I was in my ninth decade. And this rose garden was lovely. I mean, there was a general feeling of sadness and loss about the place, but also peace and well-being. And though I probably would rather have been sharing a packet of crisps with Jack Sheridan, I had done a good thing today, and there weren't many days when I could say that.

'Here he is...' said Ethel, and I braced myself for the arrival of her 'toy boy'. It was going to take some explaining back at the home.

I looked up and saw a young man walking towards us. Ethel and Gladys waved at him like lunatics. As he got closer, I realised I recognised him.

‘Jack?’ I said, ‘Is that you?’

‘Mary? My goodness, what are you doing here?’

‘This lovely lady took me out for the day,’ said Ethel.

Jack smiled at me with such warmth that I felt my stomach turn over with excitement.

‘Thank you for doing that,’ he said. ‘I usually come every Sunday to see grandma, but the guys have been giving me so much abuse about not going to the pub to watch the football that I went along for the first half today.’

I glanced at Susan, who was open-mouthed at the arrival of Sexy Sheridan. This truly was a delicious turn of events. Jack kissed Ethel on the cheek and gave her a warm hug.

‘Well, I didn’t need you today,’ Ethel said. ‘This young lady looked after me very well. She's a lovely girl.’

We sat there for a while, all five of us snuggled up on the bench, enjoying the tranquillity of the moment, only spoiled when Jack produced Ethel’s favourite toffees, which led to both Ethel and Gladys losing their false teeth. There was a clatter on the floor, followed by another clatter before Jack manfully crawled under the bench to retrieve them. Ethel wiped her teeth on her purple jacket before putting them straight back into her mouth. Gladys did the same. Then there was a chorus of clicking and clacking from the mouths of the two women, a little bit of sucking, then more clicking.

‘What are you doing?’ asked Jack.

‘I think I’ve got the wrong ones,’ said Ethel. ‘Either that or my mouth's just got bigger.’

‘Aw wour teef wav wot schmaller,’ said Ethel helpfully. ‘Mine vont vit eiver.’

‘We’ve definitely got the wrong ones,’ said Gladys, removing hers. Then, without flinching, she handed over the teeth to Ethel, and Ethel clicked them in and handed hers to Gladys.

‘All good now,’ they said.

'When we're old, we will never be sharing teeth,' muttered Susan. 'However much I like you, I'm not sharing your teeth.'

'Absolutely fine by me,' I replied.

'How about me?' asked Jack. 'Will you lend me yours if I lose mine?'

'I'll think about it,' I said, feeling myself turn plum red with embarrassment.

Then my alarm rang to indicate that it was 4.50 pm, the sound made us all jump, so quiet and serene was this lovely little garden. 'Sorry, I'm supposed to get them back by 5 pm,' I said to Jack. 'I set my alarm so we wouldn't be late.'

'Yes, they like them back for their tea at 5.30 pm,' he said. 'I'll take Ethel if you want to take Gladys?'

So, we took one woman each and drove them back to the home. We met up in the reception area.

'Thank you, you lovely girl,' said Ethel, hugging me with surprising strength for such a tiny woman. 'I think you'd make a lovely girlfriend for my Jack.'

With that, she winked and ambled down the corridor, arm linked with her friend.

'I think she's right,' said Jack. 'Fancy heading to the pub to see whether the guys are still there? Perhaps we could go to dinner afterwards? Just the two of us.'

'I'd love to,' I said.

Bernice Bloom writes funny romance and mystery novels, most notably the 'Adorable Fat Girl' series which follows Mary Brown as she goes on safari, on a cruise and immerses herself in online dating. The stories will resonate with anyone who has ever tried a fad diet or taken an ambitiously small garment into a changing room and become completely stuck. You can find Bernice at www.bernicebloom.com, https://www.facebook.com/BerniceBloombooks or @bernice1bloom

LOVE IN THE AIR AT THE APPLEBY FARM VINTAGE TEA ROOMS

CATHY BRAMLEY

'There, all clean again,' I said to Elsa, my red setter puppy, drying her paws with a towel. 'Now, please try to keep out of muddy puddles for at least an hour.'

I threw her favourite teddy for her, and she gave a yelp of joy and bounced after it, her gangly little legs flying in all directions on the kitchen floor.

The farmhouse kitchen was warm and cosy, Christmas songs played non-stop on the radio, and the fire at the other end of the room gave a comforting crackle and hiss every so often. I missed Auntie Sue and Uncle Arthur since they'd moved away from the farm into a spanking new bungalow. But if I closed my eyes, I could still picture them: Uncle Arthur's tufts of grey hair just visible over the back of the chair; Auntie Sue pulling trays of scones out of the Aga.

I sighed and picked up my mug of tea, pulling the diary towards me. It had been such a busy few days in the run-up to my friend Tilly's wedding, and I'd hardly had time to catch my breath, what with the tea rooms being so busy now that the schools had broken up for Christmas.

The Appleby Farm Vintage Tea Rooms were closed now

until after the wedding, and the staff were having a break, but in two days, it would be all hands to the pump to get the tea rooms ready for the wedding breakfast.

Today I'd spend the day catching up with a few odd jobs, and a couple was coming to view the farm as a possible venue for their wedding next autumn.

The phone rang, distracting me from my mental to-do list.

'Freya, love?' Uncle Arthur croaked. 'Can you hear me?'

My heart clenched, and I clutched the phone to my ear. 'Yes, but you sound awful; what's happened?'

'Nothing.' He gave a wheezy chuckle. 'But you know what your auntie's like: ears like a bat. I have to whisper.'

I exhaled with relief. 'Why?'

'It's our anniversary tomorrow – can I book a table at the tea rooms? That nice one in front of the window?'

I frowned. 'Anniversary? I thought you were married in the summer.'

'Yes, but we met in December, fifty-seven years ago tomorrow. This year will be the first time we haven't celebrated it on the farm.' I detected a tremor in his voice and felt my lip wobble. Fifty-seven years together, and they loved each other as much now as they did then.

'Of course,' I said, even though the tea rooms were technically closed.

'And can you make that tea loaf that she likes?'

My heart sank: the fruit had to be soaked in tea overnight, and the loaf took ages to make and cool.

'Not scones?' I suggested hopefully.

'Oh yes, scones too, you are a good girl.'

I agreed a time with him and rang off before I offered to make cream horns and a Victoria sponge, too.

. . .

At two o clock the following day, Appleby Farm Vintage Tea Rooms was ready for its VIP guests. Auntie Sue's favourite crooner, Nat King Cole, was singing softly in the background, the log burner was giving off a gentle glow, and I'd lit vanilla candles and dotted them around the room. And right on cue, Uncle Arthur and Auntie Sue appeared in the farmyard in their new little hatchback.

It took them a minute or two to park, but soon the elderly pair was crossing the courtyard, and my heart squeezed with love for them. Uncle Arthur appeared to be as proud as punch to have Auntie Sue on his arm. He looked very smart, too, in his jacket and tie, and she looked radiant in a royal blue coat that set off the colour of her eyes.

'Freya!' called Auntie Sue with a wave. 'Isn't this a lovely surprise?'

Uncle Arthur beamed and gave me a wink.

'Happy anniversary!' I yelled and then quickly dived after Elsa, who'd squeezed through my legs.

She was such a good little puppy normally and happy to stay in her basket in front of the Aga, but she'd been a bit clingy since her jab earlier that morning, and I hadn't the heart to leave her crying in the kitchen on her own.

I tucked Elsa under my arm and kissed them both, ushering them to Uncle Arthur's favourite table.

'Oh, Artie,' said Sue, her eyes looking moist as she took in the flowers on the table and the cake stand heaped with afternoon tea. 'You didn't have to go to so much trouble.'

He patted her hand. 'Nothing's too much trouble for my girl.'

I suppressed a smile as I set the teapot in front of them; all he'd done was make a quick phonecall, whereas I'd been baking all morning. Not that I minded really, I'd do anything for those two.

The sound of a second car crunching into the courtyard made us all look up.

'It's Eddy,' I said brightly. 'He's brought the couple who've come to view the tea rooms. Tuck in while I go to meet them.'

An hour ago, when Eddy the farmhand was having lunch in the kitchen, and I was putting the scones in the oven, I'd had a rather fraught phonecall from the bride-to-be.

This had been their second call. The first was from her fiancé, Josh, to say that they'd missed their train and would be late. They weren't having the easiest of journeys, by the sound of it.

'We've finally arrived, and we're at the station, but there are no taxis,' Milly, his girlfriend, said indignantly. 'Nothing. The place is deserted, and we've had to walk miles just to get a phone signal.'

So, Eddy had been despatched to collect them in the old Land Rover, but my heart had plummeted at Milly's clipped tone. Experience told me that once a bridal couple got themselves into a negative frame of mind, it was difficult to prise them out of it. Earlier in the year, we'd had an unfortunate incident with one such pair who'd timed their visit to coincide with Eddy spraying slurry over one of the fields nearest to the yard.

'I'm sorry,' the young man had said, holding his nose as he whisked his fiancé back into the car. 'But that's something I can never unsmell.'

I left the elderly lovebirds to it, with Elsa sitting hopefully under the table, and went to greet the new arrivals. Josh was in the front, staring out of the side window. Eddy's dog, Buddy, was on his knee, probably panting his hot meaty breath into poor Josh's face, so I didn't blame him for keeping his head turned away. Milly, in the back, looked equally stony-faced, and Eddy rolled his eyes at me dramatically as he got out of the car. He whistled to Buddy, who jumped down from Josh's lap, and the two of them headed off to the cattle shed.

'Welcome to Appleby Farm,' I cried, flinging my arms wide.

I plastered on a huge smile as Milly and Josh stepped onto the cobbled yard. They were in their late twenties and had dressed for the country in the way that city people always did: immaculately clean wellies, quilted jackets, and designer checked scarves. Josh attempted to put his arms around Milly's shoulders as they crossed the yard, but she ducked away and folded her arms defensively.

I sighed inwardly as I hurried forward to greet them and shook their hands.

'Now, I usually start with a trip across to see the shepherd's huts where you'll be spending your wedding night,' I began.

Milly shook her head and raised her hand firmly. 'The buffet car was closed; we're famished. We'd prefer lunch in the café first.'

'Oh, yes,' said Josh, pressing a hand to his stomach. 'Perhaps some of that soup and homemade bread I saw on your website.'

I swallowed. 'Ah. This is awkward; the café is actually closed.'

Milly pursed her lips and folded her arms again. 'There are people in it.'

Josh shot me a pleading look.

'Yes, well,' I stammered. 'Of course, follow me; I'll see what I can do.'

I led the way, my heart sinking further with every step. I might as well admit defeat – there was no way they'd be booking their wedding reception here. And frankly, as I glanced at the lovely stone farmhouse with its curl of smoke disappearing into a china blue sky, they didn't deserve it anyway.

'Ooh, look out,' Milly shrieked, grabbing Josh's sleeve as Kim, the Jersey calf, came careering into the yard in front of us.

'Grab her, lass,' Eddy yelled in his gravelly voice, stumbling along several paces behind the errant animal.

I lunged at the calf, managing to catch hold of her head-collar. She'd grown so much since she'd been born at Easter; it was all I could do to steady her.

'OK, Kim,' I soothed, handing her over to Eddy with relief.

'That frightened the life out of me,' gasped Milly, looking over her shoulder for more potential attacks by wild animals.

'Lovely beast,' said Josh, doing his best to look manly. He stepped forward and patted the calf's rump, just as Kim lifted her tail and produced a steaming poop which splashed across his new wellies.

'Oh my lord.' Milly wrinkled her nose and took a step away from her fiancé, just as Uncle Arthur appeared in the doorway of the café.

'Well held, Freya, I'll make a farmer of you yet,' he laughed and then beckoned Milly and Josh in. 'Don't stand on ceremony; come on in.'

I helped Josh out of his wellies while Milly removed her coat and Auntie Sue bustled off to refill the teapot.

'Oh, this is gorgeous,' said Milly, her face softening for the first time. 'Josh, look at these lovely old beams.'

Josh muttered something under his breath that sounded a bit like 'hallelujah'. I caught his eye, and we shared a tentative smile. It sounded like she might be thawing a bit.

'The photos on the website don't do it justice,' Josh said, straightening up. 'This is even better than I imagined.'

'Thanks.' I gulped. Hopefully, he'd still say that when I presented him with a makeshift lunch from yesterday's leftovers.

Elsa, who couldn't be more adorable if she tried, scampered up to Milly and offered her a paw.

'Well hello, little one.' Milly bent down, shook Elsa's paw, and then scooped her up, pressing her face into her fur.

'I don't normally allow her in here,' I said hastily, 'but she's been to the vets was feeling under the weather.'

'Oh, I don't mind.' Milly clasped Elsa to her tightly as if scared I would whisk her away.

Josh put his arm around Milly. 'We'd love a dog, but we live in a flat in London.'

'Come and join us; we've got plenty of cake,' Auntie Sue cried, placing a fresh pot of tea on their table. 'And tell us all about your wedding plans.'

Uncle Arthur pulled up two more chairs; I set plates and cutlery out for them while Milly and Josh told us all about their ideas for a rustic wedding.

'And where are you staying tonight?' Uncle Arthur asked, dotting more strawberry jam onto his scone.

'A tiny B&B in Cartmel.' Josh cringed, glancing at Milly. 'Made a bit of a schoolboy error there and booked a single room by mistake.'

'Oh, yes,' Uncle Arthur winked at him. 'I made the same mistake myself on our honeymoon.'

He cupped a hand to his mouth and whispered loudly, 'Accidentally on purpose.'

Auntie Sue's mouth dropped open. 'You did that on purpose? I should have known. And it's taken you fifty-six years to own up!'

Uncle Arthur laughed so hard he made himself cough,

and by the time Josh had banged him on the back, we were all laughing along with him. I noticed Milly edge her chair closer to Josh so that their arms and thighs were pressed together.

'You should have seen Sue's face when she came out of the bathroom in her long nightie, and I was already taking up all the bed.'

'Oh, Arthur Moorcroft!' Auntie Sue pressed a hand to her pink cheeks, but her eyes were sparkling at the memory.

'She got in the wrong end at first; I thought she was perhaps one of those funny foot fetish people.'

Auntie Sue chuckled. 'I came from a big family; I had to go toe-to-toe with my sister growing up.'

'Anyway, we soon sorted out what went where,' said Arthur gruffly, squeezing her hand. 'And we've been happily married ever since. We fit together like two spoons.'

'Two spoons,' murmured Milly gazing into Josh's pale grey eyes. 'How romantic.'

Elsa had curled herself up into a ball and was fast asleep on Milly's knee. She stroked the little dog's silky ear and caught my eye.

'I suppose I'd better show you around the rest of the farm?' I asked.

'No rush,' Milly smiled. She took Josh's hand and gave him such a look of love that I felt a lump forming in my throat. 'Besides, I think we've seen all we need to see, haven't we?'

Josh nodded. 'Yes, this is definitely the place for our wedding.'

Milly gave a small sigh and leaned her head on her fiancé's shoulder. 'I don't know what it is about this place,' she said. 'It's almost as if there's something special in the air.'

'There certainly is,' said Uncle Arthur shuffling his chair closer to his wife's so he could press a kiss to her cheek.

'Oh, yes, for as long as we've been at Appleby Farm, and probably a hundred years before that,' Auntie Sue reached for his hand. She squeezed it three times: their secret signal, meaning I love you. 'There's always been love in the air.'

Cathy Bramley is the author of best-selling romantic comedies including 'Ivy Lane', 'Appleby Farm', 'Conditional Love', 'Wickham Hall' and 'The Plumberry School Of Comfort Food'. Her latest book is the Sunday Times bestseller 'The Summer That Changed Us'. She lives in a small Nottinghamshire village with her family and Pearl the Cockerpoo. Her recent career as a full-time writer of light-hearted romantic fiction has come as somewhat of a lovely surprise after spending eighteen years running her own marketing agency. However, she has always been an avid reader, hiding her book under the duvet and reading by torchlight.

LAST YEAR

CESCA MAJOR

Last year you'd groaned and dragged yourself unwillingly out of bed - another cold winter day, off to make an instant coffee and de-ice the car. You'd left the room, didn't want to disturb me, walked blearily down the stairs to begin your routine.

Then you passed the window in the hall - yelped in surprise, ran back up the stairs and startled me into sitting up. You were jabbering, and I was groggy, not understanding. Then you crossed the room and opened the curtains with a flourish, exposing the view beyond.

I craned to look.

The whole world had turned white overnight. A crisp, clean layer of snow had found its way into every nook and cranny. It had spilt over gutters, piled high on fences and gates, disguising everyday objects. I joined you at the window, and you put an arm around me, pulling me close, both still warm from our bed.

Our little village was tucked in between two hills and was now cut off from the rest of the world. We made a vague effort to get into work, pushing snow off the car and successfully turning the engine over, but, as the wheels turned fruitlessly on the ice, it was obvious we were going nowhere. You had called work on your mobile phone and explained the situation. They were resigned to the fact that half their workforce was stranded in nearby villages. They'd told you to take the day off and try the next day. I'd done the same. We were both smiling as we hung up. Even the lack of electricity didn't dampen our mood. You were humming as you lit the fire, heating water in a saucepan for some tea, your face aglow with boyish enthusiasm. We toasted hot cross buns over the flames.

We dusted down the sledge from the loft and crunched up the slope of a nearby field, laughing as we got speed up. I took a camera and snapped dozens of shots of you, of running children who had the same idea, of dogs burrowing into the snow, white flakes clinging to their fur. More pictures: of trees, their branches weighed down, the blue sky peeking hopefully through.

We waded to the pub, chatting with the locals, inane talk, delighting in the day off, rubbing our hands exaggeratedly in front of the fire, the scent of woodsmoke on our clothes. On exiting, we were peppered with snowballs from waiting teens. Our squeals turned quickly to cries of revenge as we retaliated, scattering their army.

We bumped into friends on the walk home across the fields. Now and again we would dive at each other, trying to catch the other unawares, ending up in a great cold mess on the ground. I was giggling childishly, cheeks bright red with the effort, eyelashes glistening with melted flakes.

The electricity was back on when we made it home, and we spent the evening watching DVDs, stretched out under a rug, the embers glowing and bathing the room in a soft light.

The snow was still there the next morning, but the roads had been cleared and gritted in and out of the village. You gallantly cleared your car, leaving our road at a slow crawl. I watched you go, deciding to build a snowman on my own outside our gate. He would hold a sign welcoming you home so you would see him by the gate and laugh when you returned that night.

Last year was eleven months ago. The snow has started to fall again, carpeting the ground in crisp white. The branches are beginning to bend and give; little sprinkles fall from them like a sneeze. I'm sitting in our living room, knowing I should feel the usual excitement, the child-like wonder at the extraordinary scenes. Great gusts of billowing white flakes are cascading, twirling, settling on the ground. Already children are running past the window dragging plastic sledges, beckoning to their parents who are dawdling at a distance, wrapped in huge coats, knitted scarves and hats blocking out everything but their eyes. Some are holding hands, and I know they are all smiling.

I look around me. Ashes in the fireplace are waiting to be swept and cleared. The bookcase stands half-empty. A calendar still announces it is 'August'. Cushions plumped pointlessly again and again. I don't want to go out into the snow by myself. I don't want to build a snowman on my own. You are not coming home today.

I would never have let you go that day if I'd known. The snow had started again. The lorry had jack-knifed on the A road; two cars caught up in the collision. Three people were injured, one fatally. A man in a navy hatchback, around thirty, was rushed to A and E, but there was nothing they could do. He was pronounced dead just before ten o'clock.

I never made it to the hospital. Your colleague, our friend, had called asking where you were. I'd said you'd left, had left hours ago. I panicked, pacing up and down, ringing my parents, who were helpless, now upset and confused. They couldn't come. The snow. I rang your parents; they hadn't heard anything, and your mother started to cry. My car couldn't get out of our road. I tried all the taxi firms, but no one would take me anywhere; the roads were too bad. You were alone in those last moments; you would have been scared.

Now I sit by the window, hollowed out. Outside, the snow is still falling, blanketing the world in a layer of new. I sit, and I pray, pray for my fresh start. Pray that you are going to walk through the door soon. Pray that it might be last year.

Cesca Major writes suspenseful books inspired by events in the recent past and her latest, 'The Silent Hours' is an epic tale set in wartime France. Cesca worked in television and teaching before writing full time. Alongside her thrillers she writes feel-good reads under the pseudonym Rosie Blake. Cesca lives in Berkshire with her husband, son and twin daughters. She can be found on Twitter, Facebook and Instagram and at her website cescamajor.com

NO GOOD DEED GOES UNPUNISHED

CHRISSIE MANBY

Monday morning at the bus stop. Already the weekend seemed like ancient history to Karen Jones as she waited for the 452 that would take her into work. Her glasses misted over as the rain dampened everything, including her spirits. Two buses sailed past, both too full to stop and pick up extra passengers. Karen had forgotten about the tube strike that encouraged everyone to pile onto the bus instead.

Just as she was about to give up and start walking, Karen noticed an older woman struggling up the pavement with her shopping. Four plastic bags strained with the weight of the tins inside them. It was inevitable that one of the bags would split, spilling the poor woman's groceries all over the street. A tin of expensive cat food rolled off the pavement into the gutter. Leaping to retrieve it before it came to any harm, Karen was rewarded with a stream of expletives from the old woman.

'She's stealing my tins!' she cried.

In the commotion that followed, as the old woman grabbed back the can, Karen's glasses fell off into the road, crushed beneath the wheels of the first 452 to pull over at

Karen's stop since she had arrived forty-five minutes earlier. So Karen lost her glasses, and she missed her bus.

'I might be able to salvage them,' said Ed, the trainee optician, as he looked at the twisted frames. He and Karen had been on nodding terms for several months now. She usually arrived at the bank branch where she worked just as Ed was opening up the optician's shop next door. Now, at last he had a chance to talk to her, possibly even impress her by mending her horribly mangled specs, ahead of asking her how he might get a loan to start his own business in due course.

'How much will it cost me?' Karen asked. Another expense was the last thing she needed right then.

'Oh nothing,' said Ed. 'This one's on me. It'll be good practice.'

Ed certainly needed the practice. He sometimes wondered if he should have chosen to be a car mechanic rather than an optician. His fingers and thumbs felt like sausages when he wielded the tiny screwdrivers that were essential to spectacle repair. The screws that held Karen's frames together had been done up especially tightly. Ed grunted as he tried to twist them open, then his hand slipped, and he managed both to gouge a channel right across the polished surface of his desk and to tip his morning coffee into his lap.

'You need to deal with stains quickly,' said Ed's boss, passing by. 'I'd take those trousers to the dry-cleaner right away if I were you.'

Ed changed into his tracksuit bottoms – thank goodness it was a gym day – and hot-footed it to the nearest dry-cleaner with his coffee-stained slacks.

Kerry the dry cleaner sucked her teeth.

'When did this happen?' she asked.

Ed told her the story. 'How much will it cost me?'

'Aw. You can have it on the house, love,' she said. Ed reminded Kerry of her son, who was away at university. Kerry missed her eldest dreadfully.

Kerry treated Ed's trousers every bit as carefully as she would a delicate wedding dress. Wedding dresses were her speciality. That week she had three to work on; one of them was a beautiful vintage number from the 1950s with a tiny beaded bodice and a full skirt in shimmering silk. Melanie, the bride who brought the dress in, explained that it had originally belonged to her recently deceased grandmother, and she wanted to wear it on her own big day.

'I will have it looking pristine,' Kerry promised her and was very proud of the results. All it needed now was a final pressing. She'd do that after she finished Ed's trousers.

But Ed's trousers were not all they appeared to be. Though the label claimed that they were Hugo Boss, he had bought them from a market stall that specialised in knock-offs and thus the label declaring the fabric's composition was not entirely accurate either. This much Kerry discovered when she tried to press the trousers. The fabric, which should have responded well to a hot iron, instead melted like the witch at the end of the Wizard of Oz. Kerry clapped her hand over her mouth as a cloud of noxious smoke floated towards the ceiling, setting off the smoke alarm. And the sprinkler system. Which, in turn, soaked the delicate wedding dress.

Melanie, the bride, sank to the floor as Kerry told her about her grandmother's precious gown.

'Perhaps I could pay for it to be looked at by a dry cleaner that specialises in designer stuff?' Kerry suggested, though she knew that the water damage was too comprehensive for anyone but a magician to be able to make that dress look like new again.

'It was an accident,' Melanie said with as much understanding in her tone as she could muster. Minutes later, on the phone to her mother, Melanie said, 'It was an omen.'

'What on earth do you mean?' asked her mum.

Melanie took a deep breath. Weeks of pent-up anxiety about the wedding suddenly came pouring out. 'The dress...' she said. 'The dress getting ruined was Grandma trying to tell me not to marry Jason. It was a message from the other side.'

So the wedding was cancelled. It would come as a huge relief to one of Jason's colleagues, Liz, who had been having an affair with Jason since the office Christmas party. Melanie was devastated when Jason confirmed that the rumour was true, but she knew that in cancelling the wedding, she had averted a much greater dose of heartache further down the line.

The following week, Karen once again found herself face to face with the little old woman who had lost the tin of cat food. Once again, she was carrying a collection of straining plastic carriers. As she drew level with the bus stop, the old woman dropped another bag.

'I'm not getting involved,' Karen told herself, turning away and pushing her expensive new glasses further up her nose so she could get a better look at her iPhone.

However, while Karen had her back turned on the scene, another bus stop regular – a man Karen had often shyly admired - skidded on an escaping tin and ended up crashing into Karen, pressing her up against the glass of the bus shelter, breaking her glasses, her phone - and her nose.

At the time, Karen couldn't see the funny side but eighteen months later, it made a rather amusing 'first meeting' story to tell at their wedding reception.

'No Good Deed' was first published in My Weekly

Chrissie Manby is the author of over 40 novels (under her own name and pseudonyms Olivia Darling, Stella Knightley and Stephanie Ash), including Sunday Times Bestsellers 'Running Away From Richard', 'Seven Sunny Days' and 'The Matchbreaker' and her latest, 'Saying Goodbye to Tuesday' is a heart-warming tale about a ghost dog. Her work has been published in over 14 countries including Romania, Japan, Thailand and Taiwan, where her Olivia Darling debut 'Vintage' was a top-five bestseller. When she is not writing, Chrissie enjoys drawing and knitting. She is also learning to speak German. Follow her on Twitter @chrissiemanby or at her website https://christinemanby.com.

WAITING

CLARE SWATMAN

The room is quiet for now. Visiting hours are forgotten during these dark, whispery hours of the night when even the trolleys seem to squeak more discreetly, the machines begin their nocturnal dance of keeping patients alive, and I become part of the furniture, a lingering presence that's always there but barely noticed.

If I hold my hand above your mouth, I can feel your breath warming my skin, but otherwise, the only other indication that you're still with me is the rhythmic beeping of the machine tracking your heartbeat. No one is sure whether you know I'm beside you or whether you can hear me talking. But I know. I know you're here somewhere, trying to come back to me, to us.

My bladder is beginning to ache, and you look peaceful, so it feels safe to leave you for a few moments and go in search of relief and perhaps some refreshments. I stand, my joints cracking and creaking like ancient floorboards, and I'm surprised when the sound doesn't wake up the entire hospital. I stretch my arms up, then bend down to touch my toes, marvelling that I can still do that, then feel guilty that you can't. I swallow it down; my guilt is of no use to you, so why waste my energy?

I watch you for a minute more, plant a gentle kiss on your forehead, tell you I won't be long, then creep across the tiled floor and push the door open with a gentle shush.

It's almost silent out here, the nurses attending to patients or whispering among themselves in a small room behind the reception desk, and I imagine myself as the only person left in the world after an apocalypse or plague has wiped everyone else out. How long would I survive in this building of matching sterile corridors, complex machinery and limp sandwiches? I squeak along the empty hall and press the button that opens the door in and out of the ward, letting the door flap shut behind me. I feel my unease unfurl and grow as the distance between us grows, and it takes all my energy not to turn and run back to your bedside, to make sure you're still here, still breathing.

The café when I get there is empty, the shutters down, and I check my watch and sigh. Much later than I'd thought. I have a few coins in my pocket – I'm already a seasoned pro at this hospital business after four days here, I think you'd be impressed – so after a quick trip to the loo, I head to the vending machine to buy myself a plastic cup of terrible coffee and a bar of chocolate. I watch as the machine whirs to life, the insipid puddle water splashing into the cup and over the sides until it clicks off. I take a sip and wince at the heat and the taste of smoke and ash. I feed coins into the next machine, make my selection and wait while the Twix is pushed to the front before dropping down into the collection drawer with a clatter. I collect my winnings and am about to head back to the ward when I hear sobbing from a small room nearby. I hesitate a moment, stuck between wanting to make sure whoever is in there is all right and racing back to you. I know what you'd tell me even before I think it, I can almost hear your gentle voice laughing at me. *You've only been gone for five minutes, you silly sausage; nothing has changed. Go and see if they need your help.*

I take a couple of quiet steps towards the half-open door and peer through the glass, murky with greasy fingerprints. A man sits on a plastic chair on one side of the room, perfectly upright, staring at the wall. Tears run down his face, and every now and then, he takes an involuntary breath in, shuddering like a worn-out clutch.

He must sense me watching him because his head jerks up, and he fixes me with his tear-stained gaze, and that's when I wonder. Did I cry? Did I cry like this the day you were brought in here, hardly a scratch on you, yet your brain bashed around like a squash ball inside your skull when it had struck the pavement? Or had I cried when the doctor had told me, her voice kind but matter-of-fact, saying it was impossible to know whether you would ever wake up? Or how about the day Katy had come to visit and had sat at your bedside soaking the bedsheets with her tears, crying for her Mum? Had I cried with her then, or had I held them back, keen to protect our daughter from the harshness of real life even now she's a grown woman herself? I can't remember.

The man is watching me now as I step through the door, take the few short steps across the room, and sit beside him. Close up, his eyes are puffy as though he's been sobbing for days, his skin grey in the flickering overhead strip light, the pallor of the long-term hospital visitor. I know if it were you here instead of me, you'd know whether to comfort him or ask him what was wrong, or whether you could do anything to help. You've always been good that way, able to speak to anyone, in any situation, while I just hovered in the background looking like a spare part. It's the way I've always thought of myself: a spare part, not necessary but there nevertheless, in case of engine failure. But there's no room for spare parts now. The engine has failed, and I'm the only part left.

'Would you like a coffee?' I say, holding out my steaming cup of tasteless sludge. 'It's awful, but it's hot.'

'Thank you,' the man says, taking it and sipping it gratefully. He doesn't even flinch at its sheer awfulness. He takes several more sips and then puts the cup down. I'm just wondering whether to offer him my Twix when he says, 'I've never been a crier.'

'Me neither,' I say, shaking my head. We sit together in mutual understanding for a moment as the cheap clock above our heads counts the precious seconds with a plastic tick. There's no sign of anyone else around at this time of night, and I wonder whether people don't get sick after ten o'clock, or if it's just that they don't make it to this part of the hospital, clogging up A&E instead with their drunken injuries and night-time complaints.

'It's my daughter,' the man says suddenly into the empty room. I wait for him to elaborate, keen to hear about someone else's misfortune for a change rather than wallowing in my own. You would have told me off for that, of course, told me that was dreadful and that I should ask him questions, sound interested. And I'm about to obey the you in my head when he speaks again. 'She's got sepsis.' His voice is juddery, and I think he's about to start crying again, but he doesn't.

'I'm sorry,' I say and am surprised that I actually am. Despite what I'd imagined, hearing about someone else's misery doesn't make mine seem any better; it just seems to deepen the sense of understanding. Perhaps this is the first time I've understood what you mean when you tell me you like helping people, that it gives you a sense of satisfaction.

'Is she going to get better?'

I feel him shrug beside me, and he threads his fingers together so tightly his knuckles turn white. 'They don't know. She...' his voice breaks, and I wait. 'She might not.'

I don't know what to say now. I scroll back through all the conversations I've listened to you having with friends, relatives, strangers over the years. The sympathetic words you've doled out, generously, the kindnesses you've shared, and I wish I'd listened properly: really listened, and learned how to give sympathy in just the right measure, just the way you do.

'It's my wife in there,' I say, nodding my head towards the door, hoping to give the impression that I understand what he's going through.

'I'm sorry.' He sniffs loudly. 'What happened?'

It should be easy to tell him. The accident has been explained to me several times since it happened. You were crossing the road, and a car came out of nowhere, hit you side-on, sent you flying several feet in the air, and you hit your head on the kerb. Strangers helped you, had called an ambulance, and as they told me this, all I kept thinking was that I hadn't even known you'd gone into town because I hadn't taken any notice when you'd told me and had just carried on reading the paper. Just like I always do.

It wasn't until the phone rang a while later and I'd heard an official voice telling me that you were in the hospital with serious injuries that I even noticed you weren't there, pottering about in the kitchen as usual or singing along to the radio.

When did I stop paying you any attention?

When I'd arrived at the hospital it had taken me several minutes to find out where you'd been taken and even when I got there, nobody could tell me anything because you'd been taken into theatre. I can't remember how long I sat there, waiting for news, but at some point, a doctor had come out to speak to me. And that was the moment I realised what a fool I'd been. Because as he was telling me your head injuries were life-threatening and that you might never recover, he handed me a bag. It was yours. I thanked him and went to sit down again, to wait, to wait. And as I waited, I rummaged through your bag to see whether I could find any clues as to what you'd been up to, where you'd been.

And there it was.

A box. I opened it up carefully. Cufflinks. I picked them up and studied them. Our initials were engraved on them: T&E. 40 years.

Thomas and Ellie.

Forty years.

And I hadn't even remembered.

How can I tell this stranger that? How can I admit to anyone what a thoughtless, heartless husband I am? That it was my fault you'd gone out without me because you'd wanted to surprise me, even though I didn't deserve it. And that I hadn't even given the date a single thought because I'd let you slip so far down my list of priorities until you almost weren't on it any longer.

'She's in a coma,' I say now, not wanting to elaborate.

'God.' He looks at me. 'Will she come out of it?'

'I don't know.'

'How long has it been?'

'Four days.'

He nods. 'You just feel so helpless, don't you?'

I nod back.

He carries on. 'I just want to tell my girl how much she means to me. I can't let anything happen to her before she knows how much I love her.' His voice breaks again. 'I bet you feel the same, don't you?'

I can feel it then, a tingling in the back of my nose, a

tightening of my throat. And then I feel a single tear sliding down my face, and I watch with interest as it lands on my trouser leg, the tiny dot spreading out across the fabric like ripples in a pond.

What am I crying for, I wonder? For you, and for the fact you might not pull through? Or for myself, for the fact it's taken you almost dying for me to realise how much I love you, how much I need you. For the fact that it's taken this stranger, who's suffering just as much as I am, to make me realise what I need to do?

I stand suddenly, the backs of my legs bashing against the plastic chair.

'Are you all right?' the man watches me, his puffy eyes curious.

'Yes. Yes, I am, I think.'

He doesn't reply, and before I leave, I turn to him. 'I hope your daughter makes it.'

'Thank you. I hope your wife does too.'

I nod, then swivel on my toes and march back out of the room. Back along the corridor to your ward, retracing my steps as quickly as I can, drawn back to your bedside like a magnet. My heart is pulsing all over my body and I can feel my breath coming in gasps. I stop take a couple of deep breaths. I'm no good to you if I pass out now.

When the walls stop spinning, I resume my brisk walk, turning familiar corners until the door of your ward is up ahead like a mirage in the desert. It feels like the longest walk in the world to reach it, but finally, it's there, and I'm buzzing to be let in, and the door opens, and I'm hurrying, hurrying to you, imagining all the things I'll say to you as you lie there and listen to me. I hope it will bring you back to me; I hope I hope I hope.

I can almost feel your presence as I get nearer, and then I open the door to your room, and I stop dead. Because you're surrounded by people, doctors and nurses, and my heart stops, my stomach plummeting to the floor as all the things I need to tell you fall out of my mouth and scatter like petals in the wind . . .

'No,' I say, the only word left. And all I can think about in the few seconds it takes for someone to notice me are all the things I need to say to you. Like someone who's about to die says their life flashes before their eyes in their final moment, I see all the things I wish I had said to you over the years flash before mine. That you're beautiful, that you're the best mother, wife, friend; that you're kind and funny and generous and sweet and caring and. . . . I stop, panting, and then there's a hand on my arm and when I look up, I see a warm smile in front of my eyes rather than the worried look I was expecting.

'What's happened?' I gasp. 'What's happened to Ellie?'

'Oh good, you're back,' a doctor says, stepping away from your bed. She's also smiling, and I wait for her to speak, my breath held, hardly daring to hope. 'Your wife has woken up.'

I feel as though I'm going to pass out, and when I stumble, the nurse holds me and steers me towards your bedside. And then there you are, watching me.

'Ellie,' I say, and I sit down on the edge of your bed and take hold of your hand. Your skin is still cold, papery, but it feels different now, as though there's life in it again.

'He...' you try to speak, but all that comes out is a croak, and I squeeze your hand.

'We'll leave you for a few minutes,' the doctor says, and I wait, staring at you like you're some sort of miracle as the room empties and then it's just the two of us left. Me and you, the way it's always been.

'I...', I stop, unsure how to get the words out now or even which words need to come out. As I'd raced here, there had been so many things I'd planned to say to you, so many things I needed to tell you, to make up for all the things I haven't said over the last forty years, it felt like a tsunami of words and feelings building. And yet now I'm finally here, and you're listening, the words have dried up like a cracked riverbed, but it doesn't even seem to matter. Because I'm here beside you, and you're back, it's as though we both know what we want to say without having to say anything.

'I'm sorry,' you whisper, and I know what you're sorry for because I am too.

'I love you,' I reply, and then your lips turn upwards into a smile, and I think it's the best thing I have ever seen.

My girl. My Ellie. My life.

Clare Swatman is the author of three women's fiction novels published by Macmillan, which have been translated into over 20 languages. She has been a journalist for over twenty years, writing for Bella and Woman & Home amongst many other magazines. She lives in Hertfordshire. Her new novel 'Before We Grow Old' is out now.

AUTHENTIC ATHENS

EMILY KERR

Thirteen bricks high, nineteen wide. How many bricks does that make? Two hundred and something, forty-eight, is it? Maths has never been my strong point, but there's nothing much else for me to do as I languish in a stuffy jail cell two hundred yards from the Acropolis. When my boss sent me for a holiday in 'Authentic Athens', this is definitely not how authentic I thought things would get.

The day before....

I lugged my heavy suitcase from the conveyor belt and set off in search of the exit, grateful the Greek signs were translated into English letters, giving me some chance of working out where I should go in all this chaos. I was hot, sweaty, tired, and counting the minutes until I could set up my laptop on a shady balcony and check my emails whilst sipping a cool glass of white wine. After an hour and a half of waiting for my suitcase to show up, my patience was wearing thin.

I emerged into the cacophony of the arrivals hall and flinched as hundreds of handwritten signs were eagerly thrust in my direction, promising transport for Kyrios Rouvas, Mrs Jones, Leanne Kingston. I peered carefully at all the signs, but my name didn't appear anywhere. I double-checked the itinerary, which my PA had carefully printed out and colour-coded (pink for travel, yellow for accommodation, green for activities.) It definitely stated a guide would await my arrival at Eleftherios Venizelos airport and accompany me to my accommodation in the picturesque Plaka district of Athens. I checked my watch. The flight had landed on time, so there was no reason for my guide not to be here. My irritation levels increased. I'd only booked this vacation because my boss had threatened to fire me if I didn't take a break. It was meant to reduce my stress levels, not increase them. I trundled my suitcase over to a quieter area where I could phone the travel company, but as I negotiated my way through the crowds, six-foot something of blundering man careered into me, knocking me stumbling backwards into the very angular, very sharp metal seating which formed rows down the length of the building.

'Watch where you're going,' I said, my voice squeaky and shrill with pain.

'Sygnome, Kyria,' he said, briefly taking my hand, then hurrying on his way.

'That better have meant you were sorry,' I muttered, angrily waiting for my phone to connect.

'Kalispera,' a masculine voice answered. 'Hello? Can I help you?'

'Yes, hello, this is Lia Stephens. I am trying to get in touch with a Mr Sakis Papadopoulos. He was meant to have met me at the airport an hour ago, but he appears to have been delayed.'

'Ah, Kyria, I am glad you are here safe. I am Sakis. Where are you? I am in the Arrivals Hall. I am the one speaking on the phone.'

That really didn't narrow it down. Practically every person in the place had some form of electronic device glued to their ear.

'How about you wave?' he suggested.

Feeling very stupid, I reluctantly wiggled my fingers in the general direction of the ceiling. It garnered quite a few waves back. I felt my face turn pink.

'Look, I'm standing in the corner beneath a great big sign for car hire,' I hissed, 'Surely it won't be too difficult to find me?'

He made some kind of response, but the echoing din of the hall drowned it out completely. Somebody tapped me on my shoulder.

'Kyria, are you ready to go?'

I spun round to face my guide; then got a funny sensation in my stomach as I recognised the man.

'Oh great, it's the blundering giant,' I muttered, realising too late that I had said it out loud.

He looked decidedly nonplussed, then grinned. 'Yes, I am Sakis. I am sorry for bumping into you, Kyria. I was in a rush, and I had forgotten my glasses. I hope I did not hurt you.'

I raised an eyebrow. 'Well, if that's how short-sighted you are, I hope you're not driving me to my accommodation.'

'Oh no, we are not driving. It is an Authentic Athens holiday. We take the metro.'

My back twinged at the thought of having to lug my bag any further.

'The metro?' I repeated weakly.

'Yes, of course. It is the best way to travel into the city.' He picked up my suitcase as if it weighed no more than a pillow and gestured to me to follow him. 'This is where your experience of the real Athens begins.'

Oh great.

The train trundled us past mile upon mile of motorway, then slid below a line of identikit apartment blocks in the suburbs, but we re-emerged into a different world. I couldn't help gasping as I clambered the final steps out of the metro and looked up to see the Acropolis looming above me, ancient buildings of weathered marble perched dramatically on the top of the cliff.

'Welcome to my home city,' beamed Sakis, throwing his arms open expansively. I ducked to avoid being thumped by my suitcase, which he was still clutching.

'This way,' he continued, setting a punishing pace through a maze of winding alleyways. The heat was oppressive, and I swear my brain was starting to slowly cook inside my skull. I had to concentrate on putting one foot in front of the other just to keep going. I had no idea Athens was so hilly. Sakis wasn't even perspiring after the climb.

'Here we are. This is where you will be staying.'

I wiped the sweat from my eyes and blinked at the building in front of me. It was a non-descript apartment block with lines of laundry criss-crossing its balconies, a rambling, over-grown bougainvillea bush its only redeeming feature.

'This is my hotel?'

A wealth of exhaustion and general pissed off-ness made my question come out rather more forcibly than was perhaps polite, but by this stage I was beyond caring.

'No, do not worry. You are not staying in a hotel. This is Authentic Athens. My family will be looking after you.'

Before I could give my honest response to that, a wrinkled whirlwind in black rushed out and took both my hands.

'Lia, this is my mother, Penelope. Mama, this is Lia Stephens.'

'Welcome, welcome to my home,' said the old woman, 'And now it is your home too for the next week.'

She was so enthusiastic in her greeting that my demand to be taken to the nearest hotel died in my mouth.

'Er, hello,' I stammered. I turned to her son. 'Can I have a word, Sakis?'

'Let me show you to your room,' he countered. 'Mama will be busy preparing dinner, and you must be hungry after your journey.'

I pursed my lips but consented to be led upstairs, my desire to be back in my safe, uncomplicated office increasing at every step.

'Here you are, everything you could want.' Sakis gestured around the room with its single bed, desk, chair and pile of clean towels. 'And this is the best bit.' He stepped forward and flung open double doors onto the balcony. 'Before you is the real Athens.'

'Can you see the Acropolis?' I asked, refusing to look.

'No, but this view is better,' he replied, enthusiastic as a puppy.

'En-suite bathroom?'

'No, but the bathroom is only down the corridor.'

'Wi-Fi?'

He smiled. 'Why would you want Wi-Fi when there is so much to explore in the real world?'

I nearly choked. 'This is ridiculous. How am I meant to relax when I can't even check my emails?'

His olive eyes sparkled in a way which served only to increase my level of irritation.

'You never know, you may find not being able to check

them more relaxing. I will leave you to unpack, then come and join the family for our evening meal. You will feel better once you have had something to eat.'

Something to eat would make me feel better? In his dreams. The only thing which would make me feel better right now would be an air conditioned five-star room with a fully stocked mini bar. I pulled my phone out ready to make an angry call to my PA to sort out this debacle when I realised the battery had died. I actually threw my folder of travel documents across the room in frustration. I slumped down on the bed in defeat, a wave of tiredness hitting me. I would lie down for five minutes, then sort out this mess.

The clattering of a two-stroke engine in the street below woke me. I sat up, scrabbling around to find out what time it was. 8am. I must have slept straight through. Someone had removed my shoes and placed a blanket over me. I staggered over to my suitcase, but that had been emptied and thoughtfully unpacked. I hoped it had been the old lady Penelope who'd done it and not her son. I didn't really like to think what he'd make of my collection of boring old M&S underwear and business-like blouses and skirts. Not that his opinion of me mattered one jot of course. I collected the aforementioned items and padded down the corridor to the bathroom. Shower time, then find a proper hotel.

I had heard complaints about Greek bathrooms, but I'd never actually had to confront the reality of not being allowed to flush toilet paper before. Then there was the shower cubicle or rather, non-cubicle, as there was no sign of a curtain to keep the water from escaping into the rest of the room. Maybe if I stood really still whilst showering it wouldn't matter. I soon discovered my mistake. The moment I turned the tap on, water sprayed everywhere, drenching my clothes, my towel and the toilet paper. It didn't make for a relaxing bathing experience. I washed as quickly as I could, then wrapped the dripping bath-towel around me and made a hasty dash back to my room. Of course, sod's law dictated I encountered Sakis on my way back.

'Kalimera, good morning. Did you sleep well?' he asked, having the good grace at least to appear to be ignorant of my state of undress, but I still felt myself blushing like a schoolgirl.

'Fine,' I muttered begrudgingly.

'My mother has prepared breakfast, then we shall go exploring.'

My stomach gurgled in anticipation. Maybe I could put off transferring to a hotel until I'd had some food. And perhaps the exploring would help me find somewhere else to stay, somewhere with that holy grail, internet access. I dreaded to think how many emails would be filling my inbox.

I had expected to start with a visit to the Acropolis, but Sakis seemed reluctant.

'At this time of the day, it is no good. We will go tomorrow, very early. It is better then. Let us explore the Plaka first. It is the neighbourhood of the gods. Let me hold your phone for you.'

I had been surreptitiously trying to check for Wi-Fi, but it seemed we wouldn't be going anywhere unless I surrendered my phone. I reluctantly handed it over. I felt naked without it, but the stern look on Sakis's face told me there was no point in arguing with him. He took my arm and we set off down a narrow road.

Only a few streets from the main tourist areas, it was like stepping back in time. The alleyways in this area of the Plaka were too narrow for cars and so the locals had set up tables and chairs, sitting in the sunshine, chatting back and forth across the passageways. I felt like we were walking through their front rooms, but everyone we went past had a smile and a greeting for us. The friendly atmosphere was infectious and gradually I realised the unfamiliar feeling creeping over me was actually a sense of relaxation.

'This is Adrianou Street,' said Sakis as we turned another corner. 'It is the oldest street in the city. My friend is an archaeologist, and he says the road has the same layout as it did in the times of the ancient city.'

'So, we are literally walking in the footsteps of people like Socrates?' I asked, with a frisson of excitement.

He laughed. 'Yes, and breathing the same air as he did.'

'Thank you for showing me this,' I said sincerely. 'I would never have thought of coming down here.'

'That is the beauty of an Authentic Athens holiday,' Sakis smiled.

'What's with all the English graffiti though?' I asked as I spotted yet another spray mural exhorting the authorities to 'Free the people from hunger.'

A shadow crossed his face. 'That is another part of authentic Athens, but not one I normally mention to my visitors.'

That piqued my curiosity. 'Well, you have to tell me about it now,' I insisted.

He stared at me intently as if he was trying to read in my face whether I meant it or not. Whatever he saw there must have satisfied him because he took my hand and led me in a different direction. We hurried past Syntagma Square with its guards dressed in their uniform of pleated mini-skirts and pom-pom shoes and plunged once more into a maze of streets. These lacked the quaint charm of the Plaka district, instead they looked tired and rundown. Most shops were boarded up with more of the graffiti sprayed across their doorways. Finally, we came to a halt at a café which had a queue of customers snaking out down the street.

'This is 'Food for All.' It is a soup kitchen for those who cannot afford to feed themselves.'

'But there are so many people. And they look...'

The words died in my mouth. They looked so normal is what I wanted to say, but I knew it would sound rude. Sakis seemed to understand what I was getting at though.

'Yes, they are. They are former government employees, businesspeople, doctors. The financial crisis has caused hardship for many people.'

'And is this what all the graffiti is about?'

'Yes. They want the world to know the difficulties we are facing. I am a qualified teacher, but I work as a tour guide on the side, so I have money to help my mother,' he confessed. My admiration for him grew. 'There is another vote in parliament tonight. We expect the politicians will decide upon more cuts and the queues here will grow longer.' He hesitated. 'A group of us were planning to go down to Syntagma Square and wait for the result of the vote. You are welcome to join us, but I should warn you that things can get a little lively.'

'Yes please.'

Penelope didn't look happy when Sakis informed her of our plans, but she didn't say anything and instead thrust a packet of sandwiches and a scarf at me as we set off that evening.

'It's not going to get that cold, is it?'

Sakis smiled as he tied an identical scarf round his throat. He tweaked the jaunty bow I'd constructed around my neck.

'It's in case there is any tear gas. It will protect you from the worst of it.'

What was I getting myself into? The sensible voice in my head told me to turn back now, pack up my belongings and move to a hotel to continue my holiday in comfortable ignorance, but the memory of the quiet resignation on the faces of those in the soup kitchen queue stirred my conscience. I wanted to stand in solidarity with the people who had so generously welcomed me to their home and their city.

Syntagma Square shone with the light of thousands of candles held aloft by a peaceful crowd. People of all ages stood together; their gaze focussed on the parliament building in front of them where their fates were being decided. I shivered, more from the atmosphere of nervous anticipation than from the cold but didn't object when Sakis wrapped his arms round me.

Suddenly a policeman stumbled into me, knocking me flying.

Sakis unleashed a torrent of Greek, the gist of which was clearly warning the man to watch where he was going. My assailant looked like he was about to square up to Sakis. I didn't stop to think. I threw my packet of sandwiches at him, hitting him squarely in the face. I reckon I would have got away with it if I hadn't started laughing at how ridiculous he looked with tzatziki dripping down onto his pristine uniform. Soon the whole crowd were laughing along with me. They cheered as my 'victim' arrested me and led me off into the police van. I felt like a folk heroine. I may even have shouted something along the lines of 'Vive la revolution', not exactly the correct lingo I know, but the crowd appreciated the sentiment.

So that's how I ended up in this sweat box, experiencing an authentic Athenian jail cell. No Wi-Fi, no ensuite. No problem.

'248 bricks,' I call across the corridor to my fellow jailbird. He looks pretty good, even in the dim light of the cell block.

'Close. It's 247,' says Sakis.

A guard walks down the corridor.

'Lia Stephens? Sakis Papadopoulos?'

He lets us out, indicating bail has been posted.

Sakis takes my hand, and we walk out of the police station together.

'I'm afraid you're about to experience something else authentically Athenian. My mother is going to kill us.'

Emily Kerr has been scribbling stories on bits of paper ever since she learnt how to write. She works as a journalist and is based in Yorkshire. Her latest book, 'Meet Me Under The Northern Lights' is out now. Emily loves to hear from readers. You can tweet her @EmilyKerrWrites or check out her Facebook page www.facebook.com/emilykerrwrites and website www.emilykerrwrites.com.

THE WITTIEST WOMAN IN THE WORLD

GILL PAUL

Dorothy Parker was often said to be the wittiest woman in the world – or at least in Manhattan, which, as far as her writer friends were concerned, was the same thing. Newspaper columnists quoted her quips, and out-of-town visitors pestered her for autographs, approaching her at the round table in the Algonquin Hotel where she misspent most afternoons.

"Say something funny," begged a woman in plaid with a Midwest accent.

"Something funny," she replied, deadpan, and the woman fell about laughing as if it were the cleverest thing she'd ever heard.

Half the time, Dottie didn't recognise quotes that were attributed to her, but there was always the chance she'd been drunk when they passed her lips. She hadn't been a big drinker before the 1921 Prohibition laws banned the sale of alcohol, but the thrill of the illicit soon worked its magic, and now she had a close and tender relationship with Messrs. Haig & Haig.

Booze was more widely available than ever before in speakeasies, cordial stores, dance halls, and in your friends' bathtub gin stills. Taxi drivers got in on the act, charging premium prices for cheap liquor to customers with more dollars than sense. The Algonquin Hotel had stopped serving liquor, but waiters turned a blind eye when Dottie's friends topped up their water glasses from a hip flask passed around the table with all the solemnity of a church collection plate. They could have gone to the speakeasy on the next block, but they were creatures of habit, like elephants returning to the same watering hole.

Dottie felt an obligation to be funny for these friends with whom she whiled away her afternoons. How else would they fill their columns? She had a reputation to maintain, so she often rehearsed a few lines in advance, ready for an opportunity to arise. When she saw in the newspapers that Henry Ford had sold over a million cars the previous year, she tried to devise a witticism about wealth, millionaires, automobiles, production lines... All morning, she turned over word associations in her mind, searching for the perfect line.

In fact, she was able to use the resulting quip in a different context that very afternoon when someone commented on the fee author Edna Ferber was getting for the Broadway musical based on her novel Show Boat.

"If you want to know what God thought of money," Dottie said, "just look at the people he gave it to."

She spotted Franklin P. Adams, columnist at New York World, scribbling down her words, and knew it would make his column the next day. He always did her justice. She only minded when writers misquoted her and blew the punch lines. That was unforgivable. Dottie had her "wittiest woman in the world" title to think of, after all.

It was ironic when she looked at the state of her life. Her abusive, occasionally violent husband had recently left her. She'd been fired from her job at Vanity Fair for insulting the high and mighty in her – admittedly flippant – theatre reviews. And she'd lost more family members to early death than she could count on the fingers of one hand – although counting had never been one of her strengths, as her bank balance demonstrated. Truth be told, Dorothy was depressed most of the time.

'Something needs to change,' she said to herself, staring at her new bob in the bathroom mirror. 'And not just my hair.'

His name was Charlie MacArthur. He walked into the Algonquin, all chiselled cheekbones, dark widow's peak, and naughty eyes. As soon as he caught sight of Dottie, he made a beeline for her.

'That seat's taken,' she said, arching an eyebrow as he slid into the chair beside her.

'It is now,' he said, looking her up and down without embarrassment.

Close up, his eyes had huge black pupils, and he gave off intoxicating clouds of sex appeal. No one had examined her so intimately since her last full medical.

'Have you lost something? she asked sweetly.

'Yes,' he said, clutching a hand to his chest. 'I've lost my heart to you.'

'Well, that was careless.'

Damn! she thought. All her best lines had deserted her just when she needed them most. His voice was as intimate as the rustle of sheets, and it tugged deep down in her gut. She knew this man was going to be trouble – and she couldn't wait.

Charlie worked in newspapers, he said. He'd just arrived from Chicago, and, like her, he was separated from his spouse. The 'Big D' had not yet been mentioned, he said, but there were no kids, so it should be straightforward. The wife in question had never understood him. Dottie liked him enough to ignore the cliché.

There was alcohol involved, she would later say in her defence—oodles of it. Charlie was only the second man she had ever slept with. And he was excellent. The most fun she'd ever had doing anything, ever, without exception.

She lay awake afterwards, the first pincers of a hangover starting to grip her temples. He had long eyelashes, she noted. And a birthmark the shape of Africa on his calf. He snored gently, like a puppy. My god, he was beautiful.

Next morning, he awoke and clutched his head with a groan. 'Are you all right?' he asked. 'Because I'm sure as hell not.'

'Same as you, I think.' Her heart was beating hard, and she couldn't tell if it was post-alcoholic palpitations or newfound love. Her stomach was gurgling and groaning like an old water cistern, and her head was firmly clamped in an evil vice. 'It seems the wrath of ethanol has struck again.'

'Do you think a hangover shared is a hangover halved?' he asked.

'Let's find out,' she suggested and staggered out of bed to dissolve some aspirin powders in a couple of glasses of water.

Was it that first morning she'd fallen in love? Or had she already done so the night before? Whenever the arrow struck, it was a bullseye straight to her heart.

It wasn't just the fabulous sex; Charlie was smart and funny, and they played well together, like two headstrong children without any parents to rein them in. They rolled somersaults on the grass in Central Park, shocking elderly ladies in wigs and diamonds. They caught taxis all over town and once managed to have sex in the back while the driver pretended not to watch in his mirror. They got caught in a speakeasy raid, and Charlie gulped down both their drinks then claimed they'd been water while hiccuping cheap bourbon fumes over the Prohibition agents. They challenged each other in word games and free association jokes, and most of all, they made each other laugh.

'Where's hinterland?' he challenged.

'I don't know, but I suspect it's a place where they don't tell you that you smell; they just put on a gas mask when they see you coming.'

He chuckled.

'Now it's your turn,' she challenged, 'And the word you have to define is... gondolier.'

'A nasty disease you catch from boatmen, of course.' He was quick, and he was fun – so much fun.

She couldn't pinpoint when fun wasn't enough. Maybe she had always wanted more, or maybe her longing grew when he began to pull away, although the change was ever so subtle at first.

His editor sent him out on stories some nights, and Dottie was restless. She hurried home early in case he was trying to call, then sat by the telephone, sipping a highball and watching the clock. If he hasn't called by eleven, I'll try him, she thought, then at eleven, her courage failed. I'll definitely try if he hasn't rung by twelve, she decided.

She finally dialled the number and, when he picked up, she said, 'Room service. How about I arrive at your door wearing satin underwear and a big smile? I can be there in ten minutes, courtesy of New York City cabs.'

'I'm still working, Dottie,' he said. 'I need to file this story first thing in the morning. I'll see you tomorrow.'

Damn. Why had she telephoned? What an idiot she was! She'd sounded desperate rather than funny. Where was her wit when she needed it most?

And then there was a night when he didn't call, and he hadn't told her where he was going. The next day, she quizzed him, trying to keep her tone light.

'I'm going to have a word with that editor of yours,' she said, 'for depriving a girl of her lewd and libidinous requirements.'

'I'll mention it next time I speak to him,' Charlie said, but his tone was absent-minded.

'What was the story?' she persevered. 'And was it worth depriving me for?'

'Give it a rest, Dottie,' he snapped, and she jumped back as if scalded. He shook his head. 'You used to be so sweet, and now you're always on my case.'

It's easy to be sweet when you're not in love, she thought. Out loud, she said: 'I don't mean to be, angel. I think I'm a little cronky because I wrote to my husband this morning asking for a divorce. It's time for me to move on.'

'I hope you didn't do it on my behalf,' he said.

'Someone's in a mood today,' she commented, swallowing hard. 'Here' – she passed him her hip flask. 'Have some of Dottie's special medicine.'

Looking back, the alarm bells were echoing all around, like a village church on a Sunday morning, but still, it came as a shock when he announced his editor was sending him back to Chicago for a few months. Months! That was unthinkable!

'Why don't I come too?' she asked quickly. 'We could live in sin. It would be worth it just to make my bible-thumping stepmother pirouette in her grave.'

'Dottie, you forget that I'm married. I'll be living with my wife at our marital home in Chicago.' His voice was gentle but firm. His pupils were mere pinpoints against the hazel of his irises.

~

How did she get it so wrong? she wondered. She shouldn't be allowed near the opposite sex. Someone should lock her in handcuffs next time a man like Charlie walked in the room. Meanwhile, she would have to come up with some lines to explain to the Algonquin crowd why they were no longer an item.

'At the beginning, I wasn't aware of Charlie's liability,' she said. 'In other words, his skill at telling fibs.' That got a muted laugh. Some of the slower folk were still working it out, while others gave clucks of sympathy. She didn't want sympathy.

'I thought at first he had the sex drive of an animal,' she continued. 'Unfortunately, it turned out to be a sloth.' There were sniggers at that one. It wasn't true, though. All the best lines had some truth in them. Try harder, Dottie!

'Love is like quicksilver in the hand,' she said. 'Leave the fingers open and it stays in the palm. Clutch it and it darts away. In Charlie's case, it sprinted.'

She noticed FPA scribbling that down.

I should stick to what I'm best at in future, she decided. Forget about love. Forget about men who appear in a cloud of sex appeal. At least I've got words. They're not going anywhere. She opened her hip flask and had a long, thirsty slug. And neither is my beloved Haig & Haig.

~

Gill Paul is the bestselling author of ten historical novels, including 'The Collector's Daughter', about Lady Evelyn Herbert, the first person to enter Tutankhamun's tomb in modern times. Her novel 'Women and Children First' was shortlisted for the 2013 RNA Epic Novel of the Year award. Her books have reached the top of the USA Today, Toronto Globe & Mail and Kindle charts, and have been translated into twenty-one languages. Gill lives in London, where she is working on her new novel, and she swims daily in an outdoor pond. 'The Manhattan Girls', Gill Paul's novel about Dorothy Parker and her friends, is published in August 2022.

Author's Note

Some quotations in 'The Wittiest Woman in the World' have been paraphrased from printed sources, as follows:

"If you want to know what God thought of money," Dottie said, "just look at the people he gave it to."

"If you would learn what God thinks about money, you have only to look at those to whom He has given it." **Laments for the Living, by Dorothy Parker, 1930**

His voice was as intimate as the rustle of sheets, and it tugged deep down in her gut.

"His voice was intimate as the rustle of sheets, and he kissed easily." **Laments for the Living, by Dorothy Parker, 1930**

It's easy to be sweet when you're not in love, she thought.

"Oh, it's so easy to be sweet to people before you love them." **Laments for the Living, by Dorothy Parker, 1930**

"Love is like quicksilver in the hand," she said. "Leave the fingers open and it stays in the palm. Clutch it and it darts away.

"Love is like quicksilver in the hand, Sylvie. Leave the fingers open and it stays in the palm; clutch it, and it darts away." **Complete Stories, by Dorothy Parker, 1995**

HEART TO HEART

GILLIAN MCALLISTER

Sarah was early to meet him. She was always early, always factoring in imaginary crises into her day. She always left half an hour earlier than she said she would. Waiting was waiting, wherever you did it. And, anyway, she was good at it: early people always were.

She took her cardigan off. It was one of those rare summer days in early spring that somehow seemed to feel nostalgic. She enjoyed the contrast of the sharp, ice-cream cold air and the sun warming her skin. She studied her hands. She had age spots. For some reason, she'd never thought she'd get them. Not at forty-seven, anyway. They fascinated her.

He was fifteen minutes late. Sarah's skin felt hot and tight around her eyes by the time he approached. Her stomach clenched briefly into knots as he appeared before her. It was him. It was really him: the man who had written her the letter.

'Alright?' he said to her, both a greeting and a question; shorthand. She liked the economy of it. He didn't look how she had expected, which she knew was irrational, but she allowed herself to study him anyway. He was tall, lanky. He didn't eat enough, she thought, which made sense. Long, pale hands that looked blue-ish in the bright sun. Dark hair.

'Jon,' he added uselessly.

He stepped in front of her, blocking the sun. She couldn't see his face for a moment, and then he sat down next to her. The bench dipped under his weight.

'Thanks for coming,' she said.

'No problem,' he said. He dug his hands into the pockets of his fleece jacket and crossed his long legs at the ankles.

'When did you first find out?' she said.

He knew exactly what she meant. 'I got a call after I'd seen the specialist. I was at home. Just over there - Connaught Street.' He jerked his head behind them.

She turned around, though she knew she couldn't see any buildings from their bench. She could hear traffic in the distance. The parks in London pretended to be countryside, but they weren't. She hadn't come into Central London since it happened, and she was surprised that she hadn't missed it at all.

He looked at her as she turned back to him. So that, over there, that invisible building, was where his life had changed. Where had she been? She had just got into work, was squeezing a teabag inside her favourite, cracked mug. She was irritated by the call.

'Oh, Connaught Street, yes,' she said now, though she'd never heard of it.

He shifted on the bench. He was wearing aftershave, cologne maybe. A clean sweep of something lemon-scented drifted over. 'They said it was bad news. They asked if I could come in. I knew then, I guess.' He paused, then spoke again. 'I don't remember much after that. About the appointment.'

Shock. It was common. She had felt it herself, like some other-worldly horror working its way up her body, and then:

nothing. Diazepam. Whisky. Kind neighbours bringing lasagnas. She blinked and looked across at Jon, sitting comfortably in the sun, and thought he seemed fine. Good, even. Considering. She looked down at her own age-spotted hands. Hard to believe she had made it this far. Forty-seven and unscathed. She swallowed. We are so fragile, she thought. So many things could go wrong. It was amazing that it didn't happen more often.

'How long were you waiting?' she said, instead of saying all of that.

'After I was diagnosed?' he turned to her. He had neat eyebrows. Not a single stray hair. She liked that tidiness. She scanned his features, looking - nonsensically, she knew - for a familiar trait. He shifted slightly away from her, under her intense gaze, and she felt her cheeks warm.

'Yes,' she said. 'After the call at home.'

'Only thirteen weeks. It was pretty serious. I don't remember the last few weeks. Or the recovery.'

'No. I guess not.'

He crossed and uncrossed his legs. He wanted to leave: he'd done his duty.

She closed her eyes, embarrassed, and concentrated on the traffic in the distance. She found it soothing, though she knew that didn't make any sense. If he'd been driving, safe in a car . . . if he had been cycling. On the tube, or on a train. There were so many ways he could have travelled: perhaps, if she thought about it hard enough, she could bring one of these alternative worlds into existence, and he would be sitting here on the bench, right next to her. She opened her eyes. But he wasn't. He had walked. He had been walking, soft-bodied and vulnerable on the pavement.

She received the call on a Tuesday morning. A cyclist had ploughed into him. That's the word they used: *ploughed*. He had died instantly, her son, her Matt, her fifteen-year-old son on his way to school where he had double P.E. first thing, was excited because it was the last day of the term and he was going to Spain the next week.

She'd signed the forms in the hospital, leaning against the reception desk because all of the private rooms were full. Her consent was given unthinkingly. A tick in a box. Of course he would be an organ donor.

And now, here she was, eight months on, in the spring sunshine, still here - somehow - but without him, without Matt, but next to Jon, the man who had had cardiomyopathy, and in whose chest sat her son's heart, still - somehow - beating.

She reached out, across the bench, and touched his hand, just briefly. He held onto her. His grip was firm and clammy. 'Thank you for coming to see me,' she said. 'Thank you for writing to me.'

He met her gaze this time. 'No, thank you,' he said. 'And your son.'

His shirt was open, and she could see the scar. It would match Matt's, she thought.

Gillian McAllister has been writing for as long as she can remember. She graduated with an English degree before working as a lawyer. She lives in Birmingham, where she now writes full-time. She is the Sunday Times bestselling author of 'Everything But the Truth', 'Anything You Do Say', 'No Further Questions', 'The Evidence Against You', 'How To Disappear', and the Richard & Judy Book Club pick, 'That Night'. She is also the creator and co-host of the popular 'Honest Authors' podcast. Her latest book 'Wrong Place Wrong Time' is out in May 2022.

A VERY MERRY CHRISTMAS

HOLLY MARTIN

Merry hurried as fast as she dared along the icy pavement. She had so much to do before Christmas Day, and there simply wasn't enough time left to do it all. Now she had closed her shop, Sugar and Ice, for the Christmas break, she would have to work all hours to get everything ready.

It was her turn to host Christmas for her family. Her parents were coming at lunch tomorrow for the big day, but Joy, Merry's little sister and her husband Stephen, would arrive tomorrow morning, along with their three kids. Stephen was also bringing a friend who was on his own for Christmas.

While Merry hated the idea of anyone being alone for the big day, she could smell a set-up a mile away; Joy had been telling her for weeks how wonderful this man was. He wasn't the first: Joy had been trying to set Merry up ever since she had married Stephen. Joy wanted Merry to find her own happy-ever-after and, so far, had tried to set her up with her milkman, her postman, a friend from Joy's work, the librarian, the pub landlord, and so many others.

It wasn't that Merry wasn't interested in love; she just

didn't have time for it. Owning a cake shop meant very long hours, getting up early in the mornings to make the cakes and sandwiches for the day. She also made her own handmade chocolates and sold mugs, plates, candles and other homeware in her shop. She was on her feet all day, serving cakes, making coffee or hot chocolate, and when she finally left work, she would come home late and fall asleep in front of the TV or over the book she was reading.

Today was the first time in a very long time that Merry had come home before it was dark, but she had so much to do: she had to decorate the tree, wrap the last few presents, ice the gingerbread men for the kids and make the mince pies for everyone else. And even when everyone arrived, she would be busy making sure they were all happy and well-fed. She certainly wouldn't have time to flirt with some friend of Stephen's who probably had no idea he had only been invited as some kind of plus-one for her.

Merry looked up at the snow; flakes had been falling all morning. It was starting to settle now, and the roads and pavements were already covered, showing no sign of stopping. She could feel how slippery the pavements were, and she was thankful she wasn't driving in it.

Not many people drove in the tiny town of Angel Bottom, not when you could walk from one end to the other in fifteen minutes. The hills were steep, the lanes tight and twisty. It was easier all round if you walked. The only cars on the roads were tourists visiting the little seaside town or people passing through to the next town of Angel Top, where Joy and Stephen lived.

Suddenly Merry heard a squeal of brakes behind her at the top of the hill. She turned to see a green car losing control on the steep bend, the wheels locking as the driver slammed on the brakes. The car skidded, then swerved, avoiding the little house at the top of the road by inches. But just as it looked like the car had come to rest, it started sliding sideways down the hill, picking up speed as it zoomed past her. Knowing the inevitable fate of the car was to land in the small pond at the bottom of the hill, Merry found herself running to catch up with it. Seconds later, there was a loud splash and the sound of the ice cracking as the car toppled into the icy water.

The car was sinking sideways into the pond as Merry ran unthinking into the water. She gasped as the freezing temperatures engulfed her body, making her arms feel like lead as her long winter coat weighed her down. The water bubbled as the car began to slowly sink beneath the surface. Her heart was pounding against her ribs as she heaved herself onto the side of the car, although now she was here, she wasn't entirely sure what she was going to do. She peered through the window and could see a man semi-submerged, struggling to remove his seat belt. Kneeling on the side of the car, she wrenched open the door. The man looked up at her as the icy air whipped into the car.

'The seat belt,' the man gasped, desperately trying to free himself as the water level crept up over his legs. Merry tried to release the button herself, but it was jammed. Realising she still had her handbag slung over her shoulder, she rummaged around inside the soggy contents for something that would help release him. She grabbed a pair of nail scissors and leaned in to start cutting the belt away from him, but the scissors were blunt and made very slow progress in cutting the thick fabric.

'Hurry.' The man's voice was tight with anxiety and cold.

'Oh, sorry, I didn't realise the situation was that desperate; I thought I'd take my time,' she grunted with the effort. Suddenly the seat belt pinged free, and the man pulled himself out of the car and knelt next to Merry, the weight displacement making the car sink quicker.

'Come on, we have to go,' Merry said, sliding off the car into the cold waters, gasping again.

'Oh, I thought we could hang around here all day.' The man slid into the water beside her. 'Christ, it's cold.' He quickly started swimming to the bank, and Merry struck out to join him, but something held her back. Her trousers were caught on the car. The weight of her coat was pulling her down too. She ditched her coat, but it gathered around her like a giant green octopus surrounding its prey. Merry struggled against the car but couldn't move.

The man reached the bank, heaved himself out and turned around, panting with the pain of the cold water. As Merry thrashed in the water, he realised something was wrong and immediately jumped back in, pushing Merry's green coat out of the way so he could get to her.

'What's up? I thought you wanted to get out of here?' His voice shook with the cold.

'My trousers...they're stuck on the car,' Merry gasped as she vainly struggled. The man felt down her leg until he could reach the trapped part and tried to rip the trousers free.

'Damn it; I can't get it.'

'It's pulling me down.' Merry wriggled to free herself as the water crept up to her neck.

He reached round to the front of her trousers, quickly undid the flies, then yanked them down.

'Sorry,' he murmured with some embarrassment.

'I normally insist on dinner before a date gets this far,' Merry shivered, kicking her shoes off so she could get her trousers past her feet. As soon as she was free of her trousers, they swam towards the bank. The man got there first, pulled himself out, and then turned to help Merry out of the water.

They sat down on the edge of the bank, panting. The man lay down, closing his eyes and breathing heavily.

At the back of her mind, Merry was aware that the street was deserted. If anyone was going to help them, it was going to be themselves.

Merry rolled onto her front, summoning the energy to stand up.

'Get up,' Merry muttered, bending double to catch her breath.

'Yeah, in a minute,' the man said.

'Get up now, you idiot.' Merry took his arm and yanked him up.

'Great, another bloody woman telling me what to do,' the man groaned as he struggled to get to his feet.

'Come back to my home; it's just up here.' Merry started walking across the grass onto the road.

'That's forward,' the man muttered as he slowly followed her. 'Nice undies, by the way.'

Merry couldn't even find the energy to blush about her Mr Tickle pants. She could feel her body shutting down; she felt suddenly exhausted and stumbled a little on her numb legs. The man caught her arm. 'You all right?'

Merry nodded, looking down at her socks flopping uselessly at the end of her feet. Very attractive.

They staggered up the street as if they were drunk, leaving a wet snail trail behind them.

'I thought you said your house wasn't far,' the man grumbled.

'Oh shut up,' Merry said. 'We're here now.' She lifted a flowerpot with shaking fingers to get the spare key and let herself into the tiny cottage. The man followed her up the stairs. The heat of the cottage seemed to swallow her oppressively as she nudged the man in the direction of the bathroom. She turned the shower on and let the hot water run over her hands; it burnt her, and she pulled back. She adjusted the temperature down, so it was lukewarm and turned back to the man, who was already fighting out of his shirt and jacket. She couldn't help noticing the swirls and stars that circled the muscles of his left arm.

'You go first,' Merry mumbled and made to leave the bathroom, but the man pulled her back.

'Don't be stupid.'

Merry turned back with resignation; he was right. She would surely get hypothermia if she stayed in these wet clothes for much longer, and he had already seen her in her knickers.

Merry pulled her jumper over her head as the man rubbed his hands under the water, groaning with pain as he massaged his arms. She tried to undo the buttons of her shirt, but her fingers had gone numb and seemed unwilling to work properly. The man stepped out of the shower and undid the buttons of her shirt quickly, almost ripping it off her arms in his urgency to get back under the hot water. As soon as her shirt was on the floor next to his, he stepped back into the shower, pulling her with him. They stood in the shower, grunting and gasping with the pain and rubbing themselves to restore the feeling in their limbs.

He pulled his trousers off and then leaned against the wall, sighing.

Merry sat on the floor, resting her head against the tiles. He slid down the wall to sit by her. He closed his eyes, breathing deeply.

'I'm Alistair, by the way.'

She reached up to the controls to turn the temperature up slightly. 'Merry.'

After what seemed like an age of sitting in silence, the hot water pouring over them, Merry stood up and walked shakily into the bedroom. She removed her wet underwear and pulled on her fleecy pyjamas. She turned to see Alistair arrive in her bedroom wearing her robe. She still felt cold, although not as bad as before, and Alistair was clearly still feeling the effects too, as he rubbed his hands together.

She got into bed and pulled the duvet around her.

'Thank you for saving me,' Alistair said. 'I don't even want to think about what would have happened if you hadn't been there.'

Merry didn't have the energy to speak.

'I should go....' Alistair said hesitantly.

She lifted the duvet. 'Get in.'

He didn't even hesitate as he climbed under the covers with her. She shivered and cringed a little as she snuggled up against him. This was weird. He probably thought she was trying it on with him when that was the last thing on her mind, but to her surprise, he wrapped his arms around her and held her against him, rubbing his hands up and down her back. OK, it had just got a lot weirder, but she couldn't have cared less as she rested her head on his chest and closed her eyes.

~

Merry woke up in darkness, feeling disorientated. She was pressed against something warm and hard. Slowly she realised she was deep under her duvet and that her body was aching. She wrestled the duvet off her head and realised that the something warm she was lying against was Alistair. He had the deepest brown eyes, like pools of melted chocolate, and his dark curly hair sticking out in all directions made him look very sexy and dishevelled.

'Hey.' Merry swept the hair out of her face, rolling back onto her pillow.

'Hey, you all right?' Alistair asked, shifting onto his side to talk to her. He had a lovely soft Scottish accent, something she hadn't noticed earlier when their lives had hung in the balance.

'Yeah, I think so, but man, do I ache. I'm boiling actually.' Merry struggled to get the duvet off her.

'Well, it's better to be hot than cold, I suppose, though you might be running a temperature.' Alistair felt her forehead.

Merry closed her eyes at his touch, his hand feeling soft and cool on her skin. 'What about you? You took quite a knock when your car fell into the pond. Are you OK?'

'Yeah, achy, the same as you, but I'm OK. You've been asleep for hours; I didn't want to leave you in case...You were actually starting to worry me; you were asleep that long.'

'What time is it?'

'It's, er, nearly five.'

Merry groaned.

'Oh god, I have so much to do. My family are coming tomorrow, and I have nothing ready for them.'

'Are you kidding? I think you have a very valid excuse. You're a hero; you saved my life.'

'I don't feel like a hero right now.'

'Come on, let's get up and get something to eat,' Alistair said. 'Eating sweet things is a good way to get your energy back up.'

'Well, fortunately for you, I work in a cake shop. Sweet things are kind of my forte. I make my own chocolates, cakes and biscuits.'

'In that case, I think you should marry me.'

Merry laughed and climbed out of bed. Alistair did too, and she met him at the bedroom door. He was taller than she had realised and had the same build her brother-in-law had, that of a rugby player. She could see his smooth chest peeping out from the top of her robe, which was huge on her and barely fitted him. One wrong move and other things might be peeping out as well.

She mentally shook herself. What was she thinking? She didn't know the first thing about Alistair, yet he was almost naked in her bedroom. And she'd just shared a bed with him. He could be an axe murderer or some kind of con artist. Although it would have to be a very elaborate con to accidentally drive your car into a frozen pond in the hope of preying on some poor unsuspecting gullible woman. But either way, maybe it would be better all-round if he left.

'So we can eat, and then I'll call you a taxi to take you to wherever you were going,' Merry said brightly. 'I'm sure you'll have lots to sort out with the car and the insurance. Probably best if you....' She didn't say the word 'go' as that seemed rude but then chucking him out a few hours after he'd had a car accident *was* rude.

His face fell a little.

'I certainly don't want to impose, but my clothes are soaking wet. And my wallet was in the car, so I have no way to pay for a taxi.'

'Right,' Merry said. Her purse was also in her bag at the bottom of the pond, so she couldn't give him any money either, but this temporary arrangement of helping a stranger was suddenly looking a bit more long-term. 'Well, I can stick your clothes in the tumble dryer while we eat.'

'And if I can use your phone, I can call my friend to come and collect me in a few hours,' Alistair said.

OK, there was a plan. And maybe he would just watch TV for a few hours while she got on with all her jobs. She didn't need to entertain him.

'Of course you can use my phone,' Merry said, opening the door. There, she wasn't totally unreasonable, and she would just ignore the edge of guilt that was gnawing away at her. And forget the feeling in her heart that said there was another reason that she wanted him gone. There was something about Alistair that she liked, and that was not a road she wanted to go down.

Merry went into the bathroom to collect his clothes and then headed downstairs into the kitchen.

'Ooh, gingerbread men, I haven't had one of them since I was a kid,' Alistair said, spotting them on the cooling rack.

'And you're not having them now; those are for my nieces and nephew. But I can offer you a slice of Christmas cake. Or some handmade chocolates.' Merry threw his clothes in the tumble dryer.

'Both, please, I'm starving,' Alistair said.

She cut him a large slice of cake and placed the tin of chocolates next to him while she boiled the kettle. 'Tea, coffee?'

'Coffee would be great,' Alistair said, taking a huge bite of the cake and then groaning in pleasure. 'This cake is amazing. And I have to say this kitchen is like a chef's dream. You have every gadget and appliance anyone could ever need.'

'I love to bake, which is why I opened my cake shop. Do you cook, Alistair?'

'I do. I don't bake cakes or make chocolates or gingerbread men, but I love pottering around in the kitchen, trying different recipes. In fact, I could make us some soup now if you like?'

She blinked. Her last proper boyfriend had never done anything in the kitchen. He'd helped out doing other things in the house, but he'd always made excuses about cooking, saying he could never do it as well as she could.

Alistair had moved to the fridge and was looking through all her food.

'Roasted vegetable soup OK?' he asked, already loading his arms up with carrots, parsnips, potatoes, mushrooms, peppers and tomatoes. He moved back to the breakfast bar and laid down his bounty. He turned the oven on and grabbed a chopping board and a knife, and then started slicing everything up.

She'd never really had someone in her kitchen before, not in the cooking sense, moving around and using her things, and she wasn't sure if she liked it. But vegetable soup did sound amazing.

As Alistair seemed to have everything in hand, she passed him his coffee and sat down to watch him for a moment. It was quite restful to watch someone else do the cooking for a change. 'So, where were you heading this afternoon?'

'I'm spending Christmas with my friend, so I was heading round to his house.'

'Oh, do you want to call him?' Merry asked. 'He'll be wondering where you are.'

'Thank you. I'll call him shortly; he can come and pick me up. He wasn't expecting me until later anyway.'

She watched as he finished chopping and slicing the vegetables then threw them all into a colander for washing.

'What about you, what are your plans for Christmas?' Alistair asked.

'My family are coming here tomorrow, my sister and her kids and Mum and Dad will be here for the big day. I also have a wonderful man coming that my sister and her husband are trying to set me up with.'

Alistair laughed. 'Don't you just hate being set up? If you're single everyone automatically sees it as their duty to find someone perfect for you when actually you'd just prefer to be left alone.'

'Exactly,' Merry said. Finally, someone understood. 'There have been so many men I've been forced to go on dates with. They all seem nice, but...'

'Not right for you.'

'Yes! Why do you get this, but my sister doesn't? She says I'm being too picky, that I can't possibly know if these men aren't right for me after just one date, but I think you can.'

Alistair nodded as he ran the vegetables under the tap. 'Oh, of course you know. If the conversation is stilted and awkward, if you don't have things in common, if the other person terrifies you.'

Merry laughed. 'Oh god, you've had it bad.'

'There have been some memorable dates and not for the right reasons. Part of the reason I'm going to Mo's house this Christmas. He knows better than to try to set me up.'

'Well, at least none of my dates were likely to kill me in my sleep; they all seemed too boring for that,' Merry said.

'Yeah, you need to have that spark straightaway. You need someone that gets the old heart pumping, someone that you would be excited to see again.'

'Yes, it has to be someone special. I'm happy on my own and I don't have a lot of time, so if I'm going to date someone, they have to have that... magic ingredient.'

He nodded. 'When you find the right person for you, the person that you're happy to make time for, you'll know.'

She watched Alistair as he washed the chopping board and the knife and left them to dry on the draining board. There was something nice about having him here, after all.

'Do you have a baking tray or roasting tin?' Alistair asked.

Merry stood up, retrieved one from the cupboard, and then started getting everything ready to ice and decorate the gingerbread men. Alistair tipped all the vegetables into the tray and drizzled olive oil over the top. He put the tray into the oven and then came over to her side.

'Can I help?'

She smiled. 'You want to help me decorate the gingerbread men?'

'Well, I'm still hopeful I might be able to try one.'

She laughed. 'I knew there'd be an ulterior motive.'

'How many children are coming?'

'Three.'

'There are six gingerbread men; surely they don't need two each?' Alistair said innocently. 'That's bad for their teeth.'

Merry sighed theatrically. 'If you decorate them well enough, I may let you have one.'

'Now that's an incentive if ever I heard one,' Alistair said.

Merry started mixing the icing together.

'So tell me about this guy you're being set up with,' Alistair said, pinching one of the Smarties and popping it in his mouth.

'Oh, I don't know, I wasn't paying any attention when my sister was telling me all about him.'

'It sounds like you've already made your mind up that you won't like him.'

Merry sighed. 'Is that awful? This poor guy. I hope he doesn't come here expecting to find the love of his life. I'm hoping he's just coming for turkey and mince pies; otherwise he'll be seriously disappointed. It's just that I've been here with my sister before; she'll find the most tenuous link possible between me and my potential date. She set me up with a guy once purely because we both liked Garfield when we were kids. I had a date a few months ago with a man, and the only thing we had in common was that we both loved tomato soup; that was why she thought we would be perfect for each other. And this guy coming tomorrow, the one guaranteed to be the love of my life, have a guess what his name is?'

'Oh, no idea, Bert?'

Merry laughed. 'I'd take Bert, actually. Christmas, Dr Christmas.'

Alistair's eyes widened in horror.

'I know, it's ridiculous. Joy has set me up with him purely because, if we get married, I'll be Merry Christmas.'

He laughed a little. 'Now that would be silly. Although this Dr Christmas might be very nice.'

'He might be, I suppose. Joy must have mentioned that he was a doctor a hundred times. As if that makes him someone I can't possibly turn down.'

'You don't like doctors?'

Merry scooped the icing into two piping bags and handed him one.

'I don't have a problem with doctors. But you can be a doctor of pretty much anything. This guy could be a doctor of something silly like fashion or music or real estate or beer. All the title of doctor tells me is that the man likes to study. It doesn't tell me what kind of man he is. Whether he is kind or funny or great in bed.'

'That's what you're looking for in a man?' Alistair asked.

She looked up at him, and his chocolate eyes sparkled with amusement.

She blushed. 'I don't think that's too much to ask for.'

'No, I think those are great qualities.'

'And someone who can really kiss,' Merry said. 'The kind of kiss that would knock my socks off.'

She saw his eyes cast down to her lips for the briefest of seconds.

He cleared his throat. 'I think that's a very important quality too.'

Was it completely crazy that she suddenly wanted to know what it would be like to kiss him?

Alistair burst out laughing as Merry finished telling him a story about one of her customers.

He liked Merry. She was funny and easy to talk to. He just hoped the ease between them would continue once she found out who he really was. He hadn't been entirely honest with her, but it was more a lie of omission than anything else.

'That soup was amazing,' Merry said, wiping the last drops from her bowl with a hunk of bread.

His roasted vegetable soup was a recent recipe he had been playing with, so he was pleased it had worked out. Usually when he was trying to impress a woman, he would cook them steak; he'd never used soup as a way to a woman's heart before.

He paused as he took a sip of his mulled wine. Was that what he was doing? Trying to win her over?

He'd been out on a lot of dates since his fiancée had left him for another man three years before, but none of them had made an impression on him, and he had felt kind of deflated by the dating scene lately. But sitting here talking to Merry, he could feel parts of his heart spark back to life again.

'Does that mean I get a gingerbread man as a reward?' Alistair asked.

She laughed as she stood, picking one up from the tray. 'You can have this one with the wonky eyes.'

'Hey, I was going for a Picasso look.'

'Well, you achieved that.'

He smiled as he took a bite, the taste of ginger dancing on his tongue. It was soft with a slight crispiness to it.

'This is good. I can see why your cake shop does such good business, and I understand why your whole family are descending on you tomorrow.'

'Ah, I love having them here. Apart from the matchmaking, I'm very close with Joy, and Stephen is wonderful for her. The kids are at that cute age where they still believe in Santa and magic and dreams coming true. They make me laugh a lot. And Mum and Dad are brilliant; I'm very close with them. It'll be a great day, and I enjoy cooking for them. We always spend Christmas together; we just take it in turns who hosts it.' She paused while she took a sip of wine. 'Do you have family nearby?'

He smiled at the subtle question. 'Why am I spending Christmas with my friend instead of with my family, you mean?'

'Oh no, I didn't mean... Well, OK then, yes I did,' she blushed.

'My parents live in Australia, my brother and his wife live in Canada, so we don't all get together very often. I did consider staying with my parents this year, but there's something a bit weird about spending Christmas on the beach in your shorts and t-shirt. Give me cold, snowy England any day. Log fires, mince pies, I love a traditional Christmas. Mo invited me to spend Christmas Day with him and I get on well with his wife and kids, so it seemed a no-brainer. Then few weeks ago, he said they were going to his sister-in-law's house instead but that I was very much still invited. I thought it might be weird to spend Christmas at someone else's house, but Mo assured me that I'd be very welcome.'

'Some people love to fill their house with guests,' Merry said. 'The more, the merrier.'

The grandfather clock in the corner struck seven. It was a lovely old piece which seemed oddly at home amongst all the cosy, modern contemporary furniture and decorations.

'I like your clock,' Alistair said.

'It literally was my grandfather's, the only thing I have of his. He died several years ago, then my nan died a week later. I miss them both very much. They were such a big part of our lives, and they were always here at Christmas. He loved this old clock, so there was no way I could get rid of it.'

He watched her as she talked. 'Family is really important to you, isn't it?'

'Yes, it is. They drive me mad sometimes with their interfering, but I wouldn't be without them.'

He liked that.

'And I can't believe it's seven o'clock already. I need to decorate the tree. Do you need to get off, or can you stay a bit longer?' Merry asked.

He smiled. 'Tree decorating? I wouldn't miss it for the world.'

Merry placed the box of decorations on the table and pulled out a toilet-roll Santa. She passed it to Alistair, and he smiled.

'Based on the other decorations around the house, I had you pegged for the more traditional tree ornament kind of girl.'

'All these decorations have been homemade by my nieces and nephew, me and my sister, parents, and grandparents. It's become a bit of a tradition. Every Christmas Day, after the turkey has been eaten and all the presents unwrapped, we all sit around and make decorations. Whoever hosts Christmas gets the box to decorate the tree with.'

'That's a lovely idea,' Alistair said. 'So what do you decorate your tree with when you're not hosting?'

Merry giggled. 'Much more traditional decorations.'

'I knew it!'

'I love the homemade tree, it's very special, and I love it when it comes to my house. But I think part of what makes it special is that it's not here every year.'

Alistair laughed. 'Is that your roundabout way of saying you like your traditional decorations?'

She blushed and laughed. 'Yes, I do.'

She started attaching the decorations to the tree, and Alistair did the same: a sparkly pink elephant, a Rudolph with three legs, a cotton-wool snowman, a Christmas tree with googly eyes; they all were hung on the branches.

'What about your tree?' Merry asked him.

'Well, it's very small,' said Alistair. 'And I'm ashamed to say after seeing how spectacular this tree is that I just put the same baubles on it every year. When I was with Gemma, my ex-fiancée, we had all these decorations we had bought from places we had been together. When she left me after having an affair with another man, I no longer wanted to hang those decorations on the tree anymore, so I just bought a big box of red baubles, and I use them every year instead.'

'Oh no, I'm sorry, that must have been really crappy.'

'It was, but in my heart, I knew it wasn't working between us. I'm an architect, and I travelled a lot with my work, and she hated that. So I got a job more locally, but I think the damage was done by then. I think it was as much my fault as it was hers.'

Merry frowned as she placed a sparkly green T-Rex on the tree. 'I don't see you working away from home being on a par with her cheating on you.'

'No, I guess not. Definitely more her fault then,' he nodded.

Merry laughed. 'That was a quick change of heart.'

Alistair shrugged. 'Cheating on me was bad, but I was far from the perfect boyfriend. We were young when we got together; I think we just outgrew each other. We should have discussed things and ended it as grown-ups, but the result would still have been the same.'

Merry was silent for a while. She had been part of one of those grown-up discussions where her boyfriend of three years had ended things between them. It was always harder when one half of the couple wanted to stay as a couple, and the other half didn't. It had hurt—a lot. And for a long time, she thought that it must have been her that was the issue. Would it have hurt more if her boyfriend had cheated on her? Would it have helped if she could have blamed him instead of him being so bloody reasonable about it all? But Alistair was right: when two people weren't right for each other, there was no point in staying together because that just led to pain and confusion. It was probably why she had been so wary of getting involved seriously with anyone for such a long time. She never really gave any of the guys she had dated a chance because she didn't want a relationship; she didn't want to get hurt again. She looked over at Alistair. Maybe that needed to change. Or, at the very least, perhaps it was worth taking the time to get to know him a bit better.

There was a thud against her window, and she looked round to see some kids running past laughing as they threw snowballs at each other.

'God, that snow is coming down thick and fast,' Merry said, going to the window to look out. It had really settled. In fact, it appeared to be very deep. 'Your friend might have trouble coming to get you,' she said, moving to the front door, opening it and peering out. Alistair came to her side.

Fat flakes of snow danced and twirled in the air while Christmas lights twinkled in the windows of the other houses, sending a golden glow over the fallen snow. The road was completely covered, and no cars had been down it for several hours. It was easily a foot or deeper out there, and drifts of three or four feet gathered against the walls and doors of the houses. It looked magical, but there was no way she could send Alistair out in it. A frisson of excitement bubbled through her.

She looked up at him, and he was smiling at her. She wondered if he'd come to the same realisation.

'Looks like you won't be going anywhere tonight,' Merry said, biting her lip nervously.

He grinned. 'Are you asking me to spend the night?'

She laughed. 'You can sleep on the sofa.'

'The sofa is fine, although technically, we've already slept together once.'

She smiled as she shut the door. 'I don't generally jump into bed with strange men.'

'Ah, but now you know me a little better you don't think I'm strange anymore?'

'I still think you're strange, but I'm pleased you're going to be staying a little longer. I'd like to get to know you some more.'

He smiled. 'I'm pleased too. I've enjoyed chatting to you over the last few hours.'

'Oh, but what about your friends? They'll be expecting you – and your friend's sister-in-law, she'll have catered for you.'

'I'll give them a call, but something tells me I'm right where I'm supposed to be.'

Merry smiled. She liked that. 'Why don't I make us hot chocolate, and you can use my phone?'

'Good idea.'

She moved off into the kitchen and heated some milk on the stove before pouring it into two mugs with hot chocolate and squirting cream on the top. She carried them back into the lounge just as Alistair was hanging up the phone.

'All sorted,' he said. 'I'm going to see my friend and his family tomorrow.'

She pushed down the tiny sliver of disappointment that she wouldn't be spending Christmas Day with him.

She placed the mugs down and turned her attention to

the last few tree decorations. She hung a felt penguin on the tree as Alistair pulled out a decoration and went to hang it on the bottom of the tree. She caught his arm as she recognised which decoration it was—the famous mistletoe decoration.

'This one has to go on the top. The mistletoe used to be my nan's. She was a bit of a potter in her day, and she made this out of clay one year and hung it on top of the tree. My grandad kissed her for the first time under it on Christmas Eve. They were married for sixty-seven years. Nan said the mistletoe was lucky because my dad shared his first kiss with my mum under this mistletoe too. She told me I was to hang it on the tree every year as one day I would be kissed by the man of my dreams.'

She cleared her throat and blushed furiously as she realised what she'd just said. She had just been trying to tell Alistair about the silly sentimental attachment she had to this ornament, but it had sounded like she was fishing for a kiss when that had been the very last thing on her mind. Well... not the very last thing on her mind. She quickly hung the mistletoe and then busied herself with looking at the other decorations.

'Well, I don't know about being the man of your dreams part, but I like a good tradition,' Alistair said.

She looked up at him. He smiled as he gently cupped her face, and then he kissed her.

God, the taste of him was heaven. Excitement erupted inside her like snowflakes caught in a blizzard. He slid his hands around her neck, stroking her face gently with his thumbs. She moved her hands around his back, feeling the solid muscles in his shoulders. She felt the slide of his tongue against hers, and a twist of desire burst through her. This was everything a kiss should be, slow, gentle, but with a touch of passion, a promise of what would be.

He pulled back slightly and kissed her on the forehead.

'How was that? Did it blow your socks off?'

Merry laughed. 'Definitely. As first kisses go, I think that was one of the best.'

His eyes searched hers. 'And was it a first kiss?'

She leaned up and kissed him briefly on the lips. 'I hope there will be many more.'

The light of Christmas Day morning filled the room, and Merry stretched and smiled.

There would be no mince pies today; she'd had much more pressing things to attend to the night before. They had wrapped the presents together and then spent the rest of the night kissing, cuddling and talking on the sofa. She really bloody liked this man and, for the first time in a long time, she wanted to see where this went. She had the feeling he felt the same too.

'Happy Christmas, beautiful,' Alistair said sleepily, kissing her nose.

She smiled. 'I can't believe this has happened. I had no interest in a relationship yesterday, I told myself I didn't have time for one, and yet here you are, you literally crashed into my life and now... Well, everything has changed.'

'I agree, I didn't expect any of this, but I'm so glad it happened. Look, why don't we get dressed and then you can partake in one of my Christmas traditions.'

'Which is?'

'Pancakes for breakfast.'

'I like the sound of this tradition.'

He stood up and held his hand out to help her up. She stood up too. He kissed her on the cheek and moved off to the kitchen to retrieve his clothes from the tumble dryer. It would be a shame to see him in clothes again; she had enjoyed seeing him in her robe.

She walked up the stairs to her bedroom and slipped into her leggings and a black jumper dress covered in sparkly gold stars. She looked out the window. It had rained overnight and while the snow hadn't gone completely, a lot of it had melted away, and there was evidence that cars had been going up and down her hill already that morning. It looked like her family would have no problems getting through, which meant that Alistair would have no problem leaving.

Merry went back downstairs to find Alistair, fully clothed, whisking up the batter in the kitchen. His face lit up when she walked in.

'You look lovely.'

She smiled as she put the radio on and a Christmas song from Michael Bublé filled the air.

'What toppings would you like?' Alistair said, pouring some of the mixture into a hot pan.

'Bananas would be good,' Merry said.

'Good plan, and do you have any maple syrup?'

'I do actually; my nephew loves it on ice cream.'

'Max, right?'

'Yes.' She was impressed that he had remembered her mentioning her nephew's name. She didn't remember telling him, but she must have let it slip in the conversation the night before.

She started chopping some bananas into slices while Alistair dished up the pancakes. He covered them in a generous squirt of maple syrup; then she slid the bananas onto the plates too. They sat down at the table to eat them.

'These are really good,' Merry said. 'My customers would love these.'

'Well, maybe I'll have to come in and teach you how to do them.'

She smiled. 'I'd like that.'

'Listen, I have something I need to tell you. I should have told you last night, but I didn't want to ruin what we had but—'

There was a sudden knocking on the door, and the doorbell rang several times. Merry smiled, knowing it was her nieces and nephew trying to get her attention, desperate to start their Christmas celebrations.

'Hold that thought; you're about to meet the family.'

Merry stood up and went to answer the door.

Her twin nieces, Alexa and Imogen, leapt into her arms, squealing greetings of Happy Christmas, while her nephew, Max, started singing, 'We Wish You a Merry Christmas'.

She hugged them all, feeling a warmth growing inside now that her family were here.

The kids ran in as she greeted Joy and Stephen. 'Ah, I'm so glad you're here; I wasn't sure if you would make it through the snow.'

'I know, it came down so thick last night,' Joy said, hugging Merry and giving her a warm kiss on the cheek. 'The kids are delighted. I've promised them we'll go sledging later if the snow on the hills holds, or at the very least, we should make a snowman.'

Merry ushered them inside as she thought how wonderful it would be to share those things with Alistair too.

Stephen struggled in with bags of presents and dumped them all by the tree, just as Alistair came through from the kitchen with Alexa hanging off his hand and Imogen wrapped over his back. That was weird. The girls were far from shy, but they would never usually throw themselves on a stranger like that.

'Ah, Alistair, you're here already,' Joy said, kissing Alistair on the cheek. 'We were worried you wouldn't make it.'

Merry looked between them in confusion. 'You two know each other?'

Joy looked at her as if she was mad. 'Of course, this is the wonderful Dr Christmas I've been telling you about.'

Merry stared at Alistair in shock. 'You... You're Dr Christmas?'

Alistair had the good grace to look embarrassed. 'Yeah, that was what I was trying to tell you just now.'

'Wait, who did you think Alistair was when he turned up on your doorstep this morning?' Stephen asked.

'Well, that's a bit of a long story, Mo,' Alistair said.

'Mo? You're Mo?' Merry asked. This was getting even more confusing.

'It's a nickname from rugby. That's how Alistair and I know each other,' Stephen explained. 'Mo after Mo Farah on account of how fast I can run when I have the ball. The nickname has stuck for years.'

'Why didn't you tell me this last night?' Merry said to Alistair.

'Last night?' Stephen chuckled. 'Alistair, you dark horse. When you phoned last night to say you were staying at a friend's house, I wasn't expecting this. I think I want to hear this story after all.'

Joy looked between Merry and Alistair.

'Why don't we go into the kitchen with the girls, and you two can join us in a few minutes,' Joy said, peeling Imogen off Alistair's back and scooping Alexa under her other arm. She walked off in the direction of the kitchen and after a few seconds, Stephen reluctantly followed her, leaving Merry alone with Alistair.

'I can't believe you didn't tell me,' Merry said. 'I told you all about me being set up with Dr Christmas, and you never thought to mention that was you?'

'I did think to mention it, but as you had already decided you wanted nothing to do with him, and I have one of those silly doctorates, which I didn't think you'd appreciate, I didn't think I would get a fair chance if I suddenly outed myself. I enjoyed your company way too much to want to do anything to ruin it. I'm sorry.'

Merry sighed. She had told him that she wasn't interested in Dr Christmas, based purely on her sister's awful track record. She couldn't really blame him for not telling her.

He moved closer to her, placing his hands on her shoulders. 'I really am sorry.'

He kissed her on the head, and she felt herself smiling slightly. For once, her sister had got it right. The night before had been amazing and, despite her fear of getting involved with another man again, she wasn't going to push him away over this.

'It's OK,' Merry said quietly.

He searched her eyes. 'It is?'

She nodded.

'And look, I'm not sure what's going to happen between us, but if we do end up getting married, you don't need to take my name,' Alistair said. 'That would be silly. I'm a forward-thinking man; I can take your surname instead.'

She smirked at this.

'What is your surname?' Alistair asked.

'McAllister.'

He laughed. 'Alistair McAllister. It's got a nice ring to it.'

She smiled and reached up and kissed him. 'Merry Christmas sounds much better.'

Holly Martin is the bestselling author of 26 books, selling over a million books worldwide. Holly's books have been translated into French, German, Italian, Dutch, Bulgarian, Estonian, Turkish and Russian and she has been shortlisted for Best Romantic Read, Best eBook and Innovation in Romantic Fiction at the Festival of Romance. Holly lives in a little white cottage by the sea, where she is hard at work on her new novel. Follow her on Twitter @HollyMAuthor

THE MAN NEXT DOOR

ISABELLE BROOM

The scratching began on the third night.

Freya was in bed, devouring a few chapters of her latest library rental, but as soon as she heard the sound, she shot up like a meercat.

Nothing. Not a murmur.

She must have imagined it. That's what you got for reading ghost stories at night. Putting down the book, she lay back and let her mind wander instead to her favourite subject, to arms thick with muscle, to tousled dark hair, to a playful half-smile, to her new neighbour, William.

The scratching began again.

Freya gritted her teeth. She could cope with her reading being interrupted but drew the line when it came to an enjoyable fantasy.

Scratch. Scratch. Scratch.

It was in the roof, whatever it was. Or maybe even the walls. Throwing aside her covers, Freya turned and slapped a protesting hand against the wall until her palm turned pink.

There was a brief moment of wonderful silence; then the scratching began again with gusto.

She should have got a rescue cat, as her friends had suggested. A mouse would not have dared cross the threshold if she had.

If it even was a mouse that was doing the scratching...

It had all seemed so idyllic in theory – a cottage tucked away down a leafy lane, a fresh start away from the tattered remnants of her marriage and the home where she had raised her children, both grown now with families of their own. Freya was not sad; her divorce had been amicable – just two souls grown apart rather than grown to loathe one another – but she was weary. She craved a space to call her own, a place where she could write and paint, drink wine on a Monday evening just because she fancied it, have friends to stay, take long walks, even longer baths, listen to the silence, enjoy the solitude.

Freya had imagined that she would thrive by herself, but now, after a mere few days, the loneliness was beginning to itch. Far from luxuriating, she was now longing for another person. Not to help her unblock the sink or work out how to get the boiler functioning or the radiators to stop grumbling – she had done all that herself – but someone to share it with. The love may have drained out of her marriage long before she pulled out the stopper, but her ex-husband had still been there. They had still talked, and laughed, and supported. Here, there was nobody. There was nothing. Except, of course, whatever it was inside the wall.

Freya must have drifted off eventually because the next thing she was aware of was her phone ringing, its shrill cry rousing her from a dream featuring William the farmer, a barn full of hay bales, and an enthusiastically uninhibited roll in that hay. Blearily, she answered.

'Hello, Mum.'

'Hello love, are you ill? You sound all croaky.'

'Just tired.' Freya carried the phone downstairs,

grimacing as her bare feet connected with the cold kitchen tiles.

'I thought you'd be sleeping as soundly as a hibernating badger out there,' her mother went on.

'So did I,' muttered Freya, filling her mum in on the suspicious scratching as she poured hot water over a teabag.

'Shall I let your dad know? He'll be over to sort that out for you in a jiffy.'

'Thanks, Mum, but no – I am a very capable woman, remember?'

'Yes, yes,' her mum soothed. 'But this is rat we're talking about. You know – long wriggly tail, sharp little teeth, ferocious appetite –'

'Mum, I have to go. The postman's here – I'll call you later.'

Hanging up, Freya hurried to the front door. She'd definitely heard what she thought was a van, but when she peered outside, it was not the postman but a very glamorous blonde woman. Freya's eyes flickered from the stranger back to herself, then from woman's gleaming Range Rover to her own fossilised Volvo. Whoever this visitor was, she had not come to see Freya.

Closing the door, she scurried to the sitting room window just in time to see the woman reach the farmhouse next door. After a moment or two, William opened it and immediately pulled the blonde into his arms.

Freya frowned. She was not surprised that William had a gorgeous significant other, but she was disappointed. Feeling her shoulders slump in defeat, Freya stepped away from her lurking position behind the curtain and forced herself to rally. So what if the object of her lustful affection was spoken for after all? She had far more pressing issues to deal with – namely, the small problem of a rat living in her roof. No way she would risk another terrible night's sleep – no, she would deal with the problem today.

Two hours later, armed with an array of humane traps, Freya stood on her landing squinting up towards the loft. She could not believe there was no built-in ladder, or that she had not thought to check for one before she drove all the way to the nearest town.

Scolding herself under her breath, Freya fetched a chair, a stool, and the box she'd used to transport her paints on moving day, arranging one item on top of the other until she had constructed a tower. Tossing aside the pole she'd used to unfasten the latch, she clambered up as nimbly as she could until she was half-crouched in the attic. It was dark inside, and the air was musty. Freya felt around for a light switch, only realising she'd found a spider instead when it tried to scuttle out from under her hand. Screaming loud enough to take the roof clean off, she flailed wildly, her feet skidding into the rodent traps, watching the biggest teeter for a moment on the open edge of the hatch before toppling downwards.

The silence that followed the resounding crash rang... until Freya filled it with swearwords.

'Hello?'

She froze, eyes wide. Someone was in her house.

'Everything all right?'

A man – it was a man.

'Fine!' she squawked, coughing out several lungfuls of dust.

'I heard a scream.' The bannister creaked as if someone was leaning on it. 'Can I come up?'

'Er, um. OK.'

Somehow, he'd heard her muttered reply because a moment later, William's face appeared in the gap.

'Oh,' he said, looking neither amused nor surprised.

Freya tried a smile.

'I just came up here to—'

He picked up the fallen trap.

'Rodent problem?'

Freya blushed. This would all be so much less humiliating if he wasn't so handsome.

'I think so. But I found, well, a spider.'

William put his head on one side.

'You won't catch a spider in this,' he said.

Freya heard a weird noise, like a bird being trodden on, then realised it was her own attempt at a laugh.

'Want a hand?' he asked.

'I'd rather have a ladder.'

'Nah.' William scratched his chin. 'No need. I'll catch you.'

He moved into position beneath the hatch, his arms outstretched.

'Come on,' he urged, planting his feet wide. He must have taken off his shoes at the door, Freya noted. There were red hearts on one of his socks and panda faces on the other.

William was beckoning now with one of his weathered hands – hands that Freya had dreamt were running all over her body only a few hours ago.

'OK,' she said, gingerly posting her legs through the gap. 'I will lower myself slowly.'

Freya pictured it happening in a single, graceful movement, like a swan coming to land on water or a ballerina executing the perfect plié.

It was nothing like either of those things.

Thinking she would be strong enough to support her weight using only her arms, Freya eased her bottom off the attic floor only to plummet through the open hatch like an anchor, the heel of her foot connecting with William's head. As he staggered backwards, his arms still raised to catch her,

Freya somehow missed both and landed on the carpet like a splat of bread dough.

'Ouch,' she groaned.

'Oof!' said William.

Freya sat up. One of her legs had wrapped itself around William's waist.

'I'm so sorry,' she wailed. 'Is your face OK?'

'Nah.' He gave her a sidelong look. 'It's always looked this bad.'

Freya giggled.

'I like your face,' she said. 'It's nice – you have nice eyes.'

'All the better for seeing you with,' he retorted. 'Although, apparently not well enough to catch you – sorry about that.'

'It's my fault – I should learn to fall better.'

William reached out and gently removed a cobweb from behind her ear.

'This is the part where I say something witty about how you fell for me,' he said.

Freya failed to stop her smile from widening.

'You're not funny.'

'Shame,' he said blithely. 'Because in that case, you probably won't agree to let me take you on a date.'

A date? For a moment, Freya's heart tightened like a fist, then she remembered.

'I'm not sure your girlfriend would like that very much.'

'My what?'

William's face creased with confusion for a moment, then he chuckled.

'Are you referring to that blonde with the planet-destroying car and the scarily high heels?'

Freya nodded.

'Yeah, that's my sister.'

'Oh...'

Freya could have sworn she heard the crackle of electricity spark between them. Either that, or she'd managed to dislodge the TV aerial in the loft with one of her stupid flailing hands.

'So,' said William. 'About that date – when are you free?'

Freya thought about all the years she'd spent washing clothes, making beds, packing lunch boxes, ironing shirts; the long days, weeks, and months when she had run the house around a full-time job, attended to her children's every need and want. The promise she had made to herself when she bought this cottage was that now, at long last, it was her time.

Tilting her chin, she smiled at William.

'How about right now?'

'Now?' William's dark eyes flickered. 'What about the traps?'

Freya got to her feet, then reached down a hand to hoist him up. His skin was warm and rough, just as she'd known it would be.

'I've decided that the rat can stay,' she said, as his fingers tightened around hers.

'As it turns out, being all by yourself is seriously overrated.'

Isabelle Broom was born in Cambridge nine days before the 1980s began and studied Media Arts in London before a 12-year stint at Heat, the UK's top celebrity magazine. Always happiest when she's off on an adventure, Isabelle travels all over the world, seeking out settings for her escapist fiction novels. Currently based in Suffolk, where she shares a home with two dogs and approximately 467 spiders, Isabelle fits her writing around a busy freelance career and tries her best not to be crushed into oblivion by her ever growing pile of to-be-read books. Find Isabelle on Twitter @Isabelle_Broom and Instagram @Isabelle_Broom_Author

THE STEP GRAN: ONE AND ONE EQUALS SIX!

JANE CORRY

Medium-height. Reliable. Sense of humour. Widowed. Two adult children. Seeking partner to spend rest of life with.

'Sounds interesting,' says my Goddaughter. I glance at Sophie's iPad, which she's thrust in front of me.

Really?

I mean, anyone can make up anything on dating sites, can't they? You hear all sorts of terrible stories about single women being taken in by fraudsters, liars, or both. And I'm not sure I could cope with having my heart broken. I've seen this happen all too often with friends. Perhaps that's why I've remained resolutely single all my life.

Funny really. When I was younger, I'd presumed I'd get married and have children because that's what my mother had told me would happen. I even had a little dolly's pram, which I pushed everywhere with me.

Yet life hadn't worked out like that. It turned out that I was quite bright at school. Please don't think I'm being boastful here. It's just what the teachers told my parents. 'Fran is particularly brilliant at maths,' said the head-mistress. And before I knew it, my whole life was being mapped out before me. University. Top job. Long hours. No time to socialise. Not a minute to find Mr Right.

Suddenly everyone around me was either getting engaged or sending me wedding invitations, including my best friend. And that's when my life changed.

'We'd like you to be Godmother, Fran,' she said after having her first baby, a lovely little girl called Sophie.

How wonderful! I vowed to myself that I would be the best Godmother possible. I took her to the top shops when I visited; I always remembered birthdays and Christmas presents; I introduced her to the theatre; and bought her pretty clothes.

I also gave her advice on love and life, especially when my best friend passed away all too soon. I became a sort of substitute mum, and I like to think Sophie's my substitute daughter.

But now, it seems that my Goddaughter has firm ideas of her own. As I speak, Sophie has grown up into a strong, beautiful, worldly young woman whose quest, it appears, is to find a man for her Godmother.

Me.

'Of course you're not too old, Fran,' she said. 'Rather set in your ways, perhaps, but you'll have to learn to adapt. There we are. I've replied for you. You're meeting on Friday night at a restaurant in town. Don't worry. I'll ring you after an hour, and you can pretend it's a friend needing help if you want to bail. I'll also track you on my phone app.'

When did children get so bossy and savvy?

But when I met Paul, I realised Sophie had been right. He stood up, pulled out my chair for me, listened as well as talking, and made me feel comfortable. It felt – and I know this sounds corny – as though we'd known each other for years.

'Told you!' said Sophie clapping her hands with excitement when I told her.

There had to be a catch. And there was. Paul and I dated for about two months before I found out what it was. We were having Sunday lunch in what had become of 'our' favourite spots, overlooking the green. The cathedral rose up before us, its spires breaking through the clouds while shoppers were thronging past with their January sales bags. Paul and I were sitting next to a log fire, and it all felt lovely and cosy.

'You know, Fran,' he said. 'I'd like to think we're serious now.'

My heart began to beat. 'Me too.'

Please don't let him propose, I thought. My Goddaughter was right. I'm too set in my ways. But I didn't want to lose him.

'The thing is,' he said, 'there's something I should have told you.'

I knew it. He's not widowed. He's married. He's a serial killer. Well, maybe that's going a bit far. 'What?' I asked.

'I'm a grandfather,' he said.

Now that's something I hadn't thought of! 'Why didn't you tell me before?' I gasped.

He looked embarrassed. 'I felt it might put you off. I mean, 'grandfather' summons up a certain kind of picture, doesn't it? A bald old bloke with slippers and pipe.'

'Of course it doesn't,' I say, thinking of my own grandfather who'd looked just like that.

'Would you have replied to my ad if I'd come clean?' he asked.

'Definitely,' I said, crossing my fingers under the table. 'How old are they?'

Paul's face was full of love and excitement. 'Emmie is six and Sam is three. Quite a handful! They live near me, and I look after them when my daughter is working on Thursdays.'

I thought back to when Paul had been 'unable' to see me. Each time it had been a Thursday.

Paul was flushing now. 'Would you like to meet them? I didn't suggest it before until I knew we were serious.'

'I'd love to,' I said. But inside, my mind was all over the place. What should I wear? Should I take a present? What kind?

'Not chocolate,' said my Goddaughter, who's a primary school teacher. 'The parents might not approve. How about a book? Oh, and don't dress up. Children that age are into mucky stuff like finger paints.'

I was more nervous than I'd ever been - including my accountancy exams - when Paul and I rang the bell on the doorstep.

'Dad!' said a tall, glamorous young woman with long auburn hair and a very chic tunic dress.

She glanced at me, taking in my jeans and old jumper, which was hopefully paint-proof. 'Nice to meet you, Fran. Do come in.'

Suddenly a herd of elephants thundered down the stairs. 'Grandad!' screamed one of them, leaping into Paul's arms.

The other burst into tears. 'I wanted to go first.'

'Hang on a minute,' said Paul, grinning. 'Aren't you going to say hello?'

'Hi,' said the taller one. I presumed she was Emmie, although they both had long hair and looked very alike. 'Mum says Grandad's too old to have a girlfriend.'

Ouch! Paul went very red. So did his daughter. 'Of course I didn't,' she muttered.

'Yes you did, mum!' replied the little girl. 'You said she might be after something.'

'No I didn't'.'

But it was clear that she had.

'I brought you a book,' I said, breaking the awkward silence.

'We've got that one,' said the smaller one dismissively.

'Sam!' said Paul's daughter. 'Where are your manners?'

Good point. I'd like to say the rest of the day went well. But it didn't. Paul's grandchildren completely ignored me and just wanted to sit on his knee watching television.

'That didn't go too badly, did it?' he asked. Had he forgotten how rude they were? I visited a couple more times, but it was so awkward that I suggested he went alone after that. Paul seemed relieved. 'I'm sure they'll get used to you soon,' he said.

'He's right,' said my Goddaughter, who clearly wasn't giving up on her search to find me love, but I wasn't sure. Paul's grandchildren were an important part of his life, and I didn't want to come between them. It was clear his daughter didn't want her dad to have a relationship. 'It's hard for her to think of someone taking her mum's place,' Paul had said.

'But I wouldn't try to do that.'

'I know.'

Maybe it was time to end our relationship, I thought. I'd tell him this Friday.

Then, the day before, he called, sounding worried. 'My daughter has been rushed into hospital with suspected appendicitis. My son-in-law is with her. I'm in charge of the children, so I can't make our date tomorrow. I'm so sorry.'

The noise in the background was deafening. 'They're playing me up a bit,' he said. 'I'll call back later.'

'Go round,' urged my Goddaughter. 'Take chocolate, toys and games.'

'But before, you said no choc....'

'I know. But the parents aren't there, and this is your chance to get on-side!'

When I arrived, the house looked like it had been burgled. Crayons were scattered on the floor, and there was food smeared on the kitchen table. Emmie was in tears. 'I can't do it,' she sobbed.

'Do what?'

'My homework. I can't add up!'

'I can help you,' I said, sitting on the only chair that wasn't smeared with fish fingers. 'And Sam, while Grandad tidies up, you can borrow this dolly pram I brought with me.'

'I love prams!' he gasped.

I had gathered that from my last visit when he had wanted to play mummies and daddies.

'It used to belong to me when I was small,' I said. 'It's got a loose wheel after being in the attic for so long, so maybe you could fix that too.'

'Cool.'

Sam wants to be a mechanic as well as a dad when he grows up.

'Fran did my homework for me!' said Emmie excitedly when Paul finished vacuuming.

'No,' I cut in. 'You did it. I just showed you how.' I'd used pictures of pram wheels to help with adding up.

'Thank you!' she said, giving me a big hug which made me feel quite tearful in the best way possible.

Later that evening, when they were fast asleep, Paul and I were so drained that we scoffed the chocolate I'd brought for the children but luckily forgotten to give them.

Then the doorbell rang. It was Sophie and a friendly-looking young man.

'Jonny!' said Paul, hugging him. 'Fran, this is my son.'

'And this is my Goddaughter, Sophie,' I said. 'How do you know each other?''

'We've just met on the doorstep!' she chirped. 'Thought I'd come round and help. You're on my tracking app, remember?'

Still?

'And my sister asked if I could give grandad a hand,' said Jonny.

'It's all under control now, thanks,' said Paul. 'But come in anyway. We've got chocolate.'

'And a three-wheel dolly pram,' I add.

It turned out that Paul's daughter didn't have a grumbling appendix at all. She was pregnant – and luckily, all was well.

As for Jonny and Sophie, they hit it off from the word go and are now expecting triplets!

'Four more grandchildren for us to enjoy,' said Paul a few months later, putting his arm around me. His wedding ring glints in the light, a larger version of mine. 'That's six between us!'

I can't wait. But I'm also enjoying being a step-gran. Emmie and Sam are real characters. And they'd been delightful - if slightly mischievous - flower bearers at our wedding.

Meanwhile, I'm in my step-daughter's good books because Emmie is now top of maths, thanks to my coaching.

It just goes to show that it can all add up at the end!

This story was first published in My Weekly magazine.

Jane Corry is a former magazine journalist who spent three years working as the writer-in-residence at a high-security prison for men. This often hair-raising experience helped inspire her Sunday Times-bestselling psychological thrillers 'My Husband's Wife', 'Blood Sisters', 'The Dead Ex', 'I Looked Away' and 'I Made A Mistake', which have been translated into over 16 languages and sold over a million copies worldwide. Jane was a tutor in creative writing at Oxford University, is an RLF Fellow at Exeter University, and is a regular contributor to the Daily Telegraph and My Weekly magazine.

FLOWERS

JANE FALLON

They had never been the kind of couple to make romantic gestures, agreeing early on that flowers and chocolates bought with five seconds thought from a garage forecourt didn't so much mean adoration as they did lack of imagination. Spontaneity, John had always said, spoke far more than buying a gift on a particular day because some greetings card company had said you should. In the early days, they would delight in surprising the other 'just because'. A kitsch hedgehog pin cushion when Carol was in her dressmaking phase, a battered copy of Moby Dick, his favourite childhood book, that she'd found in Oxfam. It hadn't happened so much lately; in fact, Carol couldn't remember the last time. Still, they were happy. They were kind to each other. They had things in common. She just sometimes felt as if they took each other for granted.

So when Richard had started to flirt with her at work, Carol had been flattered. He would make a beeline for her office, complimenting whatever she was wearing, admiring her hair. After a while, a bunch of red roses started to arrive at her desk every Monday. No card. She knew his overtures were generic and cheesy but gradually, he wore her down. She wasn't used to so much attention.

She realised that she was talking about work more than usual at home, peppering the conversation with 'Richard this' and 'Richard that', but she couldn't seem to stop herself.

The night before she and Richard were due to go away for a conference together, she willed John to do something, anything, to make her feel special. To give her the resolve to resist Richard's advances. They cooked dinner together as they always did, watched TV in companionable silence, Carol lurching between feelings of frenzied anticipation and guilt. When she left in the morning, John kissed her on the cheek and told her to have a good time. She could barely look him in the eye.

That evening, in the hotel, after the official get-to-know-you social had finished, Richard made a beeline for her in the bar. He produced a single red rose from behind his back, and she blushed even though she knew it was a ridiculous cliché. She ordered a gin and tonic for Dutch courage. Richard placed a hand in the small of her back, and the warmth from it burned right through her.

'Do you come here often?' he said, and he laughed heartily, showing even white teeth. He looked different out of his suit, she thought. Nice. She knew that he was going to make a pass at her. That she would refuse because it was too soon, but with enough regret and frustrated longing in her voice that he would know the door was open to try again. It would move their flirtation forward. She had never done anything like this before, but she knew she had to take it slowly. To be able to remind herself later that she had thought it through and had not thrown her marriage away lightly.

'Do you know how beautiful you are?' Richard said,

holding her gaze as they finally – reluctantly - said goodnight. He put his hand under her chin and stared into her eyes. She hardly slept, thinking about the moment, about what might happen in the future.

Back at home, the weeks dragged by. Richard's roses still appeared every Monday like clockwork. One morning – a Tuesday – there was a teddy bear sitting at her desk with the words 'I can't 'bear' it when you're not around' embroidered on its chest. An unsigned card was propped up in front of it —a Valentine.

'Have you got a secret admirer?' Carol's assistant Pauline said.

'Of course not!' Carol said, blushing. 'It's just someone being silly'. But when Pauline offered to get the bear out of her way, Carol refused.

Later, Richard stopped by on the pretext of dropping off some paperwork.

'Let's sneak off for a long lunch', he said in a low whisper. Carol felt her heart flutter but shook her head. 'I've got a meeting,' she said. 'Let's do it tomorrow.'

That evening John was hovering by the front door when she let herself in.

'I've got something to show you,' he said, leading her back through to their little garden where it was already dark. The security light sprung on. 'Only, it's a bit ... well, it hasn't quite turned out as I hoped.'

He pointed to a muddy looking patch of the lawn. Carol could just make out tiny green stubs pushing up out of the earth. She stared hard and realised they formed a heart shape.

'Happy Valentine's Day,' said John, almost tripping over the words. 'They're crocuses - I know how much you love crocuses - but I didn't realise they'd take so long to grow.'

'When did you do this?' she laughed.

He looked her straight in the eye. 'The weekend you went to that conference. I wanted to do something nice for you. I know it's stupid. I know we don't do this kind of thing.'

Carol thought of him down on his hands and knees, planting what had to be close to a hundred bulbs. John hated gardening. She imagined him down there in the mud for hours while she sipped G and Ts and flirted with Richard. It occurred to her that Richard had probably just placed a regular order with the florist to deliver twelve roses to her every Monday. Maybe he'd even got his assistant to do it. She thought about John worrying that he was losing her, wanting to make a gesture. Trying to think of something original, remembering that crocuses were her favourite flower. She thought of how well John knew her.

And Carol knew she was going to cancel lunch with Richard tomorrow. Tell him it had to stop.

The security light snapped off again, and she reached for John's hand in the dark. 'Thank you,' she said. 'It's perfect'.

'Flowers' was first published in the Sunday Express.

Jane Fallon is a Sunday Times bestselling author and multi award-winning television producer behind shows such as 'This Life', 'Teachers' and '20 Things to Do Before You're 30'. Her novels include 'Getting Rid of Matthew', 'Got You Back', 'Strictly Between Us' and 'Worst Idea Ever', and have sold over a million copies in the UK.

UNDER THE STAIRS

JESSICA FELLOWES

When Henry's mother died, all she owned was in storage. She had been ill for many years, but the family had held out the hope that she might get better and would need her things again. After her death, there were years of complications with the inheritance as she died without a will, and the petty squabbles of uncles and siblings meant that what money there was soon disappeared. Anything of value was sold to pay the storage bills. At the end, all that was left for Henry were a few boxes of old clothes that he gave to charity and a large, battered leather suitcase stuffed with a jumble of letters and photographs. The bleak sadness of his mother's enfeebled final years depressed Henry for a long time, and he did not like the idea of remembering who his mother had been before; the contrast was too painful. But eventually, there came a day when Henry opened the cupboard under the stairs, saw the suitcase and thought: Now.

49 Cadogan Square, London
25th May 1936

. . .

My darlingest Kate,

A very wonderful weekend and I only hope you enjoyed it as much as I did. I have never been so happy – it's really rather frightening wondering if it can possibly last at such a frantic high pitch.

I've never met anyone quite like you before. I can't believe that I hadn't even wanted to go to the Gunnington's party and might have missed the chance of meeting you and redirecting the course of my life.

As I was writing this, I telephoned you, my most beautiful one, but the maid said you were out for a drink with Jocelyn. Thursday will soon come, my only beloved. Take care of yourself, especially your hands and feet.

Your adoring, Dominic

It took Henry a few tries, with much squinting, to read the letter. The old-fashioned writing in navy ink squiggled and jumped on the thin white paper, and it felt as if he were translating from a foreign language. Something in Henry's distant childhood memory started to try to swim to the surface, and he wondered if he should push it back down or allow it some air. With hands that had started to tremble, Henry picked another.

Fettercairn, Aberdeen.

14th September 1938

My most loved,

I long so much to see you again to delight my eyes and senses with the fullest of looks upon you. I am sorry not to have written before today; I was somehow not much in the mood for writing and have been so busy. But I took the hounds for a walk across the moors today and thought about you. My darling, the desperation I feel needing you, knowing you are still married, is ripping me apart. I know I have been no innocent in my past. The fact of a woman being married didn't vex me before; I suppose because I was quite happy to while away my time in London until I knew I'd have to come back here and take over the estate. I imagined I'd marry a nice Scottish lass, and things would tick over in a humdrum but pleasant way. But then, you.

You, who drinks like a soldier but has the unmistakable figure of a woman. You, who is brittle and witty with a martini in your hands yet softens and yields in my arms—you, the only person with whom I want to grow old and faded.

Please come up here again. I was so thrilled driving us through the village, everyone waving their hats at us as we passed. I shall buy you an owl of your own to keep in the woods, and we shall train it to fly to your hand. Other men may have bought you diamond brooches in the shape of your favourite bird, but only I can give you one with a beating heart. You already have my beating heart.

All my love darling, your adoring Dominic

Henry read the letter twice through and then looked at the dates again. It couldn't be what he thought. Could it?

Somewhere in France

17th June 1943

. . .

My beloved Kate,

It's difficult to go into paeans of praise every time I write, but please know that thinking of you makes me happier than I could otherwise be in this wretched place. Being with you on the last leave made me both exalted and terribly sad. It was almost a tease to have a few days of normalcy with you without fear of Bill coming through the door. I know it is wretched for you to have us both away fighting, but with him in another country, the simple pleasure of bringing you breakfast in bed, of us going for a walk in the park and to drinks and dancing in the Ritz... I hardly dare remember it. Here, I don't have your fingers tracing my features, but rats that run across my face as I sleep. My darling, do you think you will try to talk to Bill about a divorce when this war is over? It will be over, eventually. We have to believe that, and we have to try to plan for a future.

We move on tomorrow, and I will write again then. Pray for me.

I do love you so terribly, frighteningly much. Dominic

Rifling through the letters, photographs fell out here and there, in black and white. His mother was easy to find with her striking beauty, her dark hair with its white streak.

49 Cadogan Square, London
11th December 1946

My own Kate,

I have just put down the telephone from you, sounding somehow sad now that the decree nisi has arrived. That you should feel that way, even after everything Bill has done to you, makes things complicated again.

I know I should feel happy that the first steps have been taken, bringing us closer together as we have so long wanted to be, but we cannot deny that it has also been fraught and difficult since the war ended. Not just you and me, but the world around us. I think everyone wants to get back to how things were before, but they can't. I'm ashamed you heard me cry out in the night, but the horrors that appear in my dreams do not always dissolve in the sunlight. I yearn for nothing more than a simple life in Scotland, and I wonder, just occasionally, if that is possible. Sometimes I like it better when things haven't been right between us; it seems more real and genuine. Or am I making myself believe that? How is Michael? I know you worried that the divorce would bring shame while he was still at school. Perhaps it's more usual these days, since the war...

I will see you on Wednesday for luncheon at the Regency before I take the train home. Your own,

Dominic

Henry knew his mother had been unhappily married to his father, Bill, a man so devoid of emotional expression that he had shaken Henry's hand when he left for prep school, aged seven. But still a trickle of ice was running down his spine.

49 Cadogan Square, London

20th February 1947

Kate,

Perhaps I should telephone, but I don't want to mix up my words or forget what I mean to say. I'm going to be married to Helen Dashwood on Tuesday. I know this must seem rather sudden, but we've been close for a long time, and it's the right thing for me to do. You met her once or twice when you came up to Fettercairn. She grew up next door, as much as one does in our neck of the woods, and our families have known each other all our lives. I know you will say the decree absolute is only a few months away. But things have changed. I have not been certain we want the same things for some while now.

I shall think of you always with great fondness.

Yours,

Dominic

Henry flipped through the letters. It was important now that he find the next one in the sequence if there was one. Had she told Dominic? This took some time, deciphering the writing, ordering the dates. At last, he had it.

Paddington Station

25th February 1947

Kate

You put the wrong letters into the envelopes. You sent me the letter congratulating Helen on her wedding, with bland good wishes for future happiness. You sent Helen the letter meant for me, despairing of my fate of waking up next to such a plain woman every morning for the rest of my life. The letters arrived on Tuesday morning and Helen very nearly cancelled our wedding. I had to rush to her mother's flat and persuade her that it is Helen's fresh-faced prettiness that I adore so much. I'm writing this from Paddington station, and we are boarding the train to Scotland for our honeymoon. If you have any sense, I suggest you go straight to a church and pray for forgiveness. Even if you get it from God, you won't get it from me.

Henry put the letters back in the suitcase and put the suitcase back in the cupboard under the stairs. It was his birthday soon, the fourth of April, and he'd always wondered why he looked nothing like his brother Michael, nor his father Bill. But he would try not to think about that again. Instead, he would simply be glad that his mother had been adored once.

Jessica Fellowes is the author of the international bestseller crime series 'The Mitford Murders', based around the real-life Mitford sisters. She has a standalone novel, 'The Best Friend', published this summer in the UK and the US, which explores the binds of female friendship. Jessica lives in Oxfordshire with her family and Butch the Chicken. Her latest book 'The Mitford Vanishing' is out now.

'TIL DEATH US DO PART

KATE GRAY

Today is the day I kill my husband.

I wake with this thought on repeat. It worms through my tired brain like an irritating jingle from This Morning.

I glance over at the crumpled bedsheet, imagining the indent of my spouse's head on his expensive memory foam pillow - another desperate attempt to cure his snoring.

That's one reason for wanting him gone.

He left before I woke. The cycling obsession, encouraged by our neighbour, Pete, an equally balding middle-aged man who enjoys squeezing himself into unflattering bright lycra, shows no sign of losing its appeal. Still, I thought he might have decided against a bike ride today of all days.

When he asked me how I wanted to celebrate, he laughed at my reply. A chesty, guttural sound I hadn't heard in years. It was clear from his tone that he expected me to say something less demanding, like breakfast in bed or a supermarket dine-in-for-two meal to mark the occasion.

This is what twenty-five years of marriage feels like.

I won't see him until this evening now. He'll ride all the way to his office and get a shower there; apparently he keeps a spare suit in an employee closet. This gives me a deadline. By six o'clock, when he walks through the door, I'll have everything ready.

It's nice to have a purpose now that there are no kids to wake - our youngest son left for university last year. Since then, I've craved the chance to be useful. Most mornings, I lie in bed, the deafening silence of our empty three-bed semi pounding in my ears. Staring at the broken curtain pole beside our bed, the one he promised he'd fix five months ago. I mentally add 'failed DIY projects' to the list of reasons he has to go.

The postman knocks. He's holding a flyer for a new pizza chain and a thick cycling catalogue that won't fit through the letterbox. No cards. From anyone. I'm only going to feel disappointed if I expect anything different today.

My vow to kill my husband never strays far from my subconscious as I go about my daily chores.

Every task feels different today, monumental somehow. When I struggle to heave the bin bag out of the overflowing kitchen bin - it was his turn to change it, of course - a thought brings an unexpected smile. I wonder if you could hide a body in the refuse collection? I'm too focused on imagining stuffing him inside our green council wheelie bin to notice I've got company.

'Hello!' It's Karen, Pete's wife. She's standing beside her car on our shared driveway. A shiny runaround complete with all the mod-cons which she bought last year with her bonus. 'You up to anything nice tonight?'

'Yes, actually. He's taking me out for dinner. A table at Dovedale's,' I call back.

Her gaze travels down the length of my dressing gown. She's dressed in a perfectly-ironed blouse and too-tight pinstripe pencil skirt. Her hair looks freshly washed. I bet she's wearing perfume. She's fond of heavy, obnoxious scents that clog the back of your throat and linger long after she has left the room.

'Oh!' Her thin eyebrows rise like I know they will. 'Fancy.'

'Mmm. He's so good to me.' I simper, hating myself.

I've reserved the table myself. I needed an alibi after all.

'Well, have fun.' She gives a brief wave and then slips into her car, revving the engine as she reverses.

I move around the supermarket aisles with a renewed interest. In place of a shopping list, I'm pondering household objects which could kill my husband. Danger really is everywhere. The cleaning products aisle is a catastrophe waiting to happen. It's incredible the number of common poisons we all keep inside our homes. It would be such a pity if they were to get into the wrong hands.

The rest of the day passes in a blur.

The light fades and I hear Karen's car pull onto her driveway. I heave dirty laundry into the washing machine. At least I know how to get rid of bloodstains. Years of washing rugby kits has taught me well.

The clock strikes five. Time to start preparing dinner. I press a knife into the skin of a plump vine tomato, the scent of a greenhouse staining my fingertips. I can't help but lift the blade to the kitchen light wondering if it would be sharp enough to puncture human flesh.

A car engine pulls me from the moment. I almost nick myself as I drop the knife and quickly rush to the front door. He can't be home early? Not today; I'm not ready!

But it's not my husband. An overweight man heaves himself out of a delivery van. He's lifting a large brown box and heading towards me. I spot the local florist's logo on the side and for a brief second, I regret being caught up in such dark thoughts all day long. Have I underestimated my husband? Perhaps, after all these years, he will finally surprise me?

The driver consults his order form. I watch, tears pressed against the back of my eyes as I see Karen answer her front door. Surprise and joy merge into one on her made-up face as she accepts the box.

No, those flowers should have been for me! This has confirmed it all. This fuels my decision.

Fool me once and all that.

It started with an open day organised by his boss. A simple summer fete to thank the staff for their hard work. Part of the day included a tour of the office. I asked a young girl wearing a lanyard where the showers were. She looked at me blankly. Confused, I checked the floor plan on the company website and felt my weary heart break into pieces.

I followed him a lot more closely after that and discovered he only rode as far as the train station. I watched aghast as he heaved his eye-wateringly expensive bicycle into a steel rack and padlocked it.

Instead of catching a train, he slipped into the passenger seat of a waiting car. One with a personalised number plate, brand new. His suit (and M&S shirt that I ironed!) lying on the backseat. I never said a word. I knew that one day I'd get my revenge. It was just a matter of when.

'Honey I'm home,' he calls in an irritating voice, a throwback to a joke that failed to be funny a long time ago. It pulls me from the sting of humiliation. There's the thump of his work bag carelessly dropped on the parquet floor.

I greet him with a peck on the cheek and ask him about his day, biting my tongue as I hang his bag on the coat hook instead of it cluttering the hallway. A receipt branded with the florist's logo flutters out. He didn't notice it. I did.

'Wow. You've gone to a lot of effort.' He loosens his tie and looks me up and down.

'I wanted to give you a Valentine's day you'd never forget.' I lead him to the dining room.

'This is role play? Right?' His eyes widen at the scene in front of us.

My pathetic attempt at spicing things up. A last-ditch attempt to save our marriage. Give it a desperate kiss of life. But I've known all along that it's too little, too late. A kinky game in honour of Valentine's Day. I was the passionate femme fatale, he the gullible husband. A role he's playing exceptionally well right now.

Things may have gotten out of hand.

The colour drains from his face at the sight of the knives lined up, the plastic sheeting I've spread over every surface, the spray bottle of bleach on standby for any spots I miss.

I think about his lies. I picture Karen's face. The personalised registration on her swanky new car.

'Of course, it's a game,' I say calmly, waving a pair of fluffy red handcuffs in his direction.

His relief is immediate - he tells me how I had him fooled. How after all these years I can still surprise him. I nod along, watching him turn and shrug his coat off as an overwhelming waft of another woman's distinctive perfume fills my nose.

Yes darling, I may have said it was a game, but never underestimate the power of a wife's intuition. And it would be a shame for all this effort to go to waste.

Kate Gray is the author of 'The Honeymoon', a 'propulsive thriller' that's available to pre-order now, also writes feel-good fiction as Katy Colins. For more about Kate please find her on social media as @kategrayauthor or @notwedordead on Instagram.

PARIS SNAPSHOT

JOSIE LLOYD

The Eiffel Tower stretches to a cloudless blue sky, the wide esplanade beneath it cleaner and more spacious than Meredith remembers. It's filled with tourists; crowds wowed by the card-tricksters, people walking past the frozen man sprayed silver, skateboarders weaving past clowns on stilts, the bare-chest tumbling Capoeira dancers impressing the teens on their phones.

An accordion player in a black beret wanders over to play to the queue where Meredith waits, his fingers twiddling over the keyboard as he squeezes out an opportunistic rendition of La Vie En Rose.

Summer used to be Meredith's favourite season, but now the sun makes her feel over-exposed, and she's glad she's worn her wide-brimmed hat and long dress, which she now fans away from her sticky chest.

Meredith swears to God that her senses have changed. She used to love to spray perfume liberally, imagining that glorious French word, *sillage* – meaning 'wake' - delighting in leaving a wave of her essence behind her, but nowadays, most perfumes smell like actual silage to her. She's particularly super-sensitive to that lavendery 'charity shop' smell, and she's often paranoid that she's the source of it.

But now, the air is filled with the smell of chocolate as she steps into the welcome shade of the crêpe sellers' canopy and her stomach rumbles with anticipation.

She used to care so much about her figure, dishonestly tapping calories into the app on her phone, but when Martin left at the same time as her menopause arrived, she threw in the towel and decided to stop with the self-flagellation; she had bigger things to worry about than her spare tyre. So, she might be in the food capital of the world, but a crêpe is what she's craving - for old time's sake if nothing else – and there's no-one here to judge.

She places her order now, feeling embarrassed as the chef ignores her rusty French and replies in English. She watches the pale batter hiss onto the hot plate as he expertly pushes it around into a perfect full moon with his wooden tool.

With both her kids off doing their own thing, Meredith had faced a lonely summer and with her sister's caravan in Bournemouth being the only other option, she'd splurged her budget on a return ticket to Paris.

A sucker for Who Do You Think You Are on the TV, Meredith had always wanted to know more about the black sheep of the family, Gigi, her great aunt who'd been a dancer here in the 1920s. In her bag, Meredith has a sepia photo showing Gigi provocatively looking over her shoulder, clad in stockings and sequins.

'And do you think you'll bump into *him*?' her friend Elsa had asked last night as Meredith handed over the instructions for walking the dog.

'Don't be ridiculous,' Meredith had replied, remembering that she'd had too many G&Ts at New Year and had told the story of her ancient past to gossipy Elsa.

As the vendor hands over the hot crêpe, Meredith settles on the nearby steps and, as the chocolate oozes over her tongue, the forbidden taste instantly conjures that magical summer over thirty-five years ago.

She'd been twenty and bored in her sleepy suburban corner of Essex when she'd answered an advert to caretake a gallery in Paris. The wages had been pitiful, but she'd longed for an adventure, and Paris had felt like the perfect chance to reinvent herself.

Meredith had loved it from the very first moment. One Saturday night, she'd gone with friends to a gig in an airless basement near the Moulin Rouge, and that's when she'd first seen him. They'd done a double take at each other across the bobbing crowd, something electric already fizzing between them.

He'd flicked his head towards the door, and they'd bundled up to street level for a cigarette as if they were already friends. She'd watched the flame from his Zippo lighter dancing in his brown eyes, and her world had turned.

He was Arnauld - *Ar-noh*, as he'd introduced himself - his eyes not leaving her face. Then, before she could protest, he was leading her over the cobbles up to the steep garden in front of the Sacré-Cœur with its white moonlit domes. He said he wanted to show her the view of Paris that he loved the most and when he'd kissed her at the top of the steps, it had been like a movie moment.

In less than a week, Meredith had moved into his bohemian loft in the Marais with a view over the slate roofs and constant coo of the pigeons that nested in the chimney pots. He'd woken her up each morning with a bowl of milky coffee and yet more sex.

Arnauld had wanted to be a photographer, and he'd taken his antique Leica with him everywhere, using

Meredith as his subject, capturing her in the Tuileries Garden dipping her feet in the fountain or choosing ripe peaches in the Marché des Enfants-Rouge. On Saturdays, they'd come here beneath Le Tour on their bicycles for what Arnauld considered the best crêpe in Paris.

Two blissful years had whizzed past, and then her dream job at Sotheby's had come up in London. At that point, there had been talk of marriage and babies - Arnaud had promised to follow her in a few weeks.

At first, she'd thought something dreadful had happened when he didn't arrive at the bedsit she'd rented in Hackney. Finally, after an agonising fortnight, he'd answered her call, sounding distracted, mumbling about a job in Spain. And she'd known then that he was never coming, and her heart had shattered.

Meredith finishes the crêpe, licking chocolate from her fingers before throwing the messy tissue in the bin. It was stodgy and not quite as good as she'd hoped, and she feels annoyed with herself for giving in to her nostalgic urges. Things are never as good as you remember them.

She looks up at the Eiffel tower deciding that she might as well take a selfie. She'd planned to go up, but it's too hot to attempt it. Besides, she'd been up before with Arnauld. Back when he took endless photos. Back when she'd felt *seen*. If only she could have told her younger self that one day, she'd become invisible.

It had been no great shock that Meredith's husband had thrown in the towel when the kids had been coming up for Uni. Theirs had hardly been a passionate marriage, but it had still been galling when he'd run off with a colleague ten years younger than her. Martin had wept when he'd told her, saying that he couldn't bear to let her down but had fallen in love. She'd called him pathetic, but when he'd moved out to start his new life, she'd been the one to feel that way.

As she flips the camera screen, she spots a man on the steps behind her talking into his phone. A faint snippet of his conversation comes to her on the breeze. She turns sharply to look, taking in his linen suit, the salt-and-pepper hair, a camera strap across his back, an SLR at his hip and, as he mounts the steps two at a time, her breath catches.

It can't be...can it?

Because he's exactly the type of man, she can imagine Arnauld would have grown into. Before she knows what she's doing, she's started to follow him, but someone grabs her arm from behind and she yelps.

'Sorry,' the man says, from the step below, holding up his hands in surrender. He's wearing shorts and a Liberty print shirt and a leather satchel, and now, as he lifts his Fedora hat to reveal his sunburnt forehead, she sees that his deep green eyes are kind as they search out hers. 'I didn't mean to startle you. Only, I saw you eating your crêpe, and you looked familiar. Oh,' he winces, 'that sounds creepy. Or crêpe-ey,' he adds, with a chortle.

She glances up towards where 'Arnauld' is getting away.

'You looked like you were really enjoying it,' the man blusters on.

He clocks the look of surprise on her face.

'Oh Goodness. I never, ever, say things like this to random strangers. Sorry...sorry,' he says, clearly mortified. 'You must think I'm...'

His cheeks are pulsing now. He shakes his head, as if revolted with himself and hurries down the steps away from her.

She can see that the man – Arnauld? - has reached the top of the steps and is going down beneath the art deco

Metro sign. In a moment, he'll be swallowed into the ground. If she runs really fast now, she might catch him.

But she stays, halfway up the steps. She looks back over her shoulder to the retreating figure of the man in the fedora, her mind racing. He could so easily be a scam artist, a weirdo, but suddenly she thinks of the photo of daring Gigi in her bag.

'Wait,' she calls out, far too loudly.

The man stops, his face strained, then hopeful as she waves and hurries towards him.

'Oh, you're English,' he says, relieved. 'Thank God for that. For a moment, I thought I'd made a complete idiot of myself jabbering on at you.' He holds out his hand. 'I'm Alec. From England...Essex, actually.'

'Me too,' she says. Essex, I mean.' She shakes his hand. 'Meredith.'

'Sorry, sweaty hand. Oh, it's so hot,' he says. 'I can't bear this heat. Paris in the summer and all that, but I'm not convinced.' She notices his tanned feet and cool sandals. He flaps his hat at his face. 'Do you fancy a beer? A cold one? I was heading to a bar over the bridge. It's a walk, but...?'

'Yes,' she says, smiling right back at him. 'Yes. Why not?'

And as they set off towards the twinkling Seine, in her mind's eye, she sees Gigi in the photograph winking.

Josie Lloyd is the author of 20 novels under various pen names. Her latest novel 'Life Saving For Beginners' is published in July through HQ, as is the final part of her Joanna Rees Stitch In Time trilogy set in the 1920's. She lives in Brighton with her husband, Emlyn Rees, with whom she has written several best-selling parodies, including 'We're Going On A Bar Hunt' and the best-selling nineties hit, 'Come Together'. She is currently working on the film adaptation of her novel, 'The Cancer Ladies' Running Club', which is out now.

THE BIRTHDAY PARTY

KATIE FFORDE

'Why are we going to school on Saturday?' asked Jessy, who was nearly four.

'It's Lulla's party,' explained her older sister, Bella, who was six. 'She's very kindly invited you, too.'

Gemma, who was a single parent, could hear that Bella wasn't entirely happy about this, but personally, Gemma was grateful. There seemed to be someone's birthday party every weekend for Bella, and it was nice that this time Jessy didn't have to be left with a neighbour so Bella could go. This time they were all going and staying.

It was a pleasant walk along the country lanes to the village hall, and they left in good time. Usually, this journey was cheered up by Gemma's secret crush. She'd never spoken to him, and it was unlikely she ever would, but every day, just after half-past eight, a gorgeous man in a very smart car drove past them. Gemma would always stop and get the pushchair out of the way and make sure Bella was standing well back. He would always slow down and raise his hand as he went past. It was a small thing, Gemma realised, but it brightened her mornings. But one day, one she couldn't forget, the driver had a very beautiful, very young blonde woman with him. He'd still crept past and raised his hand, but right then, Gemma's secret dreams had died a little.

Today thankfully, there hadn't been too much stopping to examine things in the hedge, jumping in muddy puddles and generally making the journey take longer. It was a shame that Jessy's pushchair had finally collapsed, but Gemma would worry about that later. Little Jessy might be full of beans after a party or exhausted, in which case Gemma would end up carrying her.

The party was in full swing when they arrived. It seemed half the school had been invited, and the hall was full of the sounds of children rushing about and screaming along with some random pop music. Gemma gathered they were playing Musical Bumps. She fully expected Jessy to hang back and want to stay with her, but no, in she rushed, leaving Gemma free to go into the kitchen and offer help.

After she'd put sandwiches on plates, built a tower of chocolate fingers and emptied packets of crisps into bowls, Gemma asked if there was anything else she could do.

'The entertainer should be here soon,' said the harassed party-giver. 'I wish I'd booked them to come earlier.'

'If they don't come soon, we can organise some party games,' said Gemma. 'It'll be fine!'

By the time Gemma left the kitchen, having blown up extra balloons and attached string, one of the dads, was on the floor being a bear. The children were delighted.

Gemma couldn't help being a bit envious of the lucky woman who had a full-on, interactive partner. Her ex-husband wasn't horrible, he loved his children and paid his child support regularly, but he wasn't present quite as often as everyone would have liked. The thought of him romping around being climbed on by random children made Gemma smile. He'd take his own, well-behaved little girls on outings, but he wouldn't have let other people's children rumple him and possibly damage his clothes.

The bear, who was now crawling along with four small people clinging to him, had longish hair in his eyes, nearly covering his glasses. Gemma couldn't quite work out which of the children were his. She looked around the adults, trying to find someone who was obviously his partner. A few women looked at him adoringly, but any or all of them would be the one.

Gemma decided that the dad pretending to be a bear looked a bit hot and sweaty, so she went to the kitchen and came back with a cup of tea and a large cup of water. He was on his feet now, and she waded through the children towards him, making sure she didn't spill hot tea on any of them. 'You looked as though you needed a drink,' she said. 'Tea or water?'

He gave her a grateful smile, pushed his hair out of his eyes, and adjusted his glasses. 'Can I have both?'

Gemma stopped, mouth open. The Bear was The Crush. The gorgeous guy who drove past her, waving every morning was one and the same as the dad rolling around on the floor.

'Of course you can,' stuttered Gemma, handing him the drinks. Embarrassed, she

was about to move away when a little boy she recognised ran up to the man. 'Daddy!' he began, then he saw Gemma and stopped. 'You're Bella's mummy,' he said.

'Yes, I am,' Gemma agreed. 'You must be Al.'

Al, she knew, was a little in love with Bella, who, with her long dark curls and dark eyes, had a few little boys in her thrall. Al was the only one Bella liked back, though.

'And I'm Ben,' said Al's daddy. The bear. The crush.

Gemma was trying to think how to continue the conversation when the entertainer arrived, and one of the mums came up to Gemma to ask if she could help set up the tables for food while the children were in the garden, watching giant bubbles being blown.

Gemma was happy to help. Jessy was being mothered by someone in Bella's class, and Bella wanted nothing to do with her mother. As she laid out plates and folded napkins, she regretted that you could ask who someone's children were, but you couldn't say, 'which one is your wife?'

'I'm sure I know Ben from somewhere,' Gemma said to another Mum. 'But I don't think it's the school gate.'

'No, he's never there for drop off or pick up. He takes Al to the childminder first thing.'

Gemma wondered if she could ask this Mum if there was a Mrs Ben, but decided not. Everyone had been very kind and welcoming when she'd arrived in the village, a single parent with two little girls. People might be slightly less kind if they suspected her of having her eye on a single man. And he probably wasn't single anyway; she couldn't forget the beautiful girl who had been in Ben's car.

The party drew to a close without Gemma having any opportunities to find out more about Ben. She decided that the only thing she could do was to encourage Bella to invite Al for a play date.

Gemma and her girls were amongst the last to leave, and unsurprisingly, little Jessy was exhausted and needed to be carried. Gemma was staggering somewhat when she saw a familiar, elegant car pulling up next to her. In it was Ben, still looking like a dad, although his car looked just as smart as it did on weekday mornings. An excited Al was in the back.

'I went home and got the car to see if you needed a lift,' said Ben. 'Al told me you were carrying Jessy; Bella said your pushchair had died.'

Gemma hesitated for as long as it took for Al to greet

Bella. 'Thank you so much. We'd love a lift. Jessy weighs a ton!'

Ben moved the car, so it wasn't blocking the road. 'We have a spare car seat and a lap strap,' he said, just as Gemma was beginning to worry about how the car would carry three children safely. It was a very short distance to her house, but she'd always insisted on her children being safely secured, and it wouldn't be right for her to change the rules now, just because she fancied the driver.

When everyone was strapped in, Gemma got in the front. 'Now I know why I recognised you at the party. But you look so different.'

'In my business suit and contact lenses?' he laughed. 'Well, I knew who you were, straight away.'

'Bella's Mummy?'

'I didn't know you as Bella's Mummy until just now. I just thought you were the lovely young woman who walked her children to school each morning.'

Gemma felt herself flushing. 'I do have a car, but I try and avoid using it as much as possible. Just to get to work. I only work part-time,' she added but wasn't sure why.

'Dad!' said Al, from the back. 'Bella said can I go and play for a bit.'

'That's up to Bella's mummy,' Ben said.

'Gemma,' she said. 'And as long as I can get Jessy down for a nap and you don't make too much noise, that will be fine.' She wasn't expecting the playdate to happen quite so soon but was happy about it. 'It can't be for too long, though.'

'Maybe I could stay for half an hour and then take Al home?' suggested Ben.

'That would be perfect. We can have more tea and eat the birthday cake. I have a huge wedge of it in my bag.'

'So,' said Ben. Jessy was inside, asleep on the sofa, and

the older children played in the garden. Gemma and Ben were sitting on the terrace with tea and cake, keeping half an eye on them. 'Would I be right in assuming you're a single parent?'

'Yes,' said Gemma, praying she could assume the same thing.

'Me too,' said Ben. 'Can you ever get a babysitter?'

'Oh yes. My neighbour Pam is very kind. She doesn't mind popping round and watching my television instead of hers, as she puts it.'

'Does that mean, if I asked you, it's just possible you'd agree to come out for a drink with me?'

Gemma paused. There was just one thing stopping her from saying 'yes please' in an embarrassingly enthusiastic way.

'Do you not go on dates?' Ben persisted when she didn't answer.

'I would if I was asked,' Gemma said. 'But – '

'What?'

'I once saw a beautiful blonde woman in your car. I couldn't go for a drink with you if you were involved with someone else.'

Ben frowned, obviously thinking hard. 'Oh! You must mean Bethany! She's my child minder's daughter. I gave her a lift when she had a job interview.' He paused. 'She got the job and lives away from home now.'

'In which case, I'd love to go for a drink with you.'

'I am so delighted,' said Ben and gave her a beaming smile.

Gemma decided she almost preferred dishevelled 'Dad' Ben to the glamourous man who swept past her in his car every morning. And she smiled right back.

Katie Fforde lives in the beautiful Cotswolds countryside with her family and is a true country girl at heart. Each of her books explores a different profession or background and her research has helped her bring these to life. She's been a porter in an auction house, tried her hand at pottery, refurbished furniture and she's even been on a Ray Mears survival course. She loves being a writer; to her there isn't a more satisfying and pleasing thing to do. She particularly enjoys writing love stories. She believes falling in love is the best thing in the world, she wants all her characters to experience it, and she wants her readers to share those stories too. To find out more about Katie Fforde step into her world at www.katieffforde.com, visit her on Facebook and follow her on Twitter @KatieFforde.

COOL GINGER

KIRSTY GREENWOOD

Someone recently said to me that turning thirty marks the slow and final descent into a life of 'meh'. As if suddenly, on my thirtieth birthday, I would sprout hair on my chin and become magically interested in pension plans and whether my coffee beans were organic.

For me, that couldn't be further from the truth. I turned thirty earlier this week and it's made not a jot of difference. I feel exactly the same as I did at twenty-nine. And twenty-eight, come to think of it.

Exactly the same.

It is, however, my last year of eligibility on the 18–30s holidays I have loved all of my adult life and I plan to go out with a bang. Or two, depending on the talent levels this year. My best friend Jane, partner-in-crime for many years of sand, sea, sangria and sexy times, is now in a most serious relationship with Knobhead Pete, but as a birthday gift to me, she has agreed to play the part of wing-woman on a concluding clubber's jaunt to Skiathos.

I am prepared: newly single and ready to tingle (Dan wanted to do the Inca Trail. I told him I'd rather squirt eyelash glue directly into my eyeball. He dumped me.). My body is toned, honed, and perfectly fake baked, hair streaked just a little blonder, belly button freshly pierced with a stone the colour of the med, and I am flush with the most valuable 18–30s currency known to humankind: Berroca.

Scoping out the departures board, I nudge Jane, who looks up from her copy of Grazia. 'We've got at least another forty minutes until the gates open,' I say. 'Let's get another drink.'

'Ginger, I don't know,' says Jane. 'I don't want to get dehydrated. My skin will look like a flapjack!'

'Ew. But it's my birthday week. And I was just dumped! Come oooooooon.'

'Hmmm.'

'Red aftershock or green, Jane? Make the call.'

'Bleurgh,' she says, but her eyes are sparkling. 'Go on then. One of each.'

I heart her.

~

I spend the first hour of the flight heaving and spewing into a paper bag. I am possibly the most hated passenger on board. Maybe even more despised than the ten-year-old girl singing a Little Mix song on repeat and only pausing at ten-minute intervals to ask if we are in Greece yet.

Jane is stroking my head and making soothing noises with one eye on the inflight TV.

I don't know why the shots have made me so ill. They've never given me a problem before. I am the shots queen. They call me Stomach of Steel back home. The incredible Ginger with her amazing Stomach of Steel!

I heave into the bag again.

Stomach of Sadness, more like.

Shuffling to the plane loos, I squeeze myself inside and splash my face with cool water. Okay. Woman up, Ginger. Only two hours until we land. I'll put on my sleep mask and rest for the remainder of the flight. By the time we arrive in Skiathos, I'll be replenished, re-vitalised and raring to go. I am on it. It will definitely be party time. Oh yes.

Thirty can suck it.

Two hours later

Ugh. My head hurts, and my eyes are all blurry.

'It's called a hangover,' Jane says helpfully.

We've stepped off the plane into the enveloping heat and squint-inducing sunshine, and despite the pukey feeling I'm experiencing, all of the familiar excitement is flooding back. Holidaaay! Celebraaaaate! Woop! Seven days of pure, unadulterated Living. It. Up.

For the next week, I am not Ginger, bored receptionist at the world's least successful car tyre centre; I am Cool Ginger! Sexy, sparkly mastermind of fun and frolics. The girl everyone will remember fondly back in England. 'Ah, remember Ginger,' they will say, shivering in their coats and brimming with holiday nostalgia. 'Ginger MADE that holiday. Ginger was... so cool!

'This is going to be amazing,' I sing to Jane.

'AMAZING!' she replies.

I'm putting my hand luggage into the boot of the waiting taxi when I hear Jane, from inside the car, let out a blood-curdling scream.

Shit!

I dash around and poke my head inside the car door.

'Jane! What on earth...?'

I don't get chance to finish my question because there, inside the car, is a massive knobhead holding a diamond ring.

'Yes, Pete!' Jane squeals. 'Yes, I will marry you!'

Bamfreakingboozled.

'You swear you didn't know?' Pete says, cuddling Jane in the back of the cab as we make our way to the hotel.

'I swear! I had no clue!' she beams. 'For all I knew, you were at work in Manchester!'

'Definitely no idea. At all,' I pipe up from the front seat.

I try to sound chirpy. Hurrah for Jane. Really. But did he have to propose now? On my birthday? On our holiday? I mean, 18–30s is fabulous, obviously, but who proposes on one? It's like trying to have a nice afternoon tea in a strip club. I want to say something to this effect, but it's a proposal. I can't ruin a proposal.

Think positive, Ginger. The dynamics have changed but the holiday isn't necessarily ruined. Pete might be a knobhead, but there's nothing to say that he can't hang around the apartments while we go off to do our Living It Up.

'There's another little surprise,' Knobhead Pete says as the taxi makes an unexpected stop outside a seaport.

Dear Jesus. Please let the surprise be that Pete is going back to England now.

'We're not quite staying in Skiathos,' he grins.

Exsqueeze me?

Jane is looking at him like he's the most romantic fucker that ever existed. Buoyed by her adoration, Pete gets down on one knee and spreads his arms.

'Jane. We're going to the magical island of Alonissos, where our families are waiting, where we'll get married.'

Jane bursts into tears of joy. Pete grins at me like I'm in on the plan.

'Hurrah!' I give a feeble thumbs-up in return.

What a massive holiday thwarting knobhead.

~

We're aboard a gigantic ferry on the way to Alonissos, and we've just passed an island called Skopelos where the Mamma Mia movie was made. If my holiday had to be ruined by any tiny island, I'd much rather it have been one that Pierce Brosnan had visited. I ask Pete, and he tells me that precisely zero movies have been made on Alonissos.

'Penny and Andrew are waiting for us too!' Pete says.

Ugh. Penny and Andrew. Jane and Pete's sad act couply friends. Great.

'Is Katy there?' I ask. Katy is Jane's eighteen-year-old sister. She might be good for a laugh now that Jane is otherwise engaged.

'Of course she is!'

Yay! Katy will definitely come clubbing with me. I'll be the cool older mate. I will introduce her to the 18–30s lifestyle, teach her how to say 'my place or yours?' in Greek, show her how to make her boobs look twice the size with only the use of bronzing powder and four safety pins. Cool Ginger still has a chance!

'You should have told me!' I nudge Pete when Jane nips to the loo. 'I could have helped, at least.'

'I'm sorry, Ginge. The surprise was so much better because you had no clue either! Did you see her face? I've rescued her from the tacky 18–30s holiday she was dreading, and I'm going to give her the wedding of her dreams. Definitely one to tell the grandkids!'

'Dreading?'

Pete has the good grace to turn a bit red.

'Er... You know, not dreading, per se. She loves coming

away with you. It's just...the pair of you are a little bit old for all those hijinks now, don't you think?'

'I'm twenty-nine!'

'Didn't you just turn thirty, like, three days ago?'

'Oh yeah... Well, same difference,' I protest.

'Not really.'

From the ferry, we catch a cab through some scarily winding roads. I squeeze Jane's hand as we take a particularly treacherous curve with a steep drop straight into the sparkling turquoise ocean. Thankfully we don't drive off the edge, and soon we come to a village called Steni Valla, the village we'll be occupying for the week. I look out of the car window, hoping to see at least one nightclub, one shop selling bright lilos and inappropriate postcards, one British-themed pub, one person under 50. I don't see any of those things. Instead, I see trees and olive groves, hills and chickens and tiny white houses dotted everywhere. I suppose it's quite pretty if you are completely boring.

The cab takes one final turn, and we pull up at a tranquil harbour where moored boats, big and small, rock gently in the dainty breeze. And – hurrah – there is a pretty taverna, inside of which are Jane's family and friends.

They rush to hug her, squealing and yelling and twirling her around. I stand and watch, unable to keep the grin off my face at my friend's happiness.

'I can't believe it!' she laughs over and over.

'Hi everyone!' I wave to Jane's family. 'What a surprise, eh!'

'Bet you didn't think you'd get to come somewhere as glorious as this?' Penny, Jane's boring friend, says. 'They say this island casts magical spells, you know?'

'Right. Cool.'

I wonder if it can magic me back to Skiathos?

Jane's sister Katy hurries over with a map of the island.

'There are some totally amazing hikes here, Ginger. Maybe we could get up at dawn try one together tomorrow?'

My hope of Katy as a substitute Party Jane fades away like a cheap home hair colour.

I make a non-committal noise. If I see in my thirtieth year with a hilly walk, I really should give up on life in general.

Ordering myself a soul-soothing ouzo from the bar, I take a look around at the taverna. Bright Tiffany green tables and chairs fill up a courtyard lined with flowering bushes and huge pots full of basil and mint. It's not exactly pulsating with sex and energy, but I can see the appeal. Dan would like it here.

'Ginger!'

It's Jane's mum, making her way towards me with a sympathetic look.

'I heard about you and Dan. You poor lass. I really thought you'd be the next one to marry, not our Jane.'

I smile and shrug. 'Thanks. It sucks, I suppose, but it wasn't right in the end.' I sip my ouzo and grimace at its strength. 'Ah well. I'm still young! There's plenty of time.'

She tuts and pats my arm, a grimace playing around her mouth. 'Not really, love. I saw this thing on This Morning where they said wombs don't last as long these days.'

Oh God.

'Let's celebrate!' I suddenly yell to the taverna at large. 'To Jane and Knob, er, um, Pete! Ouzos are on me!'

The cheer of agreement I expect doesn't happen, but a few of the group agree that a small carafe of white wine might be quite nice.

By seven o'clock, everyone bar me has left to get an early night—tedious buggers.

I look around for someone to talk to, but everyone in here is in a couple or three times my age.

Pah.

I order another carafe of wine because I absolutely cannot go home yet; Cool Ginger is always the last to leave a party! Though, this isn't exactly a party…

Shit.

I check my phone for any tweets or texts, but wouldn't you know it – no reception. Obviously.

Well, this is rubbish, isn't it? No friends, no music, no phone reception, no hot men rubbing sun cream onto me, no 18–30s. Nowt.

Without anything else to do, I find myself looking out at the harbour and the various boats, swaying to and fro in the breeze.

To and fro. To and fro. To and fro.

'Yasou? Hello? Excuse me?'

I jump as someone pinches my arm.

'It unclips at the front!' I grumble inexplicably and sit up to find myself still in the taverna, looking into the glinting green eyes of a large tanned man wearing a navy-blue bandana.

'The bar is about to close, miss,' he says, handing me a napkin. 'You will have to go home.'

Ugh. I'm napping now? And why has he given me a napkin? I look at him and then at it and then back at him.

He rolls his eyes, takes it off me and dabs at the side of my mouth.

Sleep drool.

I bury my head into my hands. I should be at a foam party right now, twerking with an overflowing fishbowl of mai tai being supped through a willy straw. Instead, I'm napping in a strange, silent village and having my own spit wiped off my face by a stranger.

'You are sad?' the stranger says with a rolling Greek accent.

'Yeah,' I say. 'A real sad act. Don't worry. I'm going now.'

'No, no, I mean sad, like… boo-hoo sad. Boo hoo hoo. I'm so sad.'

'Alright, alright, I get it,' I huff. 'I'll be fine.' Standing up, I wobble on my heels, still tipsy.

'Where are you staying, lady?'

'Somewhere called Angie's Place.'

'I will walk you there.'

'I don't know you. You could be a murderer.'

'I won't murder you. I don't like the murder. I'm a sailor. I like the sailing.'

'Where's your boat?' I ask, lifting my chin.

He laughs. 'It is that one.' He points to the smallest, ricketiest boat on the harbour.

'Fine.'

I only agree because I have no clue where on earth Angie's Place is and getting lost here would really not be a good ending to this already craptastic day.

'Thanks,' I say and link the arm he proffers.

We stroll along the water and apart from the occasional knock of boat against the quay, it's completely serene.

'I'm Aris,' he says. 'Who are you?'

'Ginger,' I answer. 'Cool Ginger,' I mutter under my breath sadly.

'A lovely name. Like your hair, yes?'

'Yeah.'

We climb the harbour steps and about halfway up I have to stop for a breather. Wow. I'm really unfit! When did I get so unfit?

'Are you okay, Ginger?' Aris says, amusement flashing in his eyes.

I sit down on one of the steps and sigh, my bottom lip wobbling. The jet lag, combined with the ouzo, plus the fact that my best friend has abandoned me, and I can't even get up these steps without a near asthma attack leads to an embarrassing onslaught of tears.

'My friend is getting married, and I didn't know about it until today. We were supposed to be in Skiathos partying for my birthday. And now we're he-he-here!' I sob.

'Your friend has found love?' he says. 'Surely time for a celebration?'

'Of course,' I sniff. 'I'm glad she's happy but... it's all changing! Everything is changing so quickly.'

'Change, it is exciting!' he says annoyingly. 'I once heard a person say that man cannot discover the new oceans unless he has the courage to lose sight of the shore.'

'Er... thanks, I think.'

What is he on about?

He holds his hand out to help me up. It's a nice hand. Attached to a nice tanned arm. I peer at his face. It's a very nice face. Pale, twinkling eyes, light blond stubble, short beachy hair beneath the bandana. He could definitely be described as talent in any country. And I'm 99% sure there's a six-pack under that crisp white shirt.

If we were at the 18–30s in Skiathos I would just snog him without any preamble.

Well, we're not that far from Skiathos...

I grab the top of his shirt and pull him to me, planting my lips on his. I see his eyes widen in shock and then close. He wraps his arms around me and kisses me back.

Wow.

This bloke is hot.

What was his name again?

I don't know his name! Result. We could practically be in a nightclub right now! Cool Ginger is about to score.

The hottie's right hand snakes across my ribcage while the left weaves up into my hair.

A little moan escapes me.

'Do you want to come back to mine?' I pant.

He pulls back. 'I don't know you,' he says.

'So what? It's called a one-night stand, mister. It's fun! It's carefree! You'll like it, I promise.'

He frowns slightly.

'I think you are very beautiful. But no. Thank you.'

My face flushes crimson. This has never happened before. Is this... Is this my first rejection? God.

'It is lovely to meet you, Ginger. I will help you to your home now.'

'Oh. Okay.'

Mortified.

Without warning, he scoops me up in his arms and carries me up the rest of the steps, across an empty, tree-lined road and deposits me in front of a pretty white house with a wooden sign that declares 'Angie's Place'.

'You are home, Ginger,' he says and shakes my hand before turning on his heel and jogging off into the night.

~

I wake up to warm sunshine spilling into the bedroom though sheer muslin curtains. I was so tired and humiliated last night that I slumped into bed without even looking around. I rub my crusty eyes, pull on my dressing gown and head up the stairs to a large open-plan kitchen and living space.

It's gorgeous and airy; certainly an improvement on the

scratty but cheaply priced apartment I had booked on Skiathos.

While I wait for a cafetière of strong coffee to brew, I head out onto the balcony.

'Wow!' I exclaim out loud. I'm looking at an uninterrupted, panoramic view of the sea. There are hilly green islands on each side of the house and two boats sailing through the channel. If I were into this sort of thing, I would be impressed – it's pretty beautiful. I inhale and catch the scent of fresh basil growing in the garden below. Grabbing the cafetière, I sit in a large wicker armchair, face turned up to the sun. At least I'll still get a tan...

I'm thinking about what Dan's up to right now when Katy, Jane's little sister, bursts in, her face flushed and freckly from the sun.

'Morning, Ginger!' she trills. 'I came to get you for the hike this morning, but you told me to fuck off. Do you remember?'

'No. I'm sorry about that.'

'Yeah. You were totally grumpy. Hungover?'

'Only old people get hungover,' I scoff, ignoring the vague thumping in my head. 'I'm hardcore, you know? Totes.'

'There's loads to do! We're meeting down at the taverna in ten minutes.'

'What time is it now?'

'Nine a.m.'

'Ugh.'

She giggles and bounds out, full of the vim and vigour of being eighteen.

I shuffle back downstairs to the bedroom of this topsy turvy house and pull out my favourite summer dress. It's strappy and pink and has turquoise butterflies all over it. On last year's holiday, I copped off with three guys in this dress.

No rejections for me today. Hot sailor guy can go sail up his own backside.

I pull the dress over my head and down across my waist, but it gets stuck on my hips.

'What?' I ask myself with despair.

I yank the slinky fabric down, craning my neck to see if it's caught on my bra or something.

But it's not.

I lie down on the bed and, after much shimmying and panting eventually get it over my thighs.

I examine myself in the mirror. It's tight. Not obscenely so, but enough to tell me that I've gone up at least a dress size since last year's holiday.

Middle-aged spread.

What the hell is happening?

'I want to be the person who chooses which books get published,' Katy says happily, pushing a needle through a square of yellow fabric.

Katy, Jane, their mum and I are sitting around an outside table at the taverna, drinking bottled water and sewing bunting together. Katy is telling us about the publishing course she'll be doing at university in September. Her eyes are sparkling with the excitement of all that's to come.

'I wonder what I'll be when I grow up,' I muse idly, cutting off a length of duck-egg blue ribbon from a roll.

The table falls quiet.

I look up and see everyone staring at me with an odd expression.

'What?' I laugh.

'You're a receptionist at Paul's Quality Rims,' Jane chuckles. 'That's what you get to be when you grow up!'

'Ew. No!' I say. 'That's a temporary job. It's not my career.'

'You've been there for, like, five years!' Katy says, smirking a little.

I narrow my eyes and think. Oh god. It will have been five years at Christmas...

Oh dear.

'I just have to nip to the loo!' I say overly brightly and totter off in my heeled flip flops to the inside of the taverna. As if this moment isn't bad enough, the Greek guy who dismissed me last night is sitting at the bar, sipping a tiny cup of coffee.

'Hello!' he says. 'Ginger! How are you enjoying magical Alonissos?'

'Yeah! Great! Magical!' I choke before diving into the loo.

I look into the mirror and stare myself out. I can't believe I've been working at Paul's Quality Rims for five years. How did I not realise it had been that long? I sigh at myself and pull a face. Wait a minute. Is that...? I gaze more closely into the mirror. Is that a GREY HAIR? I spot the offending silver lock at the crown of my head.

It IS a grey hair!

Shit.

An odd thought occurs. Ever since I got here weird things have been happening. Rubbish fitness, low alcohol tolerance, weight gain, napping and now grey hair. I didn't notice any of these things last week. They seem to have happened overnight. Alonissos is making me old!

I almost jump out of my skin when my phone beeps with a text. That's strange. This island barely has any reception.

TEXT FROM: DAN

. . .

I miss you. I'm sorry I didn't want to come clubbing with you. But it's not my thing anymore. I'm settled; I'm happy. I wish you could be too. I still want to be with you... x

I turn off my phone.

'I forgot your name,' I say to the Greek man as I pass him on the way back out.

'Aris.'

'I need to ask you a question, Aris.'

'Go ahead.'

Gad, why does he have to be so hot? Especially since what I am about to say will make me sound like an absolute chump.

'You know how you said Alonissos is magical?' I begin.

'Yes. It is both beautiful and magical.'

'Well. Can it do bad magic? Like, for instance, if I thought bad things about it, and said I didn't want to be here, could it...curse me?'

'Curse?'

'I don't know... make me old. Make me age at a rapid pace.'

I look down, the tips of my ears growing hot. What on earth do I sound like?

Aris laughs and takes my hand. 'The Alonissos magic is only good. It gives a person clarity. The island will make you see what needs to be seen. It will also give you the courage to act on what you have seen.'

I nod slowly, taking it in.

Hmm.

'I think the island might be showing me that I'm getting

older. And that it's time to accept it and grow up before it's too late.' I pull a face.

Aris shrugs and says simply, 'It will show you what you need to see.'

At 4 pm we are back at Angie's Place and getting ready for the wedding at 6 pm. I pull on my floatiest, wedding-iest dress: a pink chiffon thingy, which, with my new middle-aged spread, is still a little tight, but the best of a too-small bunch.

Jane is sitting at the large wooden dining table while her mum fusses over her hair, curling it into a chubby bun at the nape of her neck. Katy paints her nails while I do some light, pretty makeup.

I'm brushing coral pink blusher onto Jane's cheeks when suddenly she jumps up, knocking the nail polish bottle over.

'WAIT!' she cries out. 'I don't know what I'm doing, guys!' Her eyes are wide with terror, and her hands start to shake. 'I don't know if I should get married. Shit. This has all happened so quickly! What if it's a mistake? What if we don't work out and I have to get a divorce?'

Has she seen the light? Could this be a second chance?

I'm about to tell her that we can still get the boat to Skiathos, that there is no magic on this island, that it can be just the two of us painting the town red once more.

But I don't.

I know in my heart that she wants to do this. She truly loves Pete, however much of a knobhead he might be.

'You can do this,' I say, holding her face in my hands. 'It's Pete. And it's you. And you love each other. It's all good, Jane.'

She exhales slowly, the colour seeping back into her cheeks.

'Thanks, Ginge,' she says, a smile returning. 'Blimey. I don't know what came over me.'

'I'll miss you,' I say as she runs off to get into her dress.

It will show you what you need to see.

I take my phone out onto the balcony, hold it up in the air to get reception and type out a text.

TEXT TO: DAN

I've had some time to think. I think I might want to settle down too. Maybe I'll even watch Cash in the Attic with you.

I press send. Done. I wait for the feeling of elation to come. But it doesn't.

~

My best friend is married! It was a lovely service. I cried. I think it was happy crying...

Jane is dancing with Pete, and she looks so joyful, her face flushed, her eyes sparkling with elation. Also swirling around the floor is Katy and a young, skinny Greek fisherman, next to Penny and Sue and Jane's parents. They all look so happy, so content in their duos. I clutch my glass of champagne with both hands and gaze out at the twinkling fairy lights strung all along the harbour.

I spot Aris on his boat, pulling up the anchor.

I wonder where he's going.

I wave at him, and what he said the other night pops into my head.

Man cannot discover new oceans unless he has the

courage to lose sight of the shore.

'Come and dance with us!' Jane says, dragging Pete over to me by the hand. 'You're always the first to boogie! What's up?'

'I'm just contemplating life, you know,' I say breezily. 'Sounds a bit naff, but I feel like I've changed out here.'

'It's magical, Alonissos!' Jane smiles. 'It's cast a spell over you!'

'Dan texted me,' I tell her. 'I think we're going to get back together. I'm going to apply for a promotion at work too. Think about buying a house.'

'Hurrah!' Jane claps. 'It's so great that you're figuring things out.'

'Yep!' I smile brightly. 'Arsing about without a plan is for kids. I'm thirty now. Way too old for messing around. Definitely.'

'Exactly,' Pete adds. 'And Dan's a great chap. A good, solid bloke. You know, Ginge, we're going to the Quantocks in November. We didn't mention it because it was kind of a couply thing and we didn't reckon it'd be your cup of tea, but...in light of what you've just said, it would be great if you could come. Cosy fires, great scenery, wine tasting.'

'Yeah. That'd be wonderful!' Jane says. 'Oh my gosh, they have some lovely walks there too.'

Walks?

'You'll have to book the time off work,' Pete says, excitedly. 'But Paul won't miss you, I'm sure. It's deader than disco in that tyre centre. '

No... he probably wouldn't miss me. He probably hasn't even noticed I'm on holiday.

'Ooh, we could play Couples Pictionary by the fire,' Jane squeals. How fab would that be? Dan loves Pictionary! He once told me it was number two on his all-time top list of board games. Number one was Cluedo.'

Couples Pictionary?

My stomach drops.

Man cannot discover new oceans unless he has the courage to lose sight of the shore.

I picture going back home to my life, a life where the only exciting thing to happen is the planning of a holiday I'm no longer eligible for. I get a vision of my tiny rented bedroom, the bus journey to a job where nothing happens, kissing a man who thinks I'm too excitable. Forever and ever, the end.

No.

I look out at the sparkling twilit ocean, and all at once, everything becomes clear.

'I love you, Jane,' I say, my heart beating faster. 'I do. Congratulations to you both. But I won't be coming to the Quantocks.'

Out towards the sea Aris is putting up his sail.

Thirty isn't about accepting what I have. It's about changing it.

'I have to go now!' I laugh, pulling a dumbstruck Jane into a tight hug.

'Um. What now?' I hear her ask as I hurry down the steps of the taverna and over to Aris' rickety boat.

'Hi, Aris,' I say, smiling up at his craggy, handsome face.

'Hello, Ginger. It was a good wedding, I see. You are looking beautiful.'

'Where are you going?' I say, breathless with adrenaline.

Please say somewhere good, please say somewhere good.

'I will go island hopping for a few months,' he says. 'So much beauty to explore, you know?'

Island hopping...

Island hopping!

'Are you going to the Mamma Mia island?' I ask.

'Skopelos? Yes. That is a very good idea. I will go there.'

'Aris,' I say his name quietly, nerves snaking through my belly. 'I know this is out of the blue, and we don't know each other, and it's all a bit embarrassing because I tried to sleep with you, and you weren't interested AT ALL but—'

'I was interested.'

'You were?' I feel a flush cross my face.

'Of course. You are, how do you English put it? Hot? You are hot?'

'Thanks!'

He's right. I am pretty hot.

'But you were sad. And too much alcohol. And that is not good in any situation. I like the lovemaking to be clear and free and intense.'

Clear and free and intense? I rather like the sound of clear, free and intense sex.

'Can I come with you, Aris?'

He blinks and then starts laughing, his pale eyes creased at the corners.

Shit. He thinks I'm a nutter. I ponder turning away, but I can't turn back now. Not now, when I finally see, when I finally have the courage to change things.

I stare at Aris with pleading eyes.

'I would love it, Ginger,' he says. 'You come with me. We laugh. I would love it.'

I exhale, tears springing to my eyes. This is mental. And awesome.

I'm going island hopping. Me!

'Thank you,' I whisper.

'Ginger!' I hear Jane cry from behind me. I spin around to see her dashing down the steps of the tavern, followed by the other wedding guests. 'What the hell are you doing? Come back to the wedding.'

'I'm going island hopping!' I yell, holding out a hand for

Aris to help me aboard. He pulls me up and hands me a bottle of chilled beer from a big red cooler box.

'Now?' Jane squeaks. 'You can't! This is irresponsible!'

'Irresponsible would be going back home without knowing what else is out there. It has to be now. It has to be! I love you, Jane.'

'You have none of your stuff!'

'I'll figure it out!'

'What about Dan?' Pete shouts, frowning.

'We're not right for each other. He knows that really.'

'What about work?' Katy cries.

Jane shushes her, frowns for a second and then giggles, giving me a thumbs up.

'You're bloody cool, Ginge!' she yells, shaking her head.

'I am, aren't I?' I shout back.

The engine roars and the boat slowly moves away from the quayside.

I turn to Aris, grin and take a sip of my beer. It's the best beer I've ever tasted.

'Here we go,' he smiles, clinking his bottle against mine. 'A new adventure.'

This is thirty. This is life.

And Cool Ginger lives to fight another day.

Kirsty Greenwood is a top ten bestselling author of funny, fearless and fast-paced romantic comedies about extraordinary love. A former book editor, she was named as one of The Bookseller's Rising Stars in 2016. When she's not writing books, Kirsty composes musicals, cooks new recipes with varying success, walks the blustery hills where she lives, buys too much glittery eyeshadow, sings to her dog, kisses her husband and reads all of the books she can get her grabby hands on.

TAYO'S STORY

LOLA JAYE

My name is Tayo Cole. The year is 1958, and tiny raised spots have appeared on my arms and my teeth have started to chatter. I had walked through this very airport a year ago when I first arrived in this country, and yet still, I am unable to truly embrace these low temperatures whilst marvelling at the tiny buds of white that fall from the sky.

The two people I share a house with often clutch their bellies with laughter when I try to explain my distress.

'You'll get used to it Tayo, just like we did. Just be thankful like us that you're one of the chosen ones who get to spend your life in this country. Many in Nigeria have not been given such a chance!'

I used to think they meant what they said, but when they wade through the front door, dressed in an abundance of old clothing just to keep warm, I see their faces are lined and etched with grief for the people and land they have left behind. I refuse to give in to that thought because to do so would be ungrateful. Just as my fellow lodgers implied, many, many people in my village would have given anything to have been chosen. Yet it was I who'd been given a chance to change the life of the family I had been born into, as well as the one I had started with my Adanya.

Adanya. My beautiful and graceful Adanya.

It was still hard to believe that in less than thirty minutes, she would be walking through the Arrivals gate and into my arms once again.

I knew Adanya would be my wife the moment I met her.

Seeing her beautiful face that day as she stood beside a coconut tree, I was overcome with a sense of peace I had never felt before. In her eyes, I saw the blurred faces of my future children, my home, my life, and when six months later, she agreed to my hand in marriage, I felt like I had won the entire world.

She was and is my everything.

But along with her entrance into my life came a responsibility to look after her in every way possible, for life. And I took my role seriously. I vowed to love and protect my wife and give her everything she desired. She could have had any man in the village, yet for reasons unbeknown to me, it was me she chose.

Adanya, like most girls in my village, desired three things; a husband, children and a life in England.

My family had always been divided on whether the British colonial rule in Nigeria was good or bad. Uncle Bolu insisted the country has never been the same since they arrived, whilst Aunty Kemi is always quick to announce that the country has never been better. As for me, I had never had any dreams to go to England, content to raise my family in the land I was born. Yet, the pressure from family felt so overwhelming that it overpowered anything I desired for myself. My mother often said,

'Imagine what you could do for your entire family from back there?'

So I worked all the hours God sent to save enough money for our plane tickets and initial living expenses in England. It wasn't easy. The hours were long, and when Adanya gave birth to our first child Lanre, I felt the pressure increase. The money allocated to England was diminishing further, and when our second child Mayowa was born, I knew it had to happen. Soon. Whenever Adanya complained about the children not getting the start in life they deserved, I was aware she was referring to what I hadn't done. I knew she loved me, and I was certainly in love with her - even more than the first time we met - but this only increased my sense of inadequacy; as a husband, I could not give her what she wanted. This urgency was what finally pushed me to decide to go on to England ahead of my girls.

Adanya was at first unhappy at this decision - we'd never been apart since the day we married - but with advice from her parents, she reluctantly agreed.

'Please don't cry, my love. You will soon join me in England.' I wiped her tears with my fingertips. 'I will have a good job and a wonderful house for you all to live in. This is for the best.' I tried to believe my own words. I could not.

My little girls, I would miss with a pain I had already begun to feel. Lanre at seven was so clever and could recite many of the timetables. Whilst Mayowa resembled me not only in looks but also in temperament, quiet and, at times, introverted.

The day I said goodbye to my parents, siblings and then my wife and children was the hardest day of my life. I had not cried since I was a little boy and would not start now. But If I were permitted to, tears would have fallen from my eyes and continued during the trip to the airport and until the aeroplane touched down on English soil.

Six months passed, still in England, still without my girls, knowing the letters I wrote would take at least six weeks to reach them. I once made the mistake of sending money, forgetting that poverty and opportunity can make thieves out of the most honest of men - with postal workers being no exception. It was best to wait until a friend of an acquaintance knew of someone travelling back home; that way, I could ask them to be a courier for cash to take to my family. Hoping they would not take the money for themselves.

I enjoyed my work at the factory, even though it wasn't what I had planned to pursue in England. As a trained engineer, I had hoped to work in that field and study at night. My life in England did not start or continue that way. The need for money to sustain my family back home overtook my needs, and this is where I found myself.

My boss Dave is a good man and had promised to 'look out for me' ever since that incident during my first day.

'This is the new bloke. Tayo Cole's his name.'

I tipped my hat in greeting to the five young men dressed in overalls standing by the two large machines.

'Les will show you the ropes,' Dave had said, pointing to the tallest of the men.

'Not today,' said Les.

'Why not?'

'Because I happen to be busy.'

'That is okay. I am a quick learner; perhaps you can show me...' I'd said, turning to Dave.

'No, Les will show you.' The way Dave spoke suggested it was an order. I was confused, as I could not understand why this Les was being so resistant. I just needed to learn the machine so I could get on with my work. This was my only wish.

Les did not speak at all, as he showed me the mechanics of the machine. I was aware that such a contraption could be dangerous if mishandled, so it was best to ask questions instead of remaining in doubt.

'Les, I didn't quite understand what this does,' I'd said, pointing to the red lever.

His eyes narrowed, yet still, he did not say a word. Instead, he turned his back to me and walked towards the kitchen.

That very day, I heard Les and the others use words to address me which were not my given name. I wasn't sure what the term 'Blackie' meant, but judging by his demeanour, it wasn't good. It was bad. Blackie. I rolled the word around in my head; it suggested I was of a black colour. That I could almost understand, but I was unsure of the inclusion of the 'I' and 'E'. There was so much in England I was unsure of.

I also did not understand the words; 'coloured boy' as I was neither a boy nor coloured!

The men never sat with me or engaged me in their conversations. They'd simply say the words to attract my attention and then laugh when I looked up.

Once I suppressed my loneliness - telling myself I was not in England to make any friends, that I was simply here to work - I began to feel a little better.

Dearest Adanya,

How are you all? I hope Nigeria is treating you well. As for me, England is even better than I had imagined. The roads are smooth, and the people are friendly and welcoming, just as you said they would be. Whilst there are not many here who look like us, I am not judged for this. People are more interested in my character than the colour of my skin. It is a very fair society too, where everyone is of equal value. I am allowed to get on with my life just as I let others get on with their own. The food is very tasty too. I have discovered something called the shepherd's pie. I am unsure if this was invented by real shepherds, but it is delicious. Maybe I will cook it for you when you arrive. Yes, that's right. I cook now too! I know your mouth must be wide open right now with that admission, but my love, I have had to cook for myself ever since arriving in London, and I realise that it is okay to do so. I know this is not something we are used to!

How are my two baby girls? I miss them every single day of my life. I feel only jealousy when I see other children with their parents in the street. The only thought to keep me going, to keep me alive, is the certainty that you will all soon be here with me.

I can't wait to see you again and hold you in my arms. I love you, my dear, sweet Adanya.

Until I see you again.

Tayo

The day I found a bunch of fresh bananas in my locker, I knew Les had put them there. It would be pointless to complain to Dave - I didn't want any trouble. Dave, the only shining light in my life. He and his wife had invited me to dinner on many occasions, and this kindness reminded me there was still good in this new world I lived in.

Once winter turned into a warm spring, life seemed more bearable, and with Dave offering me ample overtime, I was soon able to purchase three plane tickets for my lovely girls to join me in England.

Now, I was able to allow more light to enter my life with thoughts of her, the feel of her skin, how the corner of her eyes creased slightly when she laughed. She is the only woman I will ever love, and to know that with the purchase of three tickets, I had caused her happiness and my own felt miraculous to me!

'I couldn't be away from my lot for that amount of time,' said Dave as he drove me towards the airport and thus closer to my girls. I ignored the feeling of being judged by my best friend whilst wanting to say, 'You're lucky never to have to make that choice.'

Now at the airport, scores of people greeting loved ones, embracing, crying - my eyes have searched for them. And for a few frightening seconds, I wondered if they hadn't made the flight. Perhaps one of my girls had gotten sick and could no longer travel. What if...

I spotted my youngest first, her thumb firmly placed in her mouth, a habit I used to chastise but had missed. I had missed so much! But it was Lanre, my eldest child, who spotted me first and I became immediately overwhelmed with gratitude that she could even remember me.

'Daddy!' she screamed.

'Tayo!' shouted Adanya as she let go of our youngest daughter's hand. She ran to me yet still seemed to take an eternity to reach me. I hugged her so close, so tightly, I was scared I would injure her. Her hair smelled like fresh mango; her skin just as soft as I remembered.

'My love,' I whispered into her ear.

I stooped down, pulling both of my little girls into my arms, tears clouding my vision. Crying wasn't what a man did, but at that moment, this didn't concern me. This moment was my happiness, and nothing else could compare. I had missed the very scent of them, my nostrils drawing in the aroma of fresh black soap, my fingers twirling strands of their beautiful coily hair.

'Daddy, we missed you!' said Lanre. She had grown so

much in a year. I vowed there and then never to miss another day. I pulled Mayowa up into my arms, and with Lanre now holding onto my leg, my wife holding my hand, I had never felt more alive and more at peace.

I wasn't going to think about having been less than truthful in the letters because at that very moment, I just knew that everything would work out well. The dreams we had for our children were about to become a reality. So, as we headed into this new life together, I was filled with the wonderful certainty that a brighter future awaited us all in England.

If not, then why had I sacrificed so much?

Lola Jaye is an author, registered psychotherapist and speaker who has penned six novels and a self-help book. She was born and raised in London, England and has lived in Nigeria and the United States. Lola once gave a presentation on imposter syndrome – a subject close to her heart, because at times she's unable to believe she's an actual writer! 'The Attic Child' is her first epic historical novel. Keep up to date with Lola at www.lolajaye.com

THE RUNNING MAN

MILLY JOHNSON

There he was again, the rather portly gentleman doing his early morning run before anyone was up to see him. Margo looked out of the kitchen window while the kettle was boiling. Well, 'run' was pushing it. He sort of loped forward for a few steps, bent over to take a breath, walked on for a bit and then began the cycle again.

'Did you hear me?' said John's fierce voice behind her.

'Er, no sorry,' she'd been too engrossed in the running man to notice her husband talking to her.

John sighed heavily. 'I *said* that I'd be late home. I have no idea what time. Don't wait up.'

John had a way of speaking to Margo that suggested he was exasperated by everything she did. After ten years of marriage, there was no softness in his tone anymore. She was often on the verge of asking him why he returned to her, after his affair, if she drove him so mad. When she had gratefully – and stupidly – taken him back, even then, it had been as if he was doing her the favour. She knew she shouldn't have relented. Had it been her best friend, she would have told her to keep the door closed and not listen to anything John had to say. But it was so much easier to dish out advice than it was to take it - and Margo had been in such a low place, her ego as crushed as her heart.

Margo made herself a coffee and remembered the day when John walked in through the door and said, 'It's over, I've come home. Let's not talk about it; all you have to know is that I finished it for you. So let's look forward, shall we?' Margo had replayed that scene so many times in her head, but always with a twist at the end. Not as it happened, but with her staring blankly at him and saying, 'I'm afraid I've moved on, John. So you really shouldn't have bothered.' How Margo wished she'd been brave enough to say that to him. And thinking about it, she'd swallowed his words whole, never imagining that it might have been his bit-on-the-side that finished with him, and that's why he'd slunk home. Not until later did she start to wonder about that.

Now Margo wanted to leave John so badly, but she just didn't have the strength. At the same time, she didn't trust him anymore. He'd been 'working late' a lot recently and sometimes he arrived home hours after he should have, saying he'd been to the gym and had a shower there. Her mind instinctively went back to when John was having his affair, and he'd showered to wash the scent of the other woman's perfume from him. Of course, she did want to believe that he was working late or going to the gym, but once trust had been smashed, however much you tried to patch it up, it was never whole again.

Two weeks later, Margo was standing by the window when the running man went past again. He always came at the same time, and Margo found that she had started looking out for him. The man looked like he was running a bit now, rather than just doing that strange lurch. And he was taking it seriously because he'd bought himself a proper tracksuit. He looked slimmer too; good for him. As the runner stopped at the other side of the road to take a breath, Margo wondered what his story was, why he was pushing himself so hard. She could see how red his face was and how he needed both hands to wipe the sweat off his brow. He still looked as if he was ready for keeling over, but he shook himself and carried on up to the next lamp post, where he took another rest.

The following week, Margo found the receipt in John's pocket. Dinner for two at a restaurant you didn't go to for a business meeting. It was an intimate little Italian bistro out of town, nice and secret and very dark. Margo knew it was all starting up again. The same woman or someone else, she didn't know; the hurt was the same in either case. But Margo daren't confront him, she was scared he'd say what he said last time: that she'd let herself go, so it should come as no shock that he'd gone elsewhere.

Margo thought that maybe she'd go jogging like the running man and get herself into shape. She used to run, a long time ago - she loved the fresh morning air in her lungs - but then she'd met John and one-by-one, all the things she liked to do had fallen by the wayside.

Two months later, Margo was on her third coffee when the running man went past the window. She was having trouble sleeping. John had temporarily moved out – they needed a break, he said. He meant *he* needed a break, and she knew what he needed it for. Her heart was in pieces and her head was a mess. And sitting around stewing was doing her no good at all.

The running man didn't stop at the lamp post this time but sailed straight past it. He was running in shorts now and some very nice trainers, rather than the pumps he used to wear. He was taking it seriously and it was paying off.

Margo went into the loft and dug out an old pair of joggers - they weren't very flattering and a bit tight, but who was looking? – and she dusted off her old running shoes from the back of her wardrobe. Why had she kept them? Perhaps she'd always known, deep down, that she'd take up her old hobby again one day because she'd married a twerp who couldn't keep it in his trousers and might need the diversion. Margo knew she looked a proper sight, but she had to start somewhere, and it was early; there was no one around except insomniacs and paperboys.

...And the running man circling the block. He said good morning to Margo as he overtook her when she was leaning on the lamp post outside her house, the same one he used to lean on.

His name was Alan. She found this out a couple of weeks later when she ignominiously fell splat on the ground. He helped her up, said that the same thing had happened to him, and he'd learned to dodge that uneven slab now. She couldn't believe this was the same blobby man who used to cough up his lungs outside her kitchen window. He looked half the size he used to be.

He sat on a nearby bench with her while her nerves settled. She made him laugh by saying that when she was a kid, she used to fall over for fun, and he made her laugh back when he said he'd videoed her tripping and was going to upload it to YouTube. Margo marvelled at the sound; it was so alien. She couldn't remember the last time she'd heard herself laugh.

Sometimes Alan would catch her up in the mornings, and they'd run together. Neither of them would be chosen for the Olympic squad anytime soon, but she found that a run in the morning set her up for the day, just like it used to. And her waistbands were getting looser. Then she and Alan started meeting every morning. It was so much better running with someone, he said. He was a widower; he missed the company of a lovely lady, he said. He'd been in a bad place for a while, let himself go. His wife wouldn't have wanted him to be like that and his big sister had given him a strong talking to. He spoke about women with such respect, it was refreshing to hear. As refreshing as the morning air.

One day Alan announced he had lost exactly four stone and wanted to celebrate. Would Margo like to go out to dinner with him? Margo said she'd like that very much. She bought herself a new frock for the occasion – two dress sizes smaller than her usual. Alan treated her like a queen, and when she said as much, he replied that was how a lady should be treated. Margo knew he wasn't just spouting rubbish and that he really felt like that. John had never been so attentive, not even at the beginning when his charming veneer was still in place. They chatted as if they'd known each other forever, and Margo felt so comfortable in his presence, unjudged and accepted for who she was. It gave her a warm glow inside, and she was sure that if there had been a mirror nearby, she would have seen herself light up with an orange glow, as if she were in one of those old Ready Brek adverts.

Margo didn't know where she and Alan would end up, she thought as they finished off their lovely meal with a coffee, the candlelight reflected in his kind eyes. Maybe this was just a sweet little interlude for them both, or maybe it was the start of something long-lasting and wonderful. But what she did know for sure was that this gentle man had shown her, with his sheer persistence, what could be achieved and he'd made her feel like something of value again. And she wouldn't waste those lessons learned for anything.

That was why when she found John in her kitchen the next day, holding out his arms and saying 'Okay, I messed up, but I missed you, so I've come home,' she stayed exactly where she was, stared at him blankly, took a very deep breath and said, 'I'm afraid I've moved on, John. So you really shouldn't have bothered.'

Milly Johnson was born, raised and still lives in Barnsley, South Yorkshire. A Sunday Times bestseller, millions of copies of her books have been sold across the world. In 2020 she was awarded an Outstanding Achievement Award from the RNA in recognition of her contribution to the field of romantic fiction. Her latest novel 'The Woman in the Middle' is out now.

A CAMBRIDGE LOVE STORY

PAIGE TOON

I was seven the first time my dad took me punting. I'd gone to stay with him after the divorce, and I remember looking up at him, and my heart hurting because he was no longer an everyday part of my life. Now he's no longer a part of my life at all.

My eyes sting with tears as I lift the pole clear of the water, steeling myself as freezing-cold droplets run up the inside of my coat sleeve. I let the pole slip back through my fingers until it hits the riverbed and gently propel the punt along.

It's Valentine's Day and the Cam is full of loved-up couples. I studiously ignore two kissing under the Bridge of Sighs. Mark and I may have broken up months ago, but right now everything still feels raw. I don't actually know why I'm doing this to myself.

Dad would have been sixty-eight today if cancer hadn't got the better of him. Only my father - the least romantic man in the world, according to my mum - could have been born on the most romantic day of the year. He was nothing if not contrary.

Tucking a lock of dark hair behind my ear, I let the pole

drift up to the surface, using it as a rudder to correct the boat's position as I navigate a bend in the river. Up ahead, a group of punting novices are creating havoc outside the Wren Library. Students, probably – two couples. Their laughter carries across the water as the guy charged with pole-duty tries desperately to straighten the boat while his mate madly paddles an oar at the other end. They're currently straddling half of the river with a packed tour boat bearing down on them. I really don't have the energy for this, I think with a sigh. And then the professional punter on the tour bangs into their boat, sending it sluicing through the water towards the bank as his dozen passengers over-excitedly cry out.

Good. Now I can nip up the outside while the rookies are drifting.

My plan is sound, until the pillock with the pole gets it stuck in the mud.

'NO!' he shouts, hanging on for dear life while his friends roar with laughter.

'Let go or you'll fall in,' I command, words spilling out of my mouth of their own volition. To my surprise, he obeys immediately and his punt coasts away from the embedded pole. His hair is dark blond and a dishevelled mess, but his eyes are warm and brown and right now they're staring imploringly at me.

'Help?' he says with a crooked smile.

'Hang on,' I mutter as I go to retrieve his pole, yanking hard until it comes loose. His friends cheer.

'How do you do it?' he asks hopelessly as I slide back to his punt. Up close, I can see he's gorgeous: tall, broad and older than I initially suspected. Late-twenties, at a guess – about my age.

'Practice,' I reply with an amused shrug, handing over the pole. His fingers accidentally touch mine, making me jolt. I quickly let go, but I can feel his gaze on me as I blush and look away, inadvertently locking eyes with one of his female passengers – his girlfriend, judging by the poisonous look she's giving me.

'You're useless, Archie. Let me have a turn,' she snaps as she wobbles to her feet.

'Easy, Nessa,' he says, trying to steady the boat.

Time for me to go, I think.

'Good luck,' I call as I set off.

'Wait!' he replies, compelling me to glance over my shoulder at him. To my surprise, he appears oddly torn. 'Thank you.'

'You're welcome,' I reply.

I'm still feeling unsettled about my run-in with the stranger when I return my punt to the boatyard and walk up onto the bridge. I've barely thought about Dad which was what I'd intended this little jaunt to be about: doing something symbolic on his birthday. I'm also here to sort out his house, a task I've been putting off for weeks. I've always loved coming up to Cambridge, but Dad's cosy home feels cold and empty without him. I should go and get started, but I can't quite get my feet to move. I stare in a daze at the water below. *Happy birthday, Dad. I miss you so much.*

As I brush away my tears, I see the stranger – Archie the punter – heading towards The Mill pub. His eyes widen and his footsteps falter as he catches my eye and then he calls after his friends as they continue into the bar without him.

'Hello again,' he says as he approaches.

'Hi,' I reply, butterflies filling my stomach despite myself. His girlfriend is not going to like this. 'You made it back alive then.'

'Yeah.' He shrugs. 'My sister's friend was a natural.' Sister's friend? His smile fades and she sees my frown. 'Hey, are you okay?' he asks with concern.

'I'm fine.' I dig around in my bag for a tissue. How embarrassing.

'Want me to beat him up for you?' he offers affably. I laugh and shake my head. 'I'm not crying about a boy. My dad passed away recently.'

'Oh.' He immediately looks crestfallen. 'I'm sorry. When?'

'Just before Christmas. It's his birthday today.' I pause. 'I don't know why I'm telling you this.'

He smiles a small smile and holds out his hand. 'I'm Archie.'

'I know.' My palm tingles as our skin connects.

'And...are you going to tell me your name?' he asks with amusement.

'Oh. Matilda,' I reply, belatedly extracting my hand.

'Look, do you think...Could I buy you lunch?' he asks. 'I owe you for saving me from falling in the river.' He seems nervous, although I can't imagine why.

I glance towards the pub where his friends are. 'Shouldn't you be getting back to your friends?' *More specifically, your girlfriend?* I add silently.

'Nah, I've seen enough of them for today.' Archie leans against the bridge wall and folds his arms. 'Anyway, they're not strictly my friends. They're my sister's. Her boyfriend's at Cambridge. She and her pal are visiting.'

'Nessa is not your girlfriend?'

'Christ, no.' He looks horrified. 'No, I'm single.'

My butterflies take flight. 'Lunch would be nice.'

~

Fifteen minutes later, we're sitting at a packed bench table in Fitzbillies, near the window. It's not very private, but the atmosphere is buzzing.

'Do you live nearby?' Archie asks as he sips a raspberry lemonade.

'No, London,' I reply. 'I'm just here for the weekend to sort out my dad's house.'

He raises one eyebrow. 'You're doing that in one weekend?'

'Not likely, especially when I'm sitting here with you.' I smile at the stricken look on his face. 'No, I'll have to come back. I was supposed to arrive on Wednesday night, but my boss decided she was too busy for me to take two days off.'

'What do you do?'

'Bookkeeping.' Snore. 'You?'

'I'm a graphic designer.'

'Wow.' How cool. 'Do you live in Cambridge?'

'Yeah, I've got a flat on the other side of town. Where's your dad's place?'

'In Newnham, a few minutes' walk from here.'

'Newnham?' He looks impressed. 'You'll have no trouble selling it, then.'

'As numerous estate agents keep telling me,' I nod with a wry smile. 'They've been hounding me for weeks.'

'Bloodsuckers. Is that the plan, then? To put it on the market?'

I stare down at my fingernails. 'I have to pay inheritance tax, but I hate letting it go.'

He reaches across the table and squeezes my hand just as the waitress appears with our food, forcing us to break apart. Our cheese toasties look good, but I seem to have lost my appetite. There's not much spare room in my stomach with all the winged creatures flying around.

'If you live in Cambridge, how come you can't punt?'

Archie laughs. 'It's not a requirement by law. How did you learn?'

'Dad taught me. It's one of the things we did together when I came to visit.'

We sit there talking about our respective families and jobs for almost an hour, but at the back of my mind is the constant, pressing reminder that I have work to do.

'I guess I should be going,' I say reluctantly, as we stand on the pavement outside the café and pull on our coats.

'Do you really have to?' he asks with disappointment, checking his watch. 'We could go for a walk or something.'

'I'd love to hang out, but I have so much to do.'

'Then let me help,' he proposes. 'Two hands are better than one.' He waggles them in front of my face to demonstrate his point.

'Four hands are better than two, don't you mean?'

'Ah. I can see you're an excellent bookkeeper.'

'I can even count up to a hundred,' I smile.

He nudges my arm. 'Come on, Matilda. Just say yes. I've got nothing better to do.'

'Are you sure?' I ask hopefully. I'd love to spend more time with him, even in this depressing capacity.

'I'm sure,' he replies.

'Then so am I.'

By the time the evening comes around, I'm shattered, both emotionally and physically as we slowly work our way through Dad's house sorting and tidying. I keep reminding Archie that he can leave at any time, and he keeps insisting that he wants to be here. This task would have been a hell of a lot harder if it weren't for the hottie standing before me. I can't believe Fate has come up trumps for once.

'Thank you,' I say with sincerity, meeting Archie's beautiful brown eyes over a pile of boxes. We've talked non-stop as we worked. I've told him things that I haven't told anyone – about my life, my loves, my ambitions... I feel like I know him – really know him – yet we haven't even kissed. It's bizarre.

'Are you hungry?' I ask. 'We could order in a pizza?'

'Sounds good.'

As I go to get my phone out of my bag, he grabs my hand and tugs me towards him, making me gasp with surprise. My heart hammers against my ribcage as he stares at me intently.

'I think I've made a mistake,' he says quietly. My stomach flips. What sort of mistake? What does he mean?

'Well, once this house is packed up, you won't need to come back.' He sounds despondent.

I smile with relief and touch his hand. 'I'll still have to return. There's loads to do.'

'Why don't you quit your job and move up here permanently?' he asks.

'I can't just do that.'

'Matilda, of course you can,' he states resolutely. 'You've spent all day telling me how you hate your job, you despise your boss and how your flatmate is a nutter. Once you sell this house and pay the tax, you'll still have more than enough to buy something smaller, mortgage free. And you'll have plenty spare to go back to university and retrain to do anything you want to do.'

My head swims with possibilities. Is he right? Could I move here permanently, have a fresh start in a city that I adore? But will I still adore being here, when Dad is not? Looking up at Archie's face, I have a funny feeling that I will...

My dad might not have been a romantic who believed in fate, but he did advocate making the most of the opportunities we're given.

And right then and there, I resolve to make the most of this one.

'Do you think I can kiss you now?' Archie asks softly, cupping my face with his hands.

'Please do,' I reply with a smile.

Paige Toon is the 1.5 million bestselling author of fourteen women's fiction novels, three books for young adults and three short story ebook sequels. She writes contemporary love stories about relatable characters in often extraordinary circumstances and is one of the highest-rated romance authors on Goodreads. She loves hearing from her readers, so please get in touch on Twitter @PaigeToonAuthor, Facebook and Instagram

BETTER LATE THAN NEVER

PERNILLE HUGHES

Adam looked around the flat. He had no idea where to begin. How did you start to unravel someone's life? While he'd known this particular life for longer than he could remember, disassembling it felt like an impossible, insurmountable task.

Thank God Alex had been tidy. Everything was in its place, so Adam wouldn't have to clear a load of crap before he could start the boxing. CDs were racked alphabetically; books were confined to half a wall. For Adam, the time-saving nature of Alex's habits were a blessing; he wanted this over and done ASAP.

And yet.

If you were saying goodbye to the person who knew you longest and best, you'd want the most time possible, wouldn't you? Time to think about each item and shared memory it held. Time to think about what the thing said about the late owner. And about him.

Alex had always looked out for him; in fact, Adam felt he'd spent most of his primary years sitting on Adam's coat-tails. Uni had separated them geographically, but their dispositions remained the same; Alex had been the life and soul, while Adam had muddled along behind.

But enough of this. The boxes wouldn't fill themselves.

Adam decisively picked one up and headed for the CD shelf; it seemed like an easy start. He lifted a handful down and looked at the top one. He slid it to the back of the pile and looked at the second. He slid it back too. And again. Dropping his arms, he raised his face to the ceiling and drew a deep breath, trying to get control of the tears. Rapid blinking and a long sniff helped.

He dumped the handful of plastic cases into the box defeated. He'd sort them out at home, away from here. He'd sift out the ones he already had and sell any he didn't want. The Reggae ones could definitely go.

The silence in the room becoming unbearable, Adam hit play on the sound system, curious to know what the last album Alex had listened to.

A doorbell chimed, and it took Adam a moment to realise it was the actual doorbell, not part of the recording. It was Saturday afternoon, he thought, striding towards down the corridor, it wouldn't be the postman.

'Better late than never, right?' she said, with an apologetic smile and jazz-hands. Adam gazed at the girl standing in the doorway. She was petite until you got to her head which had an enormous pair of blue eyes and was topped by a mass of blonde corkscrew curls.

'I...I'm sorry?'

'I'm Merrilee, um...Merri. From the ad in the paper. Four o'clock.' Her confidence seemed to falter further as each additional piece of information was met with mystification on Adam's part. What kind of appointment was Alex making with girls from the small ads? Her final attempt wasn't even a statement. 'I'm buying the iPad off you?'

Finally, he got it. 'You've bought Alex's iPad?'

‘Oh, God,’ she said with a laugh. ‘I assumed you were him. I forgot to ask his name when I called. I guess I'm looking for Alex then.’

Adam looked at her, unsure what to do. He was surprised Alex was selling his iPad, but then Alex liked to upgrade his stuff, whereas Adam had a habit of hanging on to things.

’Yeah, so, is Alex here?’ The girl, Merri, peered behind him into the apartment and at the empty boxes filling the floor. Empty but waiting. Her face was inquisitive, a short vertical line forming between her eyebrows as she looked back at him.

’Not anymore,’ Adam managed, then wondered why he simply hadn't said ‘No’.

’Oh,’ she said, confused, before checking her watch. ‘We arranged it for four. I know I'm fifteen minutes late, but the bus... you know?’

This was getting a little awkward, and Adam felt a need to curtail it – for her sake.

’I'm Adam,’ he blustered, holding out his hand for her to shake, which she did, but with another curious look. ‘Alex is my brother.’

The moment he said it, he reopened his mouth to correct it to was, but shut it again. Alex would always be his brother, he reminded himself. No matter what. He was still Adam, brother to Alex. That wouldn't change, it would never change, so logically, it shouldn't change the other way either.

She made an ‘Ahh, I see’ face. ‘Any chance he left the iPad out for me?’ She dug about in her pocket and held up some twenty-pound notes. ‘I've got the cash like we agreed.’

’Look, come in. I'll see if I can find it for you.’ She followed him, stopping just inside the door.

’Is he coming back soon?’ she asked, scanning the living

room. Adam didn't think she felt unsafe, but he understood why she didn't venture in too far.

He decided just to come clean.

'I'm afraid not, Merrilee. See, Alex died.'

'Oh my god. I'm so sorry.' She appeared genuinely distressed for him.

'Thank you.'

'But...we arranged this last Monday?'

'He was knocked off his bike Tuesday morning. Stupid arse wasn't wearing a helmet.' Adam felt nausea begin to rise, but he pushed it back down again. He'd had that all week. Several times it had made it all the way.

Merrilee ran a hand through her hair, thinking.

'Look, this is the last thing you need. I'll go. I can find another iPad on eBay. This one was local, that's all.'

Adam saw she meant it. Her face was so open and warm. She tucked the money back in her pocket and started pulling her woolly gloves back on.

'No,' Adam said impulsively. 'You agreed on it with him; it's yours. He was expecting you to have it.'

'But I guess it's yours now,' she said.

'I don't need it. Honestly. I'm here to sort out his affairs and I guess you're one of them.'

That made her smile.

'I can come another time if now's not good.'

Adam looked around the room at all the things he needed to box. 'I'm not sure there's ever going to be a good time. Alex was a minimalist, but the job feels kind of huge.'

She contemplated the room, then Adam; his head was hanging forward, overwhelmed. She pulled her gloves back off.

'Say no if you want, but I'm not doing anything right now. I can help. If you like.'

He looked up, surprised. This stranger was offering him help. Did people in London do that?

'Or just company,' she tried again. 'Or not. Whatever.' She seemed genuine. He shook himself out of his stupefaction.

'That... that would be... well it would be really... yes please.' He surprised himself by accepting, perhaps because the offer came without ties or expectations.

Merrilee's face bloomed into a wide smile. Everything about her felt like a lot of big things packed into a small space. Adam sensed there'd be no end of surprises with Merri.

'OK,' she said, dropping her coat onto the settee, 'You make the tea, I'll get onto the CDs.' Only now did Adam register Alex's final album was dire, and he was slightly mortified that this girl, this gorgeous girl, might believe it was his selection.

'This was the last thing he played,' he said, accusingly pointing at the sound system.

She considered it for a moment. 'Sex music. I think your brother probably died a satisfied man.'

Adam laughed for the first time in what felt like a lifetime. A deep belly laugh that quelled the persistent nausea.

'I thought you said you didn't know him?'

'Just reading the signs; total bachelor pad, extinguished tea-lights, and there's no other excuse for playing The Weeknd.'

'Good point,' he agreed. 'I'll get the tea, Miss Marple; you pick something else to listen to.'

Rifling through Alex's cabinets, Adam supposed he should feel awkward about having a strange girl in his brother's flat. He'd be feeling plenty awkward about having a girl in his own flat; he didn't have his brother's confidence when it came to the ladies. Fleetingly he considered checking on her in case she was about to make off with something, but instinctively he knew this wasn't necessary. Opportunist thieves most likely didn't sing along to tracks as they went about their business. She was no Adele, but she got points for enthusiasm. And taste. She'd picked one of his favourites.

'I thought Evanescence might suit the mood. Reflective but with guts. Something to storm through with,' she said as Adam emerged from the kitchen, two teas in hand and a packet of biscuits under his arm.

'Ahh, Jaffa Cakes,' she said knowingly. 'The signature lure of the experienced seducer. Females are aroused by the citrus in the jelly. That's why many aftershaves have citrus notes.'

'Really?' Alex never had trouble finding girlfriends; it hadn't occurred to Adam there might be science or tactics involved.

She snorted a laugh. 'No, total lie.'

Adam felt a little foolish. And perhaps a little disappointed. After all, he'd picked them out of the cupboard; he might have discovered some latent, hitherto undiscovered, seduction instinct. He was twenty-seven. He could really do with finding one soon.

Reaching for her tea, she rewarded him with a smile before returning to her task, briskly dropping discs into a series of boxes. Her diligence prompted him to move across to the bookshelf, ready to start, but immediately hesitation caught him.

'Three piles, Adam,' called Merri. 'Books you love but don't have; books you don't have but might love, and books you know you'll never love. Pile three goes to the charity shop.' She pointed to the CD box next to her. 'Give yourself three seconds to decide for each. Read the blurb if you can't judge it by the cover.'

'I thought we weren't supposed to judge books by their covers?'

'Bollocks,' she said and took a swig of the tea. 'It's about chemistry, isn't it? Something either appeals or it doesn't. Life's too short for the rest.' An odd expression crossed her face. 'Sorry. About the short life thing. I didn't mean to be insensitive.'

''S'fine,' Adam assured her. 'It was a short life. He's my twin. He was twenty-seven. That's no age.'

'But did he use it?' she asked, slipping another load of discs into the 'Keep' box.

'Alex? Absolutely. Something was going on all the time.' Adam didn't add that the same couldn't be said of him. If he'd been the one hit by the lorry, no one would say he'd lived life to the full.

They worked quietly and diligently, humming to the music as they went. Now and again, Merri would mutter 'Dear God' and cast a CD into the Pit of Hell as she now referred to it, bound for Oxfam. She didn't stop to ask whether Adam wanted it. He didn't mind. Her criteria for book sorting was proving very successful; he was happy to defer to her music selection too. And using Merri's system, Adam finished the bookshelves quicker than he'd ever imagined possible.

'More tea?' he asked, stretching his legs. The lowest shelves had required some kneeling-action, and his long legs didn't like it.

'Could do, unless Alex wants to treat us to a beer?'

For the last week, no one, save the undertaker, had dared mention Alex by name. Merri didn't appear to suffer from such forms of unhelpful tact. Adam now found he wanted to talk about Alex, which was strange, considering Merri had never met him.

'You spoke to Alex?' he suddenly said.

Merri turned to him, understanding. 'I did. Just a short call to arrange the pick-up. He told me flat 58 and that he'd be in at four. He sounded ...well, he sounded tired, to be honest. Not the voice I'd put with the face,' she waved a finger at a photo frame on the shelf.

There was Alex and Adam, laughing together. Adam remembered that trip, learning to surf in Newquay. Alex surfed every summer after that, sometimes Newquay, but increasingly further afield and in more exotic locations. Adam hadn't quite made it. Some work thing always got in the way – when really, now he thought about it, there was nothing in the lab that couldn't have waited for a week or two. The weight of missed opportunity threatened to revive his nausea, so he looked away. He loved that photo, though. He looked young and cool and happy. He looked like someone else.

'...but that's telephones for you,' Merri was saying. 'Change your voice, don't they? You two look so alike; the voice on the phone probably wouldn't have sounded like you either.'

'Right,' Adam said vaguely, his attention wandering to the lively girl sitting cross-legged on the floor. She was wearing an all-in-one top and shorts thing over thick tights with doc martins. The yellow flowers on the black leather perfectly matched the gold curls. He couldn't think of anyone more different from the few girls he'd dated, but then they'd almost exclusively been lab technicians, who had scraped-back hair and lab coats at work, and apparently little interest in appearances outside of it. Alex had told him to look further afield, told him he was lazy. Perhaps Alex had been right; Adam had been lazy, but he couldn't see why confidence was such hard work for him when it came so naturally to Alex.

'So, do you think he would?' Merri asked.

‘Who?’ He’d been lost in his thoughts, and he’d dropped the thread of the conversation.

’Alex.’

’Would what?’

’Shout us a beer?’ She giggled at his befuddlement, then looked at her watch. ‘It's half five on a Saturday night, we’re sorting his stuff; I reckon it's the least he can do.’

Adam ran out to the black SMEG fridge. Its contents went as far as a packet of cheddar, a half-drunk carton of milk, and for some reason, a box of Ritz crackers. Adam didn't think they needed refrigerating but then linked them to the cheddar. Logical storage skills.

But at the bottom was an entire shelf of beers. Grabbing two, Adam returned to the living room with them, handing Merrilee hers.

She held it up towards him. ‘To Alex.’

Adam couldn't say it but managed a nod before clinking bottles with her.

’Nice and cold. Thanks,’ she said.

Adam felt the cold beer slide down his throat, and it seemed to wake him up from his week-long daze. ‘So how come you aren't out and about on a Saturday night?’ he asked her.

’Look like a party girl, do I?’ she asked.

’No,’ he said, worried he'd insulted her, ‘You look like someone who has loads of friends, who'd spend Saturday afternoons and evenings laughing in a pub with them... or with a boyfriend.’ Yes, he was fishing, because something in him needed to know. He hoped she hadn't noticed.

’Adam, are you trying to ask me if I have a boyfriend?’ she asked, with a huge smile now.

’I was trying to be subtle,’ he said but couldn't help laughing at his pathetic effort.

‘What if I have?’

’I think I might be a bit gutted,’ he said, quickly taking another mouthful of beer, thinking it was something Alex would have said.

‘Maybe I have a girlfriend,’ said Merri, eyebrow arched.

’Then I'm totally scuppered.’

‘Totally,’ she agreed.

A long moment passed before he ventured, ‘So am I totally scuppered, or just semi-scuppered?’ He wasn't sure it would have mattered to Alex either way, but Adam was more reserved, and he also couldn't believe a girl like this could be single.

Merri toyed with her beer bottle. ‘Actually, he and I recently broke up – apparently, I wasn’t attentive enough.’

’Really?’ Adam couldn't imagine thinking she wasn't enough – of anything. After all, she'd just given up her free time for a stranger.

‘That’s what he said when I walked in on them in our bed.’ She squidged her face in a ‘that old story’ way. ‘So we split, and he got custody of the iPad amongst other things.’

’Oh.’ Adam had forgotten about that. He got up and went to Alex's desk. The iPad lay on the top of a pile of paperwork.

’It wasn't a hint, you know. I didn't mean it like that,’ said Merri from her spot on the floor.

’I know, but it reminded me.’ He opened the flap cover.

’The ad didn’t say it came with a cover.’

’Maybe he was keeping it for his new one. Anyways, you may as well have it. I don't need a loose cover.’

He watched the home-screen pop up: a picture of the two of them as six-year-olds, arms around each other’s shoulders, with opposing front teeth missing.

He's still my brother, he thought. He'll always be my brother. If he said it enough, made it a mantra, then maybe this feeling of it all slipping away would stop. His life only felt rich for having had Alex in it.

He felt her beside him.

'I think you should keep it, Adam,' said Merri. 'There's probably all sorts of stuff on it you'll want to keep.'

Adam thought about it. Then he swiped through to the settings and deftly cleared the search history.

She looked at him. 'You weren't even tempted to look?'

'Some things should stay private, shouldn't they?' he said. It seemed a small kindness he could do for his brother, given there was precious little else he could do. How could he ever repay all the years Alex had supported him or dragged him along to places, forcing a social life on him, helping him do all the things he was too shy to do for himself.

He felt Merri's lips on his cheek and looked up in bewildered surprise.

'You're a good man, Adam,' she said. 'Alex couldn't have a better brother.'

He couldn't speak for a few moments before he took a deep breath and handed her the tablet.

'No, Adam. You keep it. Who knows what's on it that you might need?'

'So borrow it,' he said. 'Don't buy it. I have one, and you don't, so borrow this one.' Adam knew this was the right way to go. She'd done him a favour this afternoon, and here was one he could do for her. At the very least, it meant he might get to see her again.

'That's if you don't mind keeping what's on it for a while.'

She gazed at him long and hard as if mulling something over.

'You should probably have a quick run through the

photos then. Given the music, who knows what Alex used the camera for.'

Adam felt his face go hot. He hadn't even thought of that; neither that Alex might have those kinds of pictures nor that he could have used his own iPad for taking them. God, he needed to get out more.

'Right, yes,' he said, flustered.

'I'll give you some space,' said Merri, breezing back to the boxes as if she encouraged men to search through possible DIY porn on a regular basis. 'I'll make a start on the DVDs.' Flipping through the iPad's photos, Adam was constantly distracted by her mutterings of 'Jeezus' and 'Seriously, Alex?'

Five minutes later, Adam flipped the cover back on the iPad and handed it to her.

'It's all good. Nothing dodgy on it,' he said with a smile he hoped looked authentic. There were pictures he'd just deleted he'd never be able to unsee. His brother knew some very flexible women. He'd thought scrolling through the photos would be an emotional hell, but it had turned out to be an education.

'So I was thinking,' Merri said, 'How about we stop?'

Adam felt his heart drop a little. 'Oh. Sure. OK.' Fair enough, she'd given him a couple of hours; she needn't have done that at all.

Only, he really didn't want her to go.

She saw his disappointment. 'I thought we could stop and get something to eat.'

Heart soaring at the reprieve, Adam experienced a surge of courage.

'Like a date?'

She thought about it. 'If you like,' she said and gave him her gorgeous smile as she moved towards her coat. 'I'd make you split the bill either way.' That made him laugh again. Every time she did that, his soul ached a little less.

Before flipping the light switch, Adam turned to look around the room. OK, so the job wasn't finished - far from it - but it was started, which was a light-year further than he'd believed possible earlier. His eyes landed on the surfing photo again and thinking of the girl he was about to follow, Adam sensed something equally exciting was afoot. And more to the point, although it went against every bone in his scientist's body, Adam couldn't help feeling his brother had a hand in this. 'Thanks Alex,' he mouthed.

One floor down, Martin stood in his doorway smoking his cigarette, as ever annoyed he couldn't smoke in his own home. But the cleaner had asthma issues, and a tidy flat plus perfectly ironed shirts were more important to him than a nip of cold. He watched as a couple wandered down past him from the floor above. Geeky guy and a quirky girl with yellow curls. Pretty. She was laughing at something he said. Why couldn't Martin find himself someone like that? He couldn't remember the last time a girl had found him funny. The only women he ever saw were the office's efficiency drones, all sharp edges behind bland facades.

Thinking about efficiency, he looked at his watch and swore. Over two hours he'd waited in. Four o'clock, the girl had said. He'd wiped the iPad back to its factory settings and everything. Bloody timewasters. Next time he'd go on eBay and get the money upfront. He'd only used the local paper as a favour to a mate on the ad desk. He swore again, further convinced he'd been born under an unlucky star. Grinding the cigarette stub under his foot, he glanced at the couple just as the geek manned up and took the girl's hand. Lucky bastard – he was totally punching above his weight. From the doorway of 50A, Martin concluded that some people had all the luck.

~

Pernille Hughes is a rom-com author and mum, with two novels published to date: 'Probably the Best Kiss in the World' and 'Punch Drunk Love'. She used to work in Children's television which meant living in actual Teletubbyland and sharing a photocopier with Laa-Laa. Now, she lives in Buckinghamshire and shares a photocopier with her husband and their four spawn. While the kids are at school, she scoffs cake and writes rom-com stories in order to maintain a shred of sanity. Her next book 'Ten Years' will be out in August 2022. Find her on Twitter @pernillehughes and Instagram @Pernillehughes

THE INTRODER

PHOEBE MORGAN

The thing about getting divorced is that no one expects it. You don't stand at the altar wondering how you might divide up your belongings or say your vows whilst picturing a decree nisi landing on your doormat. Everyone thinks they're getting the happy-ever-after; everyone thinks they're getting the dream.

Andrew and I got divorced after ten years together. Ten years in which we had three children – Lucy, our eldest, a doctor now; Genevieve, the middle child, the one I've always worried about the most, and Noah, the baby, though he towers over me these days at six foot two. We didn't divorce acrimoniously – all things considered, I thought we did fairly well, finally managing to agree on the fact that we were better off apart. Of course, it wasn't until a few months later that I discovered his affair, and after that, things became a little more frosty. But still, I think I've always behaved with admirable decorum in the face of it all, managing not to say a bad word about him in front of the children, ensuring a smooth, easy process of joint custody, and never admitting how gleeful I was to see the back of his mother-in-law.

Yes, I'd done very well indeed.

The thing is, after the divorce, there was nobody. It was just the children and me, the four of us drawing closer together like buds on a stem, folding ourselves into a small, tight unit that Andrew penetrated every other weekend to take the kids to McDonald's (or whatever establishment he chose. It probably wasn't McDonald's. I'm possibly being unfair). I'd been single for nigh on twelve years by the time I met Charles.

The obstacle was introducing him to the children.

The three of them had grown very close to me, which I will always be eternally grateful for. In the months following Andrew's departure, they clung to me like little bear cubs, all in their own ways. Lucy, at seventeen, doled out her affection in odd moments that mounted up more and more – swift hugs in the kitchen, allowing me to link her arm as we walked in the park at the weekends. Genevieve became desperate for approval, constantly showing me her schoolwork with a heart-breakingly nervous expression on her face. Noah, still a child, nuzzled into me, his dark curls (so like Andrew's) tickling my chin, his warm breath on my neck. Andrew's absence only tightened our bond.

As the children grew older, we stayed close – I would nod along as other mothers complained that their children had not rung from university, tut in sympathy as parents told me their offspring only ever emerged from their rooms to ask for dinner, sigh sadly as my friends bemoaned their empty nests. My children never forgot to call – we spoke regularly, and not once was I made to feel like a footnote in the story of their lives.

All of this leads up to me explaining why the issue of Charles was such a tricky one for me to navigate.

I met Charles at a charity event. I'd got dressed up for it, more so than usual, putting on a new dress and even a pair of low heels. The event was a fundraiser organised by the local libraries trust. I'd been on the board a few years back and was invited for old time's sake, really. It was held in the community centre, not somewhere you'd imagine being particularly glamorous, but they did a pretty good job of sprucing the place up. Fairy lights were strung across the beams, and there were more people there than I was expecting. Somehow the prospect of libraries closing had reminded the residents of our town how much they valued them – well, that coupled with the promise of an open bar, of course.

The alcohol wasn't up to much, warm white wine in plastic glasses. Still, I sipped dutifully and even swallowed a couple of canapes, knocked up by a group of local librarians. Little salmon tartlets; delicious. It was as I was guzzling one that Charles tapped me on the shoulder.

He was very tall; that was the first thing I noticed. Andrew had always been a little bit on the short side, despite our son's unexpected height.

'What is it that first attracted you to libraries?' He asked me, appearing somewhat suddenly and causing me to splutter on the salmon, the soft flesh sticking in my mouth.

After his height, I noticed his eyes – a deep brown, in contrast to Andrew's piercing light blue ones. I don't know why I keep comparing the two of them. Silly.

'A great love of reading,' I said, eventually. He nodded; clearly, he approved of my answer.

'When I was a child, I could only get books from the library,' I continued, feeling the need to embellish my reply. The more I looked at him, the more I thought he appeared well-bred, intelligent, somebody I instinctively wanted to impress.

'Me too,' he said, to my surprise, and we began a conversation about our respective childhood libraries; mine, a small building in rural Suffolk, stocked with paperbacks clad in their plastic cases, protected by a slightly fearsome librarian who had a habit of sneaking up on you.

Charles told me about his, a large, grey building in Manchester, much bigger than mine, where he used to get lost amongst the bookcases.

'A terrible shame to lose all that,' he said sagely, and I couldn't help but agree.

Fast forward to four months later. Charles and I were having dinner, in one of our now-regular haunts, a little French bistro that served very nice wine. Since the night at the fundraiser, we had, to my great surprise, begun a courtship of sorts – a gentle one, at first, starting with walks in the park clutching flasks of tea, progressing to restaurants, and then finally to each other's homes. He lived in a large house, much more imposing than mine, but had made me feel very welcome from the first time I set foot across the threshold.

He laughed in faint disbelief when I told him how long I'd been single, as though someone like me couldn't possibly be on her own for such a long time. I tried to explain about the children, how protective we had become, the four of us, and how I hadn't felt able to put a man before their needs after Andrew left.

He had fallen quiet after that, and we'd left the subject for a while, let it lie silently between us like a crystal, something that could shatter at any point.

Until now, in the French bistro, sharing a rather lovely bottle of red.

'Are you ever going to let me meet your children?' he asked, the inner lines of his lips stained mauve from the wine. I noticed his hand shaking slightly as he took another sip, as though it didn't matter what I said in response to his question. But I knew it did.

'I want to, Charles.' I said without realising that I was going to as if my mouth had run ahead of my mind. As soon as the sentence was out, I realised how true it was – how much I wanted to merge the two separate parts of my life for the three people that mattered the most to me to meet this lovely man.

But I didn't know how to make it happen.

'I'm scared,' I confessed, looking down into my wine glass, watching the colours swirl and change under the soft lighting of the bistro. 'I haven't introduced them to anyone since Andrew left. I don't want anything to – interrupt what we have.'

'But they aren't children anymore, Marissa,' Charles said, entirely reasonably. I knew they weren't children. They were grown-ups; they had flown the nest, they didn't need protecting.

I just had to face up to that fact.

On the day they met Charles, I awoke with butterflies in my stomach – big, fierce, flapping ones that galvanised at dawn and didn't dissipate all morning. I'd chosen neutral ground for lunch, rounding up the kids in the local pub. We were seated around a relatively small wooden table, making nervous small talk before Charles appeared.

'Charles,' I said, 'Please meet my children. The three most important people in my life.'

And just like that, he did. The butterflies bid me farewell.

Phoebe Morgan is a bestselling author and award-winning editor. She has previously worked as a journalist and now edits commercial fiction for a publishing house during the day and writes her own books in the evenings. Her four thrillers can be read in any order, and her next book, 'The Trip', will publish in February 2023. She lives in London, and you can follow her on Twitter @Phoebe_A_Morgan, Instagram @phoebeannmorgan, Facebook @PhoebeMorganAuthor, or find her blog about publishing and writing at www.phoebemorganauthor.com.

NEVER TOO LATE

RACHAEL LUCAS

I tell myself I'm not being nosy – there's not much to do when you're confined to barracks for the duration of lockdown – but the truth is the comings and goings outside the garden are better than anything on television these days.

Taking my 10.30 am cup of tea, I head out of the kitchen and stroll along the cobbled path to the lavender-edged border. It's been such a warm spring. The village is so quiet without the sound of children playing in the field beside the primary school. Even though I've been retired a few years now, I can't seem to break the habit of a cuppa at what would be their morning break time.

There's a little patch of grass opposite my garden – all the estate agents call it the village green, but it's barely more than a postage stamp. There's room for a wooden bench, though, and the old red telephone box they've turned into a library, so there's always someone coming or going. I like to watch while I'm pottering around the garden.

I haven't seen these two before – working from home, I'd imagine, like the rest of the country. We're all trying to find our way in these strange times. Unprecedented, as they say on the news every half an hour. She's walking one way, tall, with long red hair tied back in a ponytail that swings as she walks. He crosses the road to the green. He's in jeans and a t-shirt, pushing back a scruff of hair from his face. It looks like he could do with a trip to the barbers – but couldn't we all? His Labrador has no truck with social distancing. It's bouncing across the grass to the Basset hound the girl's holding. He says something, and she laughs, ducking her head, so a lock of hair falls over her face. She pushes it behind her ear with a gesture that makes my heart contract. I'm pulled back to another time, with the voice in my head whispering, quiet but relentless. That was you, once, it says.

They go their separate ways – I watch them turn, as if pulled by some invisible force, and glance back over their shoulder. There's a spark there. I smile despite myself at the possibility of romance.

I head back inside. The house is tidier than it's ever been, and the garden – well, I reckon Monty Don would be impressed. But there's not much chance of him or anyone else seeing it this summer. Normally my daughter Alice would come round once a week and have a cup of tea with me, but that's off the menu. She's twenty miles away, stuck in a flat with two teenagers driving her round the bend.

Iris the cat stretches out a tabby paw and looks at me through sleepy, half-closed eyes. She's sleeping on the newspaper, but I wouldn't dream of moving her. I pick up my iPad instead and scroll through the news. The death toll keeps rising. It's heartbreaking to see all these families losing loved ones to the virus.

I wasn't always alone. Alice's mother died when we'd been married only a few years, and somehow work seemed to fill the space where love should have been.

I tell myself it's pure coincidence that I'm in the garden the same time the next morning. I trim some dead leaves away from the roses and watch as the redhead and the fellow with the Lab discuss their dogs. He points to the telephone box library, and she pulls out her phone to show him something.

The next day, he's waiting on the bench, Labrador by his side. He's holding a book. Her face lights up when she sees him, and she hesitates before sitting down beside him, picking up the book, and reading the back cover. I turn away from the kitchen window, feeling a pang of regret.

He's there the next day, too. When she arrives, they don't wait and walk towards the park, the dogs racing ahead on their leads. I read a thing about it in the paper yesterday – lockdown has made us all stop and think. All this time at home, all of us caught up in the same situation. It magnifies things. Makes you realise what you've been missing.

I keep a diary. It's an old-fashioned habit, I know, and I've no idea what anyone will ever do with a shelf full of my self-indulgent nonsense. I run my hand along the row of leather-lined books until I find one from ten years ago. It falls open at the page I want because it's not the first time I've looked at this particular entry.

Ten years ago. We met at a three-day long head teachers' conference.

'I'm Sarah,' she said, shaking my hand and looking at me with hazel eyes which danced with mischief. She scribbled 'isn't this boring?' on the notepad when an expert droned on from the lectern.

She suggested lunch, and we escaped the faceless conference hotel for a little pub around the corner. We talked about books, life, and teaching. I watched her make her way through the room and realised with a jolt that I could fall in love with her. Just like that.

We sat together for the celebration dinner that night and sat talking in the bar until well past midnight afterwards.

When she opened the door to her hotel room and paused to say goodnight, my heart caught in my mouth. Another man might have asked her for a nightcap, but I didn't have the courage.

The next morning, I was sitting at breakfast when she walked in. She paused to talk, her hand on the chair opposite mine, and it just seemed to happen that she slipped into the seat. We spent the day together. And the next. It felt effortless as if she and I had known each other for years.

And then the conference was over, and we exchanged email addresses, but I was lost for words. Everything I tried to write sounded stilted and awkward – a million miles from the relaxed and easy conversation we'd had all weekend.

A bolder man might have asked her if she'd like to meet in town, perhaps go for lunch. Instead, I just carried on working. Time – and the moment – passed.

I'm weeding the garden when they pass the next morning. Socially distanced, of course, but they're talking non-stop - it's clear they've really hit it off. I take off my gardening gloves and straighten up, stretching my back. They stop on the corner of the lane, and chemistry crackles in the two-metre distance between them. And that's when I decide.

I turn on my heel and head back into the house. I don't stop to make a cup of tea or turn on the television to see the morning news. I sit down at my desk and take a deep breath.

Dear Sarah, I begin. It's been a long time...

A shaft of sunlight falls through the window, illuminating dancing motes of dust. I stand up, pushing the chair underneath my desk and sending up a silent petition to the heavens.

I haven't even made it to the kettle before her reply pings into my inbox.

Rachael Lucas has written eleven novels for adults and teenagers, including the Carnegie-nominated 'The State of Grace', the top ten bestseller 'Sealed With A Kiss', and her most recent British bestseller 'The Winter Cottage'. Her novels have been translated into many languages, including Italian, Turkish, Latvian, Estonian, Danish and Norwegian. She lives by the seaside in northwest England with her family and two very enthusiastic spaniels. Sign up for Rachael's newsletter at rachaellucas.com, and find her on Facebook at facebook.com/rachaellucaswriter for behind the scenes news and updates.

AT YOUR DOOR

RACHEL EDWARDS

He was too dark-skinned to be of interest; his own family had told him that. Too earnest, not as tall as his youngest brother and of unreliable articulacy when over-excited. And yet, as he stood at the kerb of the road that would lead him, finally, into the heart of Scotland, Gathii felt... solid. Valid. Feet firmly connected with earth he, surely, had now earned a right to stand on.

More cars sped past. Gathii breathed their fumes – face untroubled, focused – as if it were the air swirling around the peak of Ben Nevis itself. Nothing could bother him at this moment; all worries were for tomorrow. For now, he just had to raise his thumb and get there.

His thumb stayed up for an hour and twenty minutes.

'One car!'

A young man was yelling at him from a small vehicle crammed with boys, white but otherwise just like him: menfolk in a hurry. The car did not slow down, and the shouter's eyes, tight, hard and in violent disagreement with his wide grinning mouth, did not invite a smile. Perhaps it had been 'warn car'?

The words he did not know. The roads he would not be

easily carried down. Still, not long, and he would understand, at last, what lay ahead.

Gathii lowered his long-outstretched arm, turned, and started walking.

~

'Let's say by three o'clock. No, actually two, please Sara.'

'Of course,' said Sara, successfully keeping her smile in place. After all, it was only her third week in the office, far too soon to curl her lip at the idea of working through lunch. A chance to prove she intended to stay for the long-haul. Besides, she was trying hard to care more – it made the time pass faster.

It was not that this company was the absolute worst. SkyLine Packaging was developing new eco ranges she could get behind, even though they were not going fast enough or green enough. At least they meant well, and the pay was regular. It would do for now. And months on, she was still finding her feet.

No denying it, though. How much greener and more lush had each second seemed, even in the driest season, at the Enkare Nairobi Safari Park? How much more meaning had burst from each minute when bouncing over ruts in a Jeep as they looked out for Almasi the lioness and her boisterous cubs, or when tracking any number of the charismatic creatures that populated the reserve? She dreamed often of these half-glimpsed memories, always waking to an aching feeling of loss. But a gap year was just that: a gap, holding real life at bay until you were old enough (and, her heart whispered, conventional enough) to return to home shores, and wait, and hope that real life would flood in to sweep you along in its wild and gargantuan tides.

Could happen, if you were lucky. For her, mere days

after the rush of relief at having secured her first full-time role, the flow of opportunity afforded by SkyLine already felt like more of a weak trickle, or worse, a never-changing puddle, damp with moss and stones. The river that had coursed by the staff quarters – her Kenyan home for nine months – had brimmed with Nile perch and wavy, intriguing plants; it had glittered under the bold and brilliant sun. No matter, now. By 1.45 pm, she had scanned in the required forms and sent them to the waiting inboxes. One more document to correct, and she could go grab some sushi from the canteen.

She was rising, at last, her mind set on nigiri and chilled prawns, when she saw him walk through the door into her office, redacting the silver-white light.

In came the flood.

~

Sara appeared paler than ever, standing there. It was understandable as two of the past three days' skies had drenched him, raining disapproval from above onto his hard black head. Only his throat felt dry.

As he drank her in with his eyes, he swallowed hard. He was here uninvited, never a good thing for him. But his dreams had spoken; they had blasted him awake, loud as an elephant's call, and led him to where he stood.

Now, though. The fear that had stayed at bay through the flights and through the coach journey to a town still too far away and through the long, fast walk with his one bag on his back, now that fear surged through him in one vast tide, first searing then icy, swelling his chest.

Finally seeing her, he had no words.

~

She raised her hand as a stockier shadow came up behind her man in the doorway. Security.

'Sir.' She could hear the security guard inflating his authority from across the office. He was performing to an audience. 'You don't seem to have signed in. Could you please...'

Now she was moving from behind the desk; she found herself in front of them.

'It's OK, Kenny,' she was saying, killing the ghost of applause in her colleague's thick ears. 'He's with me, my two o'clock. Sorry, I should have gone down to sign him in, running late. Come through, Mr... Gathii.'

She turned her back on the doubting eyes and walked with her visitor to a windowless meeting room.

She sat; he remained standing.

'I can't believe you're here,' she said.

'I am here.'

'This is mad.'

'You are here; that's the miracle. This was what I saw every night while trying to sleep.'

Gathii was staring at her as they had stared at the lion cubs freshly pushed into the world. With tenderness, a nervous sort of joy and disbelief that such a thing could be. His gaze took her there once more: she was trailing her hand in rushing water, bumping on hard earth, tipping her head back and closing her eyes against the sun of his smile.

'Are you OK?' he asked.

'Yes,' she replied. 'You?'

'Yes,' he said. 'I told you: this was my hope, all night long, every night.'

Sara dropped her gaze. 'I dreamed, too. But... Gathii, it's too much to take in.'

'Why?'

'It's not real life.'

'We had all the real life we could hope for.'

'I know. And it got wrecked, by me. But this can't be happening.'

He smiled then, that brilliant show of teeth and taut skin that had always stirred her. 'It is.'

She looked at him straight. 'You flew here just to find me?'

'I flew, I rode, I walked, and here I am.'

'But… why?'

He took a step closer, then another, hands spread, as if he could pull the good memories

from her:

'I could not forget so easily. Your words, that music. The songs you love, they brought me here,' he said. 'There was one you played over and over, just before you left. The men you said were from your home.'

'I don't remember.'

Gathii's shoulders dropped a touch; the hands fell to his sides.

'You don't remember?'

Sara looked away.

'Are you not pleased to see me?'

'Of course,' she said, eyes unable to settle; a glance up at the security camera in the corner of the ceiling. 'It's just so… weird… that you're here.'

He shook his head, hard, and sat in a chair opposite her, his own eyes shining.

'And why would I not be here?' he asked. 'How could I not come?

'Gathii…'

'The things we did. Sara, look at me.'

She looked.

'Us. We were together. We had a wilderness to ourselves,

day and night. Drinking down life together like cold Tusker, a whole sea of it. Am I wrong? When we touched—'

'Don't talk like this! I've got to get back to work in a minute.'

'Why are you being this way? Have you forgotten?'

Sara dug her elbows into the desk and cupped her palms to her skull.

'You don't understand,' she said.

'Tell me,' he replied.

'It's all changed since Kenya.'

'I know that,' he said. 'You think this is mad, that I am mad? No. You never answered me, and I knew that something had changed. I am not a fool. But I did not know why. When a British visitor – a white woman - disappears, she flees in the night after being so close with a man like me... When it was you – my own strange, sweet woman – that had broken away, out of the blue. How could my heart ever settle, Sara?'

Sara could not look at those eyes for another moment. She stared down at the table until Gathii was forced to say it again:

'I did not know why.'

'My father—'

'They told me he was unwell. Still. Why leave without me?'

No one spoke, neither moved for some moments.

'I thought it kindest,' she said at last, so quietly she could hear her heartbeat over her words.

'It was not kind,' said Gathii. 'It was not what I wanted.'

'Me neither.' Sara's eyes filled with tears and hope that he might understand. 'But I had to come back here, fast.'

'It was so very fast. I was sent to the north, to Lake Turkana, and when I got back, you were gone.'

'I know, but I had to take the first plane I could—'

'You could not wait for me?'

'I'm sorry, no. No time for the paperwork, not even time to think. My father was ill. My mind was all over the place. Your phone was unreachable, so I told Huso what had happened and just ran and packed and went—'

'Yes, you left—'

'I left. But anyway... anyway....'

'Anyway?' He reached out.

She shifted in her seat. 'But anyway, it was still too late. By the time I had landed, before I could even see Dad, he had gone.'

'Your father died?'

She pressed her lips together so the words would not come out.

'I am sorry,' he said.

She nodded. He waited. After a while, she spoke:

'I could not do anything, for weeks, least of all speak to you. I pushed it away, all of it. Took pills to stop... thinking. Stayed under my duvet.' Even now, her voice sounded muffled to her own ears, weighed down. 'I failed, got it wrong, for Dad, for you. Everything.'

'No,' Gathii reached out and touched two fingers to the soft underside of her chin. 'Never everything. You are here. You wrote to Huso for a reference. Why, if Africa was only good for forgetting? You knew I would hear of this; you always knew. Now, let us be kind, both of us, to you. It is not too late.'

Sara and Gathii looked at each other. As the tears wet his fingers, first a trickle, then a flood, he smiled. She pulled back, rose, and walked around the office table. Then she sank, folding herself into the warmth of him, sinking deep onto his lap, forehead pressing into the nook between shoulder and neck, arms around his chest. Holding on.

'Thank you, Sara.' he said, speaking low. 'I knew this was the truth.'

She could not move her head nor shift in the slightest way from the heat of him.

'It was those Scottish men,' he said.

'Mm?'

'The Scottish men, in my dreams. Your music. I knew I should not come, that it was not possible, but you used to play that song about walking five hundred and many more miles....'

She choked on a laugh. 'The Proclaimers? The bloody Proclaimers brought you all this way to my office?'

'You seemed to love that song. One time, you danced, jumping up and down in that red T-shirt, waving your arms, around the campfire. So happy...'

'I remember.'

'I never forget it.'

When her lips moved to him, tear-damp and pressing, he once again had no words.

After a while, she drew back and nodded towards the door.

'I suppose we had better go, then.'

'I know,' he said. 'You have your work.'

'No, I don't,' she said. 'It doesn't matter, that's the point. So few things actually matter, Gathii. Home, please.'

'Where is your home from here?' he asked, set to rise and walk as far was needed. 'Is it very far?'

'Very,' she said. 'Let's go.'

Rachel Edwards is an alumna of King's College London where she read French with English. She won an Arts Council award for her fiction and worked as a freelance writer for over 12 years prior to publishing her debut novel 'Darling' with Fourth Estate, HarperCollins. Her articles feature in the national press, including The Guardian and The Sunday Times, and she is a regular guest at literary festivals and on BBC radio. Her second novel, 'Lucky', is out now.

SALLY SAYS NO

TAMMY COHEN

The assertiveness course was Mick's idea. 'Are you going to be pushed around all your life?' he said. 'Do you want to walk around with 'pushover' tattooed on your forehead?'

That's how Mick speaks - asking questions that he already knows the answer to. By the time I cottoned onto that, we'd already been married five years, and it was a bit late for second thoughts.

What triggered the whole thing was the mug incident. In the office where I work, everyone has their own mugs. We bring them in ourselves, and generally they tend to have funny things on the side like 'I'm no Mug' or 'Shopaholic'. Marketing Liz has one with Ted Lasso on it. 'Hot Brown Water,' it says. Mine has a photo of Mick and me on holiday in Paphos. He had it done for our anniversary in one of those high street photo places. He got a mouse-mat with it on too, as part of a special deal.

Anyway, a couple of weeks ago, when I came into work, my mug wasn't in the office kitchen cupboard where it always is. I was gagging for a cup of tea, but even though I looked everywhere, I couldn't find it. 'That's weird,' I said to

Accounts Mel. 'I know I put it back after washing it up yesterday.'

In the end, I had to use one of the office mugs that no one ever uses on account of they're stained and have chips around the rim.

Later that morning, Reception Suzi sidled up. 'I know who took your mug,' she said. 'It was Nobby.'

Nobby isn't my boss, although he thinks he is. And his name isn't really Nobby.

'I saw him with it last night after you'd left. I bet he used it and broke it. He's always breaking things. You should say something to him.'

But the thing was, what would I have said? Did you use my mug and break it? He'd only have lied, and then what would I have done?

But Mick was furious when I told him.

'Didn't that mug have sentimental value?' he said. 'Wasn't it symbolic? Why didn't you confront him?'

'I didn't want to make a scene,' I said.

That's when Mick started on about the assertiveness course. He went online that same night and Googled it. Mick Googles everything. Sometimes he Googles 'What's the weather like?' even though he could just look outside and know what the weather is like.

Some of the assertiveness courses he found on Google were out of the question. A lot were in London, which we never go to because Mick says it makes him unable to breathe. And some were residential weekends away that cost more than a fortnight in Nerja. Eventually, he found a course at a further education college two miles away, one evening a week for five weeks. Concessions apply.

To tell you the truth, I didn't want to go. Meeting new people has never been one of my fortes. 'That's because you lack assertiveness, isn't it?' said Mick and I had to admit he had a point. Also, it was on Tuesday, which is my Holby night. But I didn't say that.

The further education college was tucked away just off the high street – one of those newly built red brick buildings with disabled ramps everywhere. It stank of bleach, and the classrooms all had numbers like 1:3 and 4:7, which was really confusing and meant I got lost. By the time I found the right room, I was too flustered to go in. The door had one of those panes of safety glass with wire squares, and through it, I could see everyone sitting down like they'd already started. I was just turning to leave when a woman approached, eyes flitting from side to side as if she too was looking for the exits.

'Is that the assertiveness class?' Her voice was quiet as if it hadn't been used in a while, and I had to lean towards her to catch what she was saying.

'Yes, I was just going in,' I lied.

When we entered, everyone looked at us and immediately looked away again, like they were finding something interesting on the ceiling or through the window.

'Welcome!' said a bearded man sitting on a table at the front. 'Grab a pew.'

They weren't really pews – just regular Formica tables with plastic chairs, but that was how he talked. The bearded man introduced himself as Ben, the course tutor. I'd have preferred to know his surname, so I could have called him Mr so-and-so. Calling someone by their first name doesn't give you much confidence in them, I don't think. It's like having a lesson from Mick or Nobby. You can't be sure they know what they're talking about.

The first thing Ben did was put us into pairs – I was with the whispery woman from outside – and get us to tell the other person about who we were. Then you had to introduce your partner to the rest of the group. The whispery woman was called Miriam. I asked her what she did, and she said, 'not very much'. Then I asked her if she was married or had children and she said 'no'. Eventually, I said, 'there must be something interesting about your life!' She thought for a while and said, 'When I was younger, I didn't leave the house for eight years.' So when it came to my turn to speak, I said, 'This is Miriam, and when she was younger, she didn't leave the house for eight years,' which was a lot more interesting than most people who just said things like 'This is Mark, and he's a data analyst' or 'This is Penny, and she's divorced.'

Ben was very keen on role-play. That's where you pretend to be in different situations, and you tell him how you would normally act, and then he tells you how an assertive person would have acted and then you do that instead.

The second week, I had to role-play being on a crowded bus where someone was taking up a double seat, and I had to ask them to move up so I could sit down. That was my idea, actually. Ben asked for suggestions of when we'd felt we weren't assertive enough, and I remembered being on the bus home from work the day before and having to stand because a man had his bag on the seat next to him. 'Good one,' said Ben, and I felt a little burst of pride.

A woman called Fiona played the part of the man on the bus because there were so many more women than men in the class. She seemed like the kind of woman who wouldn't say boo to a goose, but when she was role-playing, she suddenly became really aggressive. When I asked if she could please move, she said 'eff off grandma', and I know she was only being in character, but it still wasn't a very nice thing to say, because I keep myself in good shape and am almost certainly younger than Fiona is. I was almost crying by the time Ben told us to stop.

Ben seemed very impressed with Fiona's performance. When she'd finished, he said, 'move over Meryl Streep!' which was a bit of a stretch, to be honest.

'Can anyone tell me where Sally went wrong?' he asked the class, meaning me, and lots of people put their hands up to say things like 'attitude' and 'confidence' and 'deep breaths'. Breathing is very important when it comes to assertiveness; that's one thing we learned very early on. When you're confronted with 'a situation' - Ben always uses his fingers to make speech marks in the air when he says 'a situation' so we know he really means 'a difficult situation' - you have to take a deep breath, right into your tummy and let it out before reacting. That calms you down and gives you time to think. Another thing that's important is body language. How you stand, what gestures and eye contact you make can decide how seriously other people will take you.

Ben put his arm around me to move me closer to Fiona, who had put her bag on the chair next to her, to make the scene more authentic. Then he put his hand under my chin and tilted my face, so I was looking directly at Fiona and not slightly above her head, which is where I had been looking before. When he touched me, I felt like I was burning all over and hoped I hadn't gone red. Then he said, 'I think you're afraid of the word 'no', Sally,' and he made me stand there and shout out 'no, no, no, no, no' until I was almost shaking.

He also said I still didn't believe I was entitled to respect, and I should practice saying to myself in the mirror: 'My name is Sally. I'm a human being, and I am entitled to respect.' I felt a bit silly repeating that after him, and I could see Fiona smirking, but he told me not to worry about what anyone else thought and to start realising that I was important too. He made the whole class repeat that one: 'I am important' and 'I matter'.

At the end of the third class, Ben set us homework. He told us we had to look out for situations where in the past, we would have allowed ourselves to feel intimidated. Then we had to force ourselves to confront whatever it was that was scaring us. He asked us for examples, and we all said things like 'someone pushing in front in a queue' or 'a shop assistant not giving you a refund'. Fiona had a long, complicated scenario that involved being sent around lots of different departments in the council housing office, but no one really understood it, although a few people nodded as if they did, so that she wouldn't feel silly.

'Go forth and be empowered!' Ben told us before we all filed out.

The class finished at eight o'clock, and as usual, I went straight to the bus stop on the high street. Ben's words had left me all excited and I was a bit disappointed when no one tried to push in front of me getting onto the bus, and there were plenty of empty seats. It was only when I was nearly home that I remembered we needed more milk. Mick is a strictly-mornings-only person when it comes to milk, whereas I like a milky drink before bed. I always have done. A hot chocolate or a Horlicks or something.

I decided to get off the stop after mine to go to the corner shop, which is open 'til all hours. It's one of those shops that's a bit of everything: newsagent, off licence, grocers. They've even got a whole refrigerated shelf full of something called Power Drinks, which always makes me chuckle.

As the bus went past the shop, I could see all the lights on and people moving around inside, so I gathered my things together and got off the bus. But when I got to the shop door and pushed it halfway open, a man stood blocking the way.

'Shop's closed,' he said, rudely.

Well. The shop was most certainly not closed. I could

make out the shapes of people down the far end. Normally I'd have turned around and gone home milk-less and let off steam by complaining to Mick about it. But I could still hear Ben's voice in my head. 'I matter,' I said to myself. 'I am entitled to respect.'

The man had turned away, clearly expecting me to clear off and for some reason, that really got to me. I took a deep breath, right into my tummy, and let it out. Then I gave the door a big shove, catching the man by surprise, and pushed my way in.

'The shop is obviously open, and I'm going to get some milk,' I told him, brushing past.

He looked shocked, and even though my heart was hammering in my chest, I felt exhilarated as I strode towards the chiller cabinets at the back of the shop, making sure to keep my head tilted up.

It was only when I'd got halfway down the cereal aisle that I noticed how the few customers at the back were standing frozen to the spot, their mouths slightly open. At the same moment, I also noticed how very quiet it was in the shop. Normally the two boys behind the till are chatting about something in a language I don't recognise, and there are couples asking each other whether they want pasta or rice for dinner or mothers telling their kids to put the chocolate biscuits back. But that night, it was so quiet you could have heard a pin drop. And they did sell pins – in the far aisle, next to the toiletries.

'Why did you let her in?' yelled a man.

When I turned around, I could see it belonged to a young man standing at the checkout wearing a hood over a baseball cap. I've never really understood that look. Surely one of those things is enough. Why would you need them both? Then when I looked at him properly, I could see he was holding something in his right hand. Something peculiarly gun-shaped.

'The silly bitch barged straight in!' said the man who'd been standing by the door.

'Well, now we've got another one to deal with,' his friend said to him.

By that time, all the exhilaration that I'd been feeling had well and truly evaporated and I was feeling a little faint.

'Everyone line-up over by that door,' shouted the man at the checkout, pointing the gun-shaped thing towards the back of the shop where the owner and his wife usually come in and out carrying bumper packs of Pot Noodles, or plastic trays of sliced bread.

'Move!' yelled the man by the door, who seemed to think shouting louder would make up for his mistake in letting me in.

All the frozen customers defrosted themselves and started shuffling towards the door, me included, even though my legs were suddenly so shaky, I worried they might actually give way.

'Backroom?' the man in the hood said to the boy behind the counter. Then he repeated it, really slowly and exaggerated: 'Do. You. Have. A. Back. Room?' though I know for a fact the boy behind the counter got an A star in his English GCSE because I happened to go in there on results day, and his mother told me he got A stars in everything. She even showed me the piece of paper with his grades on it, as if I might not believe her.

The boy who, I noticed, wasn't looking very well, nodded slowly.

'Go on then, Baz,' said the man in the hood. 'Get them in there!'

The man by the door looked furious.

'What you want to use my name for?' he demanded.

'I didn't,' said the man in the hood. 'I said Daz. And that's not your name is it, Daz?'

The man by the door looked less angry then, although his friend clearly had said 'Baz' and we'd all heard it.

There were five of us standing nervously by the back door – two teenage girls, who were still clutching the fizzy drinks they'd been about to buy, an old lady with one of those wheel-along shopping trolleys, and a man in his thirties who looked strangely detached, as though he was watching the whole thing on telly. The old lady was shaking all over, but I couldn't tell if that was because she was frightened or if she had one of those neurological diseases.

Baz/Daz came up to where we were standing by the door and scowled at us as if we were purposefully making his life difficult. When his eyes fell on me, he looked even more upset. 'I gave you a chance to piss off,' he said, sounding quite hurt. 'You could be back home right now, safely tucked up with your Horlicks.'

Well. I was already in a state on account of the man by the checkout pointing the gun-shaped thing in our direction, but when Baz/Daz said that about the Horlicks, I thought I would be sick. How on earth did he know? I wondered.

But there was no time to think about it because we were being herded through the door and into a storeroom at the back which was piled high with stuff – six-packs of baked beans, cases of beer. They didn't seem to have much of a system going, the shop owners. As far as I could see, it was all piled up higgledy-piggledy in no particular order at all.

'What do I do with them now?' called Baz/Daz. I was getting the feeling that he was definitely the junior partner in this team.

'Tie them up,' shouted the man in the hood. 'And be quick!'

Tying us all up was no easy matter. First, Baz/Daz tried cutting the plastic twine from a giant cardboard box, but it was too thick to tie. Then he found some string sitting on a desk where the shop owners did their paperwork, but it wasn't long enough. Finally, the detached male customer pointed out a roll of gaffa tape hooped over the door handle we'd just come through.

'That'd probably do the trick,' he said.

'Cheers,' said Baz/Daz, then he made us all put our hands behind us with the wrists touching, and he tied each of us individually, tearing the gaffa tape with his teeth after each one. The shaky old lady was the trickiest on account of she wouldn't let go of her trolley.

'For fuck's sake,' said Baz/Daz, prising her fingers off. 'It's right there. No one's going to steal it!'

When he was done, he got us to stand back-to-back, and then he gaffa-taped us all together, going from shoulders down to feet in one continuous roll.

Afterwards, he stood and looked at us with his head on the side, as if he'd just made us in pottery class and was assessing us to see if we were wonky.

'That'll do,' he said, but I could tell he was quite proud.

As he went back into the main shop, he slammed the door behind him, and we were suddenly plunged into darkness. For a while, no one dared speak, and we stood there in silence, all of us vibrating slightly on account of being tied to the shaking-all-over lady. We could just make out muffled shouts through the closed door, and then it was all quiet. Still no one spoke. I tried to summon Ben's voice in my head, but I couldn't. I expected my mind was so full of fear that there was no room for anything else.

Finally, I became aware of another noise – a police siren-type noise. As it got nearer, I could tell the others heard it too because there was a general rustling and fidgeting. Finally, one of the teenage girls broke the silence.

'Oh my God!' she whispered.

That set her friend off.

'Oh my God!' squeaked the friend, more loudly.

Then everything happened at once. The detached man was trying to detach – literally – by wriggling his body to shake himself loose from the tape. The teenage girls were still 'oh my God-ing', and the shaky lady was asking in a quavering voice 'did he take my trolley?' Meanwhile, there were lots of shouts from the shop, before the door swung open to reveal several uniformed policemen and women peering in at us.

Well. Someone found the light switch and then the boy behind the counter brought a pair of scissors and snipped us all free. As we were led out of the room, my legs actually did give way beneath me, and if it wasn't for a quick-thinking policeman, I'd have fallen in a heap right there on the floor.

'You're all right, love,' said the policeman, who didn't look old enough to be a policeman. I know it's a cliché to say that, but in this case, it was true.

The police fetched a couple of chairs from behind the counter, and the shop owners came down from their flat upstairs with a few more. We all sat there for a while, trying to breathe properly while one of the policewomen brought us water, and another policeman got out a notebook and asked us questions. We all had to go through what had happened to us one by one. When it came to my turn, and I told him about Baz/Daz saying the shop was shut and me pushing through anyway, the policeman asking the questions looked like he was about to smile so I didn't tell him about the assertiveness course. Or about Ben's voice in my head.

When we'd all said our piece, the policeman said they'd drive us home, as we'd had such a shock. He said we'd need to give a proper statement the next day, but it was probably enough excitement for one night. The teenage girls looked disappointed when he said that, but I was relieved. I just needed to be in my own house, surrounded by my own things.

I was sharing a police car with the old lady and her trolley. The policewoman in the front seat tried to make conversation with us, but it was obvious neither of us was in the mood for chit chat.

My house was nearest, and when we pulled up outside, the policewoman asked if I wanted her to walk me to my door. It was nice of her, but I said no. After being tied up with the other customers in that storeroom, I could do without being in close proximity to any more strangers, thank you very much!

I'd thought Mick might be waiting for me in the hallway, pacing with worry wondering where I'd got to, but as soon as I got through the front door, I heard the television blasting out. The History Channel, probably. Mick always liked to watch documentaries about the war. Preferably one of our wars, but if not, someone else's war would do. I walked into the living room, expecting him to leap up from the sofa, but instead, he hardly glanced up.

''Xpect you went for a drink with all your new assertiveness mates, did you?' he asked. 'There'll be no stopping you now, I imagine.'

Then he chuckled as if he'd said something funny. And that's when Ben's voice popped back into my head.

'No!' I said to Mick. 'No, no, no, no, no, no!'

Mick looked up then, all right, his mouth open in a little round 'o'.

'I matter,' I told him. 'And I'm entitled to respect.'

Mick made a little whimper of surprise, and I felt a whoosh of something unfamiliar come over me. Empowerment. That's what it was. And it felt good.

'I'm going to bed,' I told him, turning to leave. 'And by the way. There's no milk.'

Tammy Cohen has written ten novels under her own name, including six psychological thrillers, the latest of which is *The Wedding Party*. She has also written three historical novels under the pseudonym of Rachel Rhys including the Richard and Judy pick, *'Dangerous Crossing'*. She lives in London and browses Rightmove in her spare time.

CONNECTIONS

TASMINA PERRY

Alice stood on the concourse, watching the departures screen blink and refresh.

Cathay Pacific flight CA782 *Hong Kong. Delayed. Expected departure: 18: 45.*

There was a collective groan as her fellow travellers turned away, trudging off towards the cafes and duty-free. The Hong Kong flight wasn't hers, but Alice could sympathise: she had a long wait too. Here in Amsterdam, it was 10.30 in the morning, and she was facing eight hours of plastic seats, overpriced coffee and the endless rumble of suitcase wheels.

Schiphol airport was the classic lay-over hub, and Alice had been through it many times, always heading east. There were no surprises for her here: Alice knew where the toilets were, which cafes sold peppermint tea, which fashion outlets would let you try things on without getting snooty. When she booked her trip and found an indirect flight to Bangkok via Amsterdam for less than £500, an eight-hour layover hadn't seemed a problem. But now, it felt an awfully long time to be hanging around.

She turned to the big picture windows where planes

were taxiing and taking off. Out there, the sun was shining. Out there were canals and tulips and blonde Dutchmen called 'Pieter'. She looked at the screen again.

'Screw it,' she whispered and headed for the escalators. Schiphol had a train station, a proper one, not a branch line like in Heathrow or JFK, but on the mainline between Rotterdam, Antwerp and all points east, which meant regular trains and...yes!

'Bing-bong...Train at platform five for Amsterdam Centraal is about to depart.'

Alice began to bound down the steps, breaking into a run, Converse trainers slapping the concrete – but by the time she reached the train, the doors were sliding shut.

'Hang on!'

A hand shot through the gap and pushed the doors aside. She looked up into blue eyes peeking out from under a dark fringe.

'Quick, I think they're going to arrest me,' said the man as an urgent 'ping-ping-ping' alarm sounded. Alice grasped his hand, and he hauled her inside as the doors hissed closed.

'We'd better hide, or the train cops will be on us.'

Still panting, Alice followed him into the train and flopped down on the seat opposite in the quiet carriage. 'Thanks,' she managed.

'You're welcome.' He was mid-thirties, English accent, and had a mischievous smile to go with the eyes. Sadly, he was wearing a suit, which was a black mark as far as Alice was concerned.

'Holiday?' he asked.

'Layover,' said Alice, finally getting her breath back. 'I've got a connecting flight this evening. Thought I'd see some sights rather than hang around the airport.'

'Me too. It was supposed to be a short stop in Amsterdam, but the next flight is delayed, so I thought I'd make the most of it.'

'Where are you heading?'

'Hong Kong. You?'

'Bangkok.'

'Backpacking?'

She glanced down at her skirt and blouse, the dangling bracelets and Alice bristled. The skirt had come from a village outside Marrakesh in the foothills of the Atlas Mountains. Maybe it made her look like a hippy student, but it was her favourite.

'And what about you? Job interview at a bank?' she asked.

Those blue eyes sparkled as he grinned.

'Look, can we start over?' he said, offering her a hand. 'I'm Ben.'

'Alice.' She said crisply, turning towards the window. She wasn't sure she wanted to spend the twenty-minute journey into Amsterdam talking to some cookie-cutter rich boy. But then he *had* saved her from eight hours in Burger King.

'So you're going to work in Hong Kong?' she asked.

'Maybe. If I get offered the position.'

'Do you want it?'

He looked surprised at her question.

'I'm travelling six thousand miles for an interview.'

'That doesn't mean you want to uproot your life and move to the Far East.'

Ben looked thoughtful.

'It's a great opportunity. I've spent my whole career working towards this. University, The City, onto Wall Street, then back to The City. Hong Kong is the next step. It's a big promotion.'

'Sounds like you've spent half your life doing things you're supposed to, not things you want to,' she replied.

Watching him shift in his seat, she felt guilty. She hadn't meant to get so personal.

'You never answered my question,' she said, more kindly. 'Do you want the job?'

Alice found she was genuinely interested in his response.

'I love London,' he said. 'I'll miss it. Family, friends, people I work with. But it's an MD position. I'd be the youngest senior executive at the company.'

Alice laughed. 'Oh dear. You really *are* the banker cliche.'

She wasn't sure why she was being mean to him, especially when he was being so open.

'What about you, Alice?' he asked, undeterred.

'As you guessed from my attire, I'll be doing some backpacking in Thailand, but then I'm heading down to a spa in Koh Samui to work. I'm a yoga teacher. It's good work, decent money and lets me travel.'

'Do you enjoy it?'

'Yes. Although I miss my family too. I miss home.'

She closed her eyes, trying not to think about why she had gone back to Scotland. Her mum's illness. It had been an emotional few weeks; the smell of the hospital, how Mum had looked with all those wires attached. And that feeling of time running out, like she was stuck on a holiday that had gone on too long while real life passed her by.

'*We are arriving into Amsterdam Centraal....*'

Shaking herself from her thoughts, Alice stood and shouldered her bag.

'Well, good luck in Hong Kong, Ben the banker.'

'Enjoy Thailand,' he replied.

She nodded and walked away, forcing herself not to look back until she was out in a wide-open square. The sun was bright, and Alice slipped on her shades. Now, this was better than staying in the departures lounge. She crossed to a bridge over a canal, feeling the excitement of being in a new place. No palm trees or tuk-tuks here, but oh – she loved the smell, the way the light was different. This was why she had started travelling in the first place.

'It's beautiful, isn't it?'

She turned to see Ben standing at the rail next to her.

'Are you following me?' She'd meant it to sound light-hearted, but she saw him take a hasty step back.

'Sorry,' he said, 'It's just you looked as if you knew where you were going.'

Alice shook her head.

'I've never been to Amsterdam before.'

'Me neither, but two heads are better than one. Fancy teaming up?'

Like a magician, he pulled something from inside his jacket.

'You have a *guidebook*?' she smiled. 'That's supposed to win me over?'

'...And a map,' he added, pulling one from the other side.

Alice couldn't help laughing.

'So, what does the guidebook say we should do?'

Ben gestured towards the water.

'It's Amsterdam; it's built on canals. Let's take a boat trip.'

Alice pulled a face. She prided herself on doing things on her own terms, and those hop-on, hop-off tourist barges looked so cheesy.

'Come on. My treat,' said Ben with such enthusiasm, she couldn't help giving in.

'Why not?'

There were dozens of open barges lined up along the dock, and Ben led her to the first, handing over a fistful of

Euros. He helped her on board with ironic gallantry, and the captain immediately began to cast off, going into a well-rehearsed commentary about the sights. Alice found she was enjoying herself, even if it was very touristy. Being a card-carrying bohemian could wear you down when everything had to be authentic and free-range. And Amsterdam was glorious, whatever angle you saw it from.

'To our right, ladies and gentlemen,' said the captain through a crackly PA, 'Are the famous Damrak Dancing Houses, built in the 17th century, so-called because they appear to lean against each other.'

The boat swung in a graceful arc into a narrow canal flanked on either side by thin gabled houses with tall white windows. A sense of calm came over Alice; she hadn't realised how tense she'd been.

'Isn't this great?' she said, closing her eyes, feeling the sun warm her face.

'I've passed through Schiphol airport loads of times, but I never seem to get further than duty-free. Which isn't like me,' she said, opening her eyes. 'I've been travelling since I was 17. I like to go where the wind takes me.

'Seventeen. Wow. You were brave.'

'Naïve maybe, but I was hopeful that there was something better out there for me. I grew up in a pretty deprived area,' said Alice thoughtfully. 'There weren't many opportunities, so I decided to make some. I was 16 when I decided to leave home. I didn't care where I went. I just wanted to *go*. So I worked all summer in a cafe, saved every penny, then I took off.'

'To Thailand?'

'Greece,' she said with a wry smile. 'It was all I could afford, but after a few weeks of island hopping, sleeping on the ferries and making friends on the road, I was hooked. And from there, I just kept going: Turkey, Israel, Egypt.

India, Nepal, down to Southeast Asia, where I did a yoga teacher-training course.'

'What freedom,' said Ben with a look of admiration. 'I wish I'd had the nerve to step off the conveyor belt.'

She nodded. Alice had met many high-flying business executives like Ben before. They came to the yoga retreats where she worked looking for spiritual enlightenment or a lifestyle reboot, but most of them couldn't even put down their iPhones long enough to take a Pilates class.

'So if you did step off the treadmill, what would you do?'

'You mean if I quit finance?'

He hesitated, as if he was thinking, then pulled out his phone and, after a few taps, passed it over to Alice: a photograph of a beautiful apartment.

'This is your place?' she said, opening her eyes wide. The whole place was gorgeous. Modern but cosy, it looked like something that might be featured in Architectural Digest. Clearly, The City paid well - and its owner had taste.

'I love the art,' she said. She zoomed in on the image – a huge abstract painting hanging above the fireplace.

'It's incredible. Those colours shouldn't go together, but they do.'

Ben gave a shy smile.

'Well, that's why I was showing you. The art is mine. It's what I do in my spare time – and my spare room, actually. I've converted it into a studio.'

'You're an *artist*?'

'I wear a suit, so I can't be creative?' he said, raising a brow.

'No, I mean....' but he was right. Alice hated people judging her, but she did it too. Everyone did. 'You're really talented, Ben,' she said and stood up.

'Where are you going?' he asked.

'Come on,' she said, 'We're getting off.'

They were just about to pass under a bridge where the canal narrowed.

'You can't just get off,' spluttered Ben. 'The guidebook says....'

Alice snatched the book from his hand and flung it, fluttering into the canal.

'Hey!'

The boat slowed down as it skirted the embankment. Alice jumped off the boat, then beckoned to Ben to follow her. Throwing a nervous look towards the captain, he leapt towards the bank, crash landing into Alice.

They froze, face to face. Awkwardly, they untangled and exchanged sheepish smiles as the barge sailed away.

'So where to now?'

'That's the point,' said Alice. 'We can go anywhere we choose.'

'In which case, I know where I want to go,' he said, pointing with his map. 'Follow me.'

He turned down a narrow street with cool boutique clothes shops and antique emporiums. Crossing another bridge, dodging the ever-present cyclists, they followed a canal until they came to a grand building with twin towers perched over an archway.

'Is this a palace?'

'The Rijksmuseum,' said Ben. 'It's like the Dutch version of the British Museum, but it also has some of their greatest art: Vermeer, Rembrandt, all the old masters. Fancy it?'

'I'd love to see some Van Gogh.'

Ben looked back at his map.

'In which case, this way,'

They crossed into a busy pedestrianised plaza. In the distance was a building that resembled a saucepan with an ill-fitting lid.

'The Van Gogh museum,' he said. 'Want to go?'

His blue eyes were bright as he looked at her. He looked like a kid on Christmas morning.

'Come on then,' laughed Alice breaking into a run, weaving through the crowds, her bangles jangling. Ben kept pace, his tie streaming behind him.

She stopped in her tracks when she saw the queue. Snaking out of the museum's entrance four-deep, it stretched around the corner and out of sight.

'Great,' he panted, his smile gone. 'It'll be time to board the plane by the time we even get in.'

Dejected, they wandered back across the square and into a little sunken park next to the Rijksmuseum.

'Wait here,' said Alice, leaving Ben sitting on a bench. She crossed to the stalls next to the museum, then came back with two bags.

'Here,' she said. 'A present.'

Ben sniffed.

'Waffles?'

'Something else too,' she said, handing him a small paper bag. He peered inside, then pulled out a pencil and a small sketch pad with Van Gogh's sunflowers on the cover.

'I reckon you can do better than Vincent,' she said, sitting down and biting into her waffle. 'Go on, get to it.'

'I can't just...' he protested.

'Come on. Sunflowers,' she grinned.

Warming to the challenge, Ben nodded and disappeared into the park while Alice sat there smelling the freshly mown grass. The waffle was good too, hot, sweet and buttery, but Alice knew she was enjoying this because of Ben. She missed this sort of easy companionship. Yes, her life was flexible, nomadic, free, but it meant that she didn't have a core group of people in her life – just acquaintances that passed through. People who didn't stick, who never really felt like friends.

'There you go.'

Alice looked up as Ben tore a sheet from his sketchpad and handed it to her. 'It's me,' she gasped as she looked at his drawing. Her heart swelled in her chest. He had sketched Alice sitting on the bench; one foot tucked carelessly under her, food cradled in her hands, surrounded by flowers. In just a few lines, he had caught the moment perfectly. It was beautiful, intimate – and for some reason, it made her uncomfortable.

'We'd better head back,' she said, handing the sketch back and standing up. She needed to get away. Away from this garden, away from Ben, away from everything. She screwed up her waffle wrapper and strode back towards the canals. What was the point of all this? Said a voice in her head. Yes, Ben was fun and handsome, but he wasn't her boyfriend. They were just two strangers whose paths had somehow crossed. By seven o'clock, she would be on her way back to Thailand, back to paradise. Back to her peripatetic life.

They walked back through those same elegant streets, but somehow the stardust had gone for her. The shadows seemed longer; the people all looked the same.

'One last quick stop,' said Ben, as he led her along the side of a canal into a marketplace.

'The Bloemenmarkt,' he said, waving the map. 'It's the floating flower market.'

'Wow,' breathed Alice. It was like Disney had decided to create the perfect florists. Tulip bulbs piled up in baskets like new potatoes, racks of seeds like paint samples. Alice wandered through the colourful bloom-filled stalls, carried away by the heady fragrances of freesias, gardenia and hyacinth.

'For you.'

Ben handed her a delicate pink poppy, shot through

with purple and blue. Alice gratefully took it, then kissed him on the cheek.

'Thank you,' she said, her voice catching.

'It's just a flower, Alice.'

'No, I mean, thank you for spending the day with me. I'm sorry for being such a grouch.'

'My pleasure,' he said simply. 'And you're not a grouch.' He gave her a smile that melted something inside of her.

'I don't think we have to head back to the airport just yet,' she said.

Using Ben's map, they circled back through the pretty neighbourhood of Jordaan, just talking. For Alice, it was like a dam had burst. She told him about her mum and the illness that had brought Alice back to Scotland six weeks earlier. Ben told her about his job and feeling trapped in a hamster's wheel. He told her how he secretly liked opera, and she told him how she missed salt and vinegar crisps. The sun started to dip in the sky, and lights from the tall houses came on, shimmering on the canals.

They stopped on the bridge next to the station, the point from which they had set off, leaning on the rail, elbows touching.

'I always used to think you had to go a long, long way to have an adventure,' said Alice with a sigh.

'So why don't you plan some adventures closer to home?'

Alice glanced at him, liking how he made it sound like an offer. Talking about her family had made her realise how much she missed them. And her itchy feet weren't anywhere as itchy as they had been at 16. Now they just felt tired.

But how could she come home? If she wasn't a boho wanderer, what was she? Who would she *be* back in the rainy lowlands?

'And what about you, Mr Career Path?' she said,

deflecting the conversation away from her life. 'You started the day telling me you were on your way to take up a job you don't want.'

'I think *you* said it was a job I didn't want,' he replied, with a half-smile.

'But why don't you just give up banking and do your art?'

'It's not as easy as that,' he said, looking serious again.

'Why not?'

'There are lots of things I do like about my job,' he said as if he was convincing himself.

'Name three things,' said Alice.

'The sense of achievement.'

'You mean the status.'

'Okay, I like having a prestigious career and financial security. I mean, if I gave it all up to become a painter, how would I pay for that gorgeous flat you liked?'

'Forget the flat. They'll be smaller, cheaper ones that are just as nice. And who's to say you won't make a fortune from your art? At least it will be more fun getting there.'

He let out a long breath. 'I guess I'm scared of change.'

'We're all scared, Ben. The trick is not to let fear win.'

They stared down into the water, their reflections looking back at them. The air had turned cold, and Alice shivered.

'I should get back,' said Ben, glancing at his watch. 'My flight is that delayed 18.45 to Hong Kong. Knowing my luck, they've bumped it back up the schedule, and I've missed it.'

'Would that be such a bad thing?'

He gave a sad smile.

'What about you, Alice? Are you staying?'

'I wish I could, but my flight leaves at seven, so I should be getting back too.'

'You don't have to keep on moving, you know.' He said it

quietly, and she was sure he had moved a fraction closer to her.

'Perfect moments don't last,' she whispered. 'You can't hold onto them. I guess that's what makes them special. That's why you have to keep going, keep finding new things, going new places.'

Ben sighed.

'But don't you just want to stop, Alice? Just put down roots, have a place and people you can call your own?'

'Sure,' she looked away. 'But that's not me.'

They barely talked on the train back to Schiphol, each looking out the window, yellow lights blurring past in the emptiness, lost in their thoughts. At the airport, they rode the escalator in silence and walked across to the departures monitor.

'My flight's on-time,' said Ben.

'Mine too. We'd better get moving.'

They went through security together but didn't say much. Alice didn't like the feeling that something was ending. Ben's gate was at the other end of the airport to hers.

She looked at Ben with a weak smile. 'So, I suppose this is it. Thanks for coming with me.'

'You came with me, remember?' he winked, then leant over and kissed her, soft lips on her cool cheek.

Before Alice could respond, Ben had turned, heading down the concourse. She watched him go, feeling bereft like something was being crushed inside her chest. They hadn't even exchanged phone numbers.

She shook her head angrily. What was she so upset about? It wasn't as if anything had happened between them.

Head down, she walked into the Ladies and stood at the sink, fumbling out her make-up bag. If she had to get on that plane, she was damn well going to look her best.

A girl joined her at the mirror, and Alice glanced across.

The girl was wearing a blouse and skirt just like Alice's, her wrists bright with bangles. She smiled at Alice.

'Bangkok?' she said. 'Me too. We'd better hurry.'

Alice watched the girl leave, then, shaking her head, went to dig out her boarding pass, but her fingers touched something else. A slightly creased sheet of paper, a sketch of a girl sitting on a park bench eating a waffle, one foot carelessly tucked under. She looked goofy. She looked *happy*. Then Alice flipped the paper over and saw Ben had written something on the back. 'Be you', it said. *Be you.*

Alice burst out of the ladies, almost falling over a man in shorts and, muttering an apology, she ran over to the monitor, holding her breath as it refreshed. *Cathay Pacific flight CA782 to Hong Kong...gate closed.*

She ran to the big window, pressing her hand against the glass, watching as a plane began to taxi. Was Ben inside? Maybe. It didn't matter. It still felt as if something had just shifted in her universe.

'*Last call for KLM435 to Bangkok leaving from Gate 31...*' came the announcement over the PA. Alice watched a plane soar into the sky, and suddenly she knew what she had to do.

She strode back to Security, words tumbling out of her mouth as she explained to the officer why she needed to get back to the landside part of the airport.

After being waved through, she made straight for the British Airways ticket counter. Never had she felt more clear-headed and purposeful.

'Can I help?' asked the saleswoman. Alice drew herself up to her full height.

'I'd like to buy a one-way ticket to London, please,' she said.

There was a cough behind her.

'Yes, me too.'

Alice whirled around, her mouth wide open. It was Ben, that beautiful smile lighting up his face.

'Ben? You're not on the plane,' she gasped.

'No, I'm not.'

'Why?'

'You were right. I don't want to live in Hong Kong. I just needed someone to ask the question, to tell me to find the life I want. What about you?' he ventured.

'I don't want to go back to Thailand either,' she said, 'I just needed someone to remind me it was time to go home.'

Their eyes met, and Alice felt something so powerful, it almost knocked her over.

A connection.

'Do you still want the tickets to London?' said the woman behind the counter. 'We do,' said Alice and Ben in unison.

'And is there any chance you can sit us together?'

Tasmina Perry is the Sunday Times bestselling novelist of sixteen novels including 'Daddy's Girls', one of the biggest debuts of the noughties. Her books have been translated into twenty languages and have sold over three million copies worldwide. A former lawyer and award-winning magazine journalist, she has edited several national titles including In Style and More. She also writes psychological thrillers under the pseudonym JL Butler. JL Butler's debut thriller 'Mine' has been optioned by Sony Pictures and is in development with Original Film. Tasmina also founded Sunflower & Co, a female-focussed media company with a brief to take on Hollywood and an office with a soothing view of the swans on the River Thames. Keep up with her news at Tasminaperry.com, follow her on Instagram @tasminaperry or join her writing club at writewithme.co.uk

THE RELUCTANT GRANDMOTHER

VERONICA HENRY

'That's ridiculous. You can't possibly be having a baby. You're far too young.'

Of course, Amanda meant that *she* was far too young - to be a grandmother.

'Mum. I'm twenty-four. The same age you were when you had me.' Holly smiled. She knew her mother well enough to see the issue. Amanda was in constant pursuit of eternal youth. And she managed it well. A trim figure, a smooth brow, a mane of golden hair. A grandchild would completely blow apart her image. 'If you're not lying about your age.'

'Of course I'm not.' Amanda was only too aware she was staring fifty in the face and was already panicking about what to do about it. She couldn't stop it happening, but was she going to have to start adjusting her birthdate? Having a five at the front of her your age was a whole different ball-game. It smacked of middle-age and menopause. Forty-something still had a bit of the sexy MILF about it. Fifty-something was another story.

She had two years before that hurdle, but in the mean-time, this was panic stations. Being a grandmother would be living proof that she was over the hill. If the truth came out, no one would want her as a brand ambassador. Her image was of a youthful, carefree, independent woman. Grand-motherhood conjured up images of frilly aprons and flat shoes and elasticated waistbands.

'Well, don't rely on me for childcare. I don't have a spare minute these days.' Amanda knew she was being curt, but she didn't like surprises. Holly could have prepared her for this bombshell and hinted that she and Joe were thinking about starting a family instead of just dropping her due date into the conversation. Five months away! Her daughter was over four months pregnant. Of course, Amanda was happy Holly had passed the danger barrier and that all was well. She wouldn't have wished her or the baby any harm. But she would have liked a bit more preparation.

After all, everything in her life was micromanaged these days. Nearly a million women looked to her for advice on clothes and hair and make-up with her online tutorials. There were no accidents on YouTube. Everything was planned, down to the last eyelash.

'Was it an accident?' she asked as that possibility occurred to her.

Holly rolled her eyes with a patient smile. 'No, mum. We want to start a family sooner rather than later, that's all.'

'What about work?'

'We're going to share the childcare. We can both work from home.'

Amanda raised a perfect micro-bladed eyebrow. 'I don't think you have any idea what it's like.'

'No. Probably not. But it's no reason to be put off. People have babies all the time. We'll just have to be organised.'

Amanda sighed. She could remember it only too well. The sleepless nights, the sudden responsibility. The fear.

The fact you couldn't walk away from the little creature that was one hundred per cent reliant on you.

And the overwhelming love that came from nowhere, a hot, fierce tidal wave that swallowed you whole.

Of course, she hadn't had anyone to help her with Holly. She hadn't had a kind, lovely Joe to share the feeds with. She had no one to give her a break when her eyes felt raw, and it was all she could do to drag her heavy limbs out of bed.

Holly was so different from her. Laid-back. She let everything wash over her and went with the flow. She certainly hadn't got her laissez-faire attitude from Amanda, but somehow, Holly had managed to drift through life, and everything had landed in her lap. Everyone adored her, not least her partner Joe, and no doubt she would embrace motherhood with her trademark calm.

'Of course I'll help if and when I can.' Amanda added hastily, realising she was being less than gracious. 'But you know my business is twenty-four seven. I'm not going to be able to drop everything.'

'Mum. Chill. We'll manage.'

Amanda felt hurt then, like she wasn't needed. And she knew she had come across as selfish. But Amanda could barely admit to herself how much she was struggling. Everything on her YouTube channel radiated success and happiness, but she felt hollow and empty inside. Unlovable. This was proven by the fact that she'd had no interest whatsoever from any of the matches she'd made on the upmarket dating website she'd joined. She was too bloody old now to find love. And being a grandmother would make her even less enticing as a proposition.

Well, she didn't have to broadcast the fact on her channels or her social media profiles. After all, most people in her line of business hid the truth and kept their private lives tucked away. Success was all about presenting an image of a gilded lifestyle, and Amanda had become very good at it. She started her Instagram posts five years ago, 'Saturday Splurge', showcasing her weekend purchases and trying them on with an irreverent sense of humour that people seemed to respond to. She didn't mind standing in her bra and pants and slipping on a slinky wrap dress or a streamlined jumpsuit, showing her viewers the little tricks that would turn them from frump to fabulous.

Now she was an ambassador for any number of clothing lines and make-up products and procedures. It was incredible, the amount of money she could be paid just for posting a photograph of her with a particular handbag on her arm or a two-minute tutorial with the latest eyebrow pencil. She was in high demand for chat shows and televised makeovers. Amanda was a phenomenon.

But to realise that success, she had a punishing twenty-four-hour regime that started at six-thirty AM with a strenuous yoga workout, and she couldn't remember the last time she'd gone over her twelve hundred calorie a day limit. She was a slave to her phone. It chirruped nonstop with notifications and reminders. She logged everything. Every step she walked. Every crumb she ate. Alarms would go off if she missed a target or went over a limit.

But the messages she received reassured her that her self-punishment was worth it. Her feed was filled with compliments from the women who followed her, and if she ever flagged, she sat down and took time to read through them, replacing her anxiety with a sense of wellbeing.

Fabulous look. Inspiration. Stunning as ever. Gorgeous lady.

She couldn't survive without them. It was worth the hard work and the sacrifice.

Over the next few months, Amanda worked harder than ever. Holly's news had given her the fear. Time, she knew, was running out, and she couldn't keep up the façade forever. And as Holly's bump grew and her daughter glowed with impending motherhood, Amanda wondered if she had got it wrong, pushing her image of perfection.

Was it time to refresh her brand? Morph into something more relaxed, something softer and kinder? Embrace the wrinkles and the extra pounds and reassure her viewers that age was not something to be feared?

But how? That wouldn't make her money. Her entire brand was predicated on holding back the years. Of course, some influencers had made grey hair chic, but their gleaming silver bobs took a huge amount of time and money to maintain. It wasn't a question of letting yourself go and not caring. If anything, it was more work than a head of golden highlights.

As Holly's due date approached, Amanda worked hard to show an interest and help her with preparations. She tried to engage her daughter in kitting out her nursery, but Holly insisted they didn't need much. She'd got a few things second-hand, and the baby would sleep in a basket in her bedroom.

'You're making life very hard for yourself,' said Amanda, waving brochures for bottle warmers and baby alarms and changing bags with a million pockets. 'I'd have given my right arm for most of these things.'

'If I need something when the time comes, I'll get it,' Holly told her. 'But I'm taking it a day at a time, mum. Stop fussing.'

Amanda couldn't help feeling this baby was going to come between them. Holly was being naïve, and she was trying to help by seeing off possible problems. But Holly obviously didn't want her interfering, so she backed off. If she were needed, she would be there; of course she would, but in the meantime, she had her own life to get on with.

And then, one morning, eight months into Holly's pregnancy, she had a phone call.

'I've gone into labour,' Holly told her, her voice very small. 'Mum, I'm really scared.'

Amanda was about to go into the studio to film a segment: The Ten Best Jeans for The Perfect Bum. She took one look at the pile of denim in front of her – boot cut, boyfriend, paper bag – and ran out of the studio. With shaking hands, she started the car and headed for the hospital. Four weeks early. Would the baby be all right? Would Holly be all right?

Joe was there, outside the delivery suite. 'She wants you with her,' he said.

'Is that ok?' Amanda didn't want to step on his toes. There was a certain etiquette to giving birth these days, and even she knew you couldn't elbow the dad out of the way.

'Of course,' he said, and she thought he looked slightly relieved not to have to go through the ordeal of seeing Holly in pain. 'She needs her mum.'

'Oh,' said Amanda, pink with pleasure. How wonderful to be wanted and appreciated for something other than your ability to put on flicky eyeliner with a steady hand.

And so Amanda found herself holding her daughter's hand as the next generation shot into the world, a red-faced bundle whose furious roars reassured all the staff that there was nothing whatsoever wrong with her. A girl, slightly over six pounds, with pixie ears and long fingers and a little mouth that pursed in disapproval when something was not quite to her liking. A princess in the making. A dictatorial duckling. A delight.

Holly looked wiped out but content as she lay back on the pillows.

'Thanks, mum,' she said. 'I'm going to need you, you know. I'm not as laid back about all this as I pretend to be.'

Amanda hugged her daughter. She was the one living a lie, not Holly. But not anymore. She vowed from that moment on not to pretend anymore. The truth was what mattered. She wasn't going to cover it up with shiny gloss and a flattering filter a minute longer.

That evening, she posted a picture of herself and her granddaughter on her social media. She still couldn't believe the overwhelming love she had felt as she held her. It was the sweetest feeling in the whole world, better than a million likes, and nothing would come between them. She had no make-up on in the photo, her hair scraped back in a ponytail, and no filter.

The new love of my life, she put in the caption. *#grand-mother #newchapter #watchthisspace*

Veronica Henry is the Sunday Times bestselling author of 14 novels including 'The Beach Hut', 'How To Find Love in a Bookshop' and 'The Long Weekend'. She has a background in writing television drama including Heartbeat and Holby City and also worked on The Archers where she was taught 'Make 'em laugh; make 'em cry; but above all, make 'em wait!' These days she lives by the sea and heads to the beach every day with her dog Zelda. Find her on Twitter @veronica_henry, Facebook or Instagram @veronicahenryauthor

ABOUT THE DEC UKRAINE HUMANITARIAN APPEAL

At the time of publication, at least 3 million people have fled their homes to escape conflict in Ukraine. Leaving behind jobs, belongings and loved ones, they now face an uncertain future.

Intense conflict in Ukraine is threatening the lives and livelihoods of civilians across the country. Families have been separated. People have been injured. Lives have been lost.

Critical infrastructure such as health facilities, water supplies and schools have also been damaged or destroyed.

At Ukraine's borders with Poland, Romania, Hungary, Slovakia and Moldova, huge numbers of people are arriving with only what they can carry.

DEC charities are in Ukraine and neighbouring countries meeting the needs of all refugees and displaced people:

£30 could provide essential hygiene supplies for three people for one month.

£50 could provide blankets for four families.

£100 could provide emergency food for two families for one month.

Please consider donating to the appeal - and thanks for your support so far, it does make a real difference.

www.dec.org.uk

Printed in Great Britain
by Amazon

80515108R00161